Beatrice the Sixteenth

Beatrice the Sixteenth

Being the Personal Narrative of Mary Hatherley, M.B., Explorer and Geographer

Irene Clyde

MINT EDITIONS

Beatrice the Sixteenth: Being the Personal Narrative of Mary Hatherley, M.B., Explorer and Geographer was first published in 1909.

This edition published by Mint Editions 2023.

ISBN 9781513136219 | E-ISBN 9781513136462

Published by Mint Editions®

MINT EDITIONS

minteditionbooks.com

Publishing Director: Jennifer Newens
Design & Production: Rachel Lopez Metzger
Project Manager: Micaela Clark
Typesetting: Westchester Publishing Services

CONTENTS

I

The Desert

Desert so far as the eye could reach. Only, on the skyline, a tuft which might be a clump of palms. Overhead, the sun industriously burning up everything visible.

I raised myself on my elbow and looked round. Then I remembered what had happened. The blow from the camel's hoof had stretched me senseless. Of course I remembered. But where was my Arab escort of the morning? And who were these unknown figures standing round me?

My first thought was for my revolver. But it had disappeared. Nor was it possible to think of flight from the surrounding assemblage.

So I spoke to them in Arabic. Who were they? Where was my escort? How far was it to Wady Keirân? Were they friends? None of them answered, and they talked among themselves in a tongue which was certainly not Arabic, nor Turkish, nor Persian. Who were they, these clean-shaved, fair, smiling people—all in kilted brown robes with a broad yellow stripe across the front? It was useless to speculate. The nearest to me proceeded to make signs in the burlesque manner of those who are not accustomed to it, and it was clear enough that the party wished me to proceed with them. There was, indeed, nothing else for it. I joined the caravan, only too thankful to be in no worse company. A smile is a sign of good intentions all the world over.

Most were walking, of the twelve or fifteen who made up the party. A few pairs of mules supported full baskets between them, and some of these had riders. Science asserted her sway, and I endeavoured to find out something about the language spoken by my companions. Addressing myself to a tall, striking-looking personage, with a profile like an old cameo of Odysseus which once hung near my fireplace in a Surrey house—far away now—I began to acquire a few nouns and verbs. But my education had not proceeded far when night overtook us, and the caravan prepared to bivouac.

I know no more of what happened that evening, for sleep came suddenly and irresistibly, and I sank into the folds of a rough, soft rug, as a child nestles into its pillows.

By early morning we were moving. But the palm-like tuft on the horizon grew no nearer after three hours of steady walking. We halted for a meal of flat cakes and excessively sweet wine, and proceeded on our way, a seat being found for me in one of the mule-baskets, for my head still ached violently. Gradually I fell into an uneasy dose, with that accompanying sensation of uncertainty and danger which is so disquieting when one sleeps on a journey. I could have felt certain once or twice, in a dreamy way, that something had passed my lips. But I wakened fresh and alert towards evening, when I found no preparations for resting, but the whole company steadily pressing on. There must have been a halt during the day to enable them to walk as they did. For myself, I lay down in my capacious basket, Tapped my rug more closely round me, and watched the moving figures in the bright moonlight, until a deep, restful sleep came upon me, which lasted until morning.

And then I saw the explanation of the palm-like tuft against the sky. There towered before us a magnificent obelisk, the very base of which was; the size of a palace. Perfectly simple, its entire plainness had a unique and lonely grandeur. Its solemn finger, as we neared it, pierced more and more into the blue. It was the discovery of an eighth wonder I know no more of what happened that evening, of the world. But how had it remained so long for unsuspected in solitary majesty? As I thought of the generations of Arabs who must have so well guarded the secret, of the many explorers who must have passed within an ace of finding it out, I could not repress a smile. The impulse was infectious. The kindly faces of my conductors beamed with pleasure, and the very mules seemed to start with fresh energy.

I soon saw why. Seven or eight miles away, so far as I could judge, appeared the serrated edge of a low range of hills, towards which we were evidently directing our course, to everybody's high satisfaction. An hour's further journey, and the stony desert melted into fresh green pasture. Feathery-topped, graceful trees appeared; the scorching heat itself gave place to a pleasant coolness; one caught sight of figures moving behind the foliage, and paddling light craft past the rushes. Finally, we stopped at two huts, for no reason that appeared. Here there came out to us the most surprising ostlers that, of many strange beings, it had been my lot to meet. Tall, lithe, brown, with a swinging step and a free carriage—so far they were commendable, but not uncommon. The singular thing to me then was their extreme beauty, and the fact that everyone of them was clothed in ivory silk, of a perfectly Grecian fashion.

These remarkable personages performed our mules' toilet, watered and fed them, and offered us various kinds of fruits and honey, which most of my companions were nothing loth to accept. Still, when all was disposed of, and even conversation flagged, we waited on. It occurred to me that some of the white-garbed people might know a little Arabic, and as I was increasingly uneasy as to my whereabouts, I selected a particularly intelligent looking subject to inquire of. But my inquiries were met with a bland stare of regret, and a minute later with a response delivered with a stately kind of diffidence, as though the speaker thought it right to answer, but hardly expected to be understood. Nor did I understand for a while, but some familiar chord in my memory was set working. Bits of old school day learning came back to mind, and as the strange people chatted with each other, I knew that their speech was a near relative of Latin, with a strong infusion of an element more resembling Greek. The blood rushed to my head—I could understand them; I could speak to them!

Only the first and third declensions and conjugations were used. The words were not spoken according to any modern system, though very nearly as in the Italian method. And to those broad vowels for classical speech I was well accustomed from days long past, when I had pored over Cicero and Horace, with some big Scottish cousins in a Dumfriesshire garden. When shall I ever forget those old Dumfriesshire mornings? The low, incessant undulations of the mossy, bent-covered earth; the damp pools; the distant mountains; the silver Solway, shining far away like the glint of its own salmon! And inside the red-brown walls of the garden, a tangled maze of larkspur and snapdragon and marigolds, and a dozen more flowers whose names we did not know, nor cared to; for we three were in the Senate watching Cataline, or listening with Plato to the last words of Socrates.

"Ulinde venitis?" The words forced themselves to my lips, and no sooner were they spoken than there ensued a most laughable scene of confusion. everybody joining immediately in animated colloquy, difficult from its rapidity to understand—the more so as my first friends did not speak the Italo-Greek dialect among themselves, but a language entirely different and totally unintelligible. And, besides, the traveller I addressed, after a sharp turn with an emphatic nod to a neighbouring muleteer, began to reply to my questions. The pronunciation was not quite easy to follow, but in a few minutes I had made out that my acquaintances were merchants, bringing country produce to town across the desert, and escorting travellers, who had business or other engagements in the city. Of these there were five or six among their number.

The city, they said, was large and populous, though its extent seemed to me exaggerated; still, I knew the wide area an Eastern city will cover. The people were engaged in trade and in manufactures, so far as I could gather; they were acquainted with the arts, and were hospitable to strangers. But when I inquired their relations to the Turkish authorities and to the desert tribes, the most impenetrable density met every question. "Arabes," "Syria," "Alexandria," "Parthii," and "Nilus"—a shake of the head met every reference to these, and the eyebrows would rise inquiringly and innocently, without a quiver.

"It is all very well," I thought to myself; "our excellent friends have reasons, doubtless for keeping their own counsel as to their knowledge of the world and the best thing I can sec at present is to humour them."

Accordingly, I waived the delicate subject, as I inferred it to be, and proceeded to inquire, what was my next point of concern, how they had come across me. But I did not succeed in obtaining the least clue to my position. They had stumbled on me lying absolutely alone, and had not been much surprised, as travellers were frequently found to be overcome by heat or weariness, and for this reason generally availed themselves of the merchants' escort, and travelled in their company.

"And were you not struck by my odd appearance? Had you ever seen a European before?" I asked.

No; they were well aware that foreign nations had each their own customs. Very likely their own seemed absurd to strangers. I glanced at the ivory silks, and then at my own tailor-made garments, and I hardly felt the comparison justified their surmise.

I changed the subject. What was the name of the great obelisk we had passed? Was it a bird, then, they said, that I had ventured to cross the Stony Desert, without knowing the use of the Index Maxima? If my guides had abandoned me without explaining its use, nothing could be bad enough for them. Words failed to express the hopelessness of the position in which they must have left me.

"But I was not intending to come here; I was going to Wady Keirân," I explained; whereat, the polite stare of incomprehension again and an awkward silence. I would have inquired the name of the city, and how far we were distant, when two horsemen came briskly up, and were at once surrounded by the travellers. These five new arrivals were well armed, but, so far as I could see, not with rifles. They were certainly nothing like Bedouins; for one thing, although they rode easily and well, they had not the air of being constantly in the saddle. Their long dark cloaks covered their dress, but the metal helmets which they wore had so classical an appearance that I half expected to see them arrayed in corslet and lorica, like a Roman *eques*. Their real attire, however, turned out to be a much simpler dress; and the idea faded which for a moment had possessed me—that these people were the relics, preserved like flies in amber, of some Romano-Syriac civilisation. Still, I was no nearer as to what they were.

The newcomers scrutinised carefully all the members of the caravan, and continually referred to parchment rolls which they carried with them. They talked for sometime to the principal spokesman, than air of friendly authority. Suddenly the young looking of the two dismounted, and came swiftly, but quietly and naturally, to where I was standing.

"Let us sit down and talk whilst matters are being arranged." My arm was taken, a pair of eyes looked into mine, and I found myself resting on the spicy herbs with a hospital figure beside me.

"You see, we generally require strangers to be provided with credentials before they are admitted into Armeria. Otherwise, they have to spend sometime in quarantine outside the gates before they can be let in, so that we may make inquiries about them; but I am expecting that, you being evidently from very far away, and having hurt yourself and—and—needing care, we may take you in without waiting (Can you understand me? I am afraid I speak too fast. No?) Have you friends in Alzôna?"

I explained that I had no intention of visiting Alzôna, and that where I wanted to be was Wady Keirân. Much, therefore, as I desired to see the beauties of the city in question, I would not think of the laws being stretched to enable me to do so, and would be much obliged to be put in the right track as soon as convenient.

An impatient movement of the graceful figure, otherwise so courteous, warned me once for all to give up speaking of Wady Keirân. "You will come to Alzôna first," was the persuasively uttered reply. "There are doctors there, and—I hope I haven't been rude!"

Well, if people thought me a lunatic, at least *protem*. I must just make the best of it. Very likely I should be no worse off by going. And the voice in my cars was very persuasive, and, I began to realise, very sweet.

I thought I would take the edge off my presumed lunacy by a little rational conversation on the subject of the Index Maxima.

"When was it built?" I said. "And why do you not use the compass?"

"Everybody hasn't got a compass," was the laughing reply. "And sometimes it is dark; then, you know, the light shines from the top, when you could not see a compass-card without a fire. But the obelisk was built five hundred years ago. Without it, we could have scarcely any intercourse with Zûnaris—and no figs."

Five hundred years! How easily traditions are distorted! The monument must have been five thousand years old.

A shout from the crowd, however, recalled us at this moment to the huts, in front of which the train was duly marshalled to proceed. A horse was found for me, and I noticed that it was kept carefully between those of the newcomers, who brought up the rear of the procession. For a few minutes we passed through a belt of trees, and then emerged on a plain, across which, not half a mile away, rose a solid mass of buildings, whose square towers hung over long ranges of battlemented wall and rows of pinnacled rampart. The material of which it was constructed seemed to be a dark grey stone, so far as I could judge at the distance. On the first glimpse of it, the merchants showed the liveliest signs of pleasure, pointing to various features of the place, and talking volubly to each other, with considerable urging of the mules.

"That reminds me," I said, "of the scene there was when I first spoke to your countrymen."

"They had been debating greatly," the elder horseman replied, "as to whether you were a native of some civilised country or an outer barbarian. Your clothes, they thought, argued the latter, though"—politely—"every nation pleases itself; but your manners were, of course, not those of a barbarian. As they are inveterate lovers of an argument, and argue all the more to prove themselves right the more clearly they are shown to be wrong, your knowledge of our language started the game afresh; and if we had not come, they would certainly have been disputing now."

"Then, they are not of your own race?" I observed.

Here the younger horseman struck in: "I hope not! Good creatures they are; and, for all their arguments, they never quarrel, which, they say, spoils the zest. Still,—of our race!"

"If you are such a stranger," said the other, in explanation, "you do not, perhaps, know that Alzôna is the capital of a State, say eighty by one hundred miles in extent; that the kingdoms of Uras and Kytôna lie next it on the east, and a series of little States—we call them the Mountain States—on the south, together with the Hyroses Mountains.

Then, on the west are Cryosis, Agdalis, and Cranthé; beyond them, others for a thousand miles. Eastward, past Uras and Kytôna, there are others too, but they do not reach so far. And these States are a group by themselves, so that for any stranger to come from outside their limits is a novelty indeed. Only we have these merchants, who come to us from Zûnaris; and the people of Orôné, far to the west, make voyages to sea. For the rest, the desert and the mountains form impassable barriers—or, at least, there is no temptation to cross them."

I could not believe my ears. A kingdom eighty miles square, here! It was simply impossible. As for the other countries, they must be distorted versions of the well-known divisions of the map. The sea to the west was natural enough. And I did not doubt that the geographical ideas of these people were considerably confused, and far from being anything like as accurate as Strabo's, say, or Ptolemy's. But a kingdom eighty miles square!

Still, there was the mass of buildings before me.

"And how are you governed in your city?" I proceeded.

My companion's head was thrown back a little.

"We are free," was the answer.

"But is there no Sheikh, Consul, Decemvir, at the head of things?"

"Yes, certainly. We have our queen."

"And who is she?"

"Beatrice the Sixteenth."

A dynasty in this out-of-the-way corner of the globe, then! And probably a more or less veneered version of an Oriental Court.

"I do not know," went on the elder of the riders, "whether you have queens in your country. But our line has lasted, as history tells us, seven hundred years, when the royal family of Uras first gave us a sovereign. And now we are not the best of friends with Uras."

"I hope you are not bound for Uras," said the younger horseman abruptly."

"On the contrary, nothing is farther from my wishes," I returned, though I had qualms of conscience, for I did not know but it might turn out that Uras was Persia, or Bassorah, or Aleppo.

"Uras has behaved disgracefully badly; they are not treating us rightly—" But a sign from my right-hand neighbour checked the political confidences which were impending.

Just then a sight presented itself which for a moment did not strike me in its full significance, but which immediately began to produce in me a sensation of bewilderment, culminating in a physical shudder.

Before us ran, in placid flow, past the now imminent walls of the town, a river, which was spanned by a fine stone bridge, and whose waters were broad and deep.

Wild surmises crossed my mind. An affluent of the Tigris? An arm of the Persian Gulf? The Euphrates? I knew perfectly well that all these were impossible. A river where no river could be, it seemed. I did not notice the boats on its surface, nor the vegetation on its banks; my agitated thoughts made me dizzy. With an effort, I refused to dwell on them. Feeling very much like bidding farewell to Europe forever, I watched the caravan file over the bridge. The two youngest travellers; the mules, in pairs, with their drivers; the merchants, with their staves, in stately order; the other travellers who accompanied them; we three on horseback—so we moved on to the causeway, and ended the last furlong of our journey.

II

THE CITY

I magine a long, low, square room, with walls of polished black wood. Give it a ceiling of gilded arabesque and a floor of red cedar, on which are inviting masses of bright mats and rugs, and tall bronze vases, with taller palms and lilies. Let there be a low table near the centre for all the furniture, save that round it are set forms, on which sit a dozen silent figures in scarlet. Light there should be in plenty from a large curiously-wrought lamp that swings above the table, and from numerous lamplets on slender pillars in various parts of the room. Add a very tired, very dusty, English-clad traveller, prone in a corner. Such was the picture that the chamber presented where the solemn question was argued of my admission to Alzôna. I am told that when a member's exclusion is debated in the House of Commons the individual in question politely withdraws meanwhile, out of an altogether touching consideration for the feelings of those speakers who are unfortunately compelled by conscience or party to deprecate his claims to a seat. But it was far from the designs of the Alzônians to lose sight of me for a moment; only they discussed the matter in low tones-mainly, indeed, in silent contemplation of maps, with a word or two interjected occasionally.

Counsel was not darkened by this queer process. It was not very long until the bright, grave figures gathered themselves up, and, with half-Japanese coos of salutation, glided out of the apartment. My friend of the horses came up to me—the younger, whose name, it seemed, was Ilex.

"Come, that is well! This is the Palace of the Warders; and Brytas and I, who are on duty, can entertain our friends here; so I can find you quarters without a minute's trouble. The inns are closed: my own house is miles away—three, I think—and people will mostly have got to bed."

An arm was put round me, and we wandered across the room to an opening, where a heavy curtain, pushed aside, admitted us to an open passage, which led between two wings of masonry to a low flight of steps. All was entirely silent. At the foot of the steps we entered a small covered courtyard or large balcony, with a massive and rich balustrade to the right, over which the sky could be seen. It was a faintly moonlit night, and there seemed to be a perfect forest of treetops outside. A sudden fright seized me next. I had thought we were quite alone, when Ilex's call, "is there a light in your quarters?" brought a sharp and startling response from quite near me, and I saw a dim, gigantic body two feet away, which turned out to be a fully armed sentinel.

Ilex thrilled with a sympathetic vibration.

"How stupid I always am! I really am not fit for my place."

I had no time to reply. We entered a garden crowded with flowers, though it must have been near the summit of the building. It was much lighter than the dark balcony, and just at our right was a door, at which we stopped. It opened at a touch. We were in a small room, furnished almost as little as the immense hall we had left. But the walls were covered with soft hangings of dark blue cloth. In an alcove a brazier was rapidly heating an urn; a kind of bureau in the centre was uncovered, disclosing in its various divisions spices and eatables of different kinds; a rich service of plate and dishes of fine porcelain stood between it and the alcove.

"Brytas has done what I said: things seem all ready for us," observed my companion, putting off the scarlet robe of state and laying it on one side. "We shall have coffee in a minute. In the meantime—a *carusna*?"

This, I found, was a banana, and by the time it was eaten and the coffee made, Brytas, under which name I recognised the other rider, came in. The orthodox thing appeared to be to lie on the woolly rugs and cushions that spread the floor. Both my hosts threw themselves down without hesitation, and I followed their example. We sat by the glowing embers, and ate and drank I do not in the least know what— only it was all delicious—Ilex sprang up and cleared the things into a corner, and produced a little cithara.

"Brytas plays so well." And, indeed, for the next half-hour the room was full of the sweetest tinkling music, elaborately Æolian—the very lace-work of cord and plectrum. The performer ended with a quiet smile, put the instrument down, and would not play more. It was extraordinary how this matter-of-fact official personage, from whose face the light of youth had faded, had the power to call up such fairy-like visions at a finger's touch. For there was nothing of romance in the conversation we had after that, or such as there was—was dropped in sportively by Ilex. We talked of the ways of the city—of its market days, its twenty Governors, its wide orchards, its walls and terraces. And they told me of its fertile environs, and of all the towns that flourished in its territory; of the arts, and the special excellence of each. I heard of the neighbouring kingdoms again—of Uras and Kytôna, Cranthé and Agdalis. I listened with vain expectation to their stories of the western sea and the outer barbarians.

I thought, with a rush of sudden emotion, of the river, swirling like an oceanic torrent, as I had seen it sweep past the wall, in such mysterious volume.

"Where does it rise?" I asked.

"That is unknown to us," Brytas answered. "But it flows eighteen hundred miles from the east, and divides us from the desert. All past the northern boundary of Uras and our own country it runs, and past them, through other lands, to the sea. In the upper part of its course it traverses barbarian countries which are pretty well known; but eighteen hundred miles from the sea it flows through the Pass of Hylis. Beyond that are fierce barbarians, whom we keep safely on the farther side, neither venturing amongst them nor letting them come through."

Well, was my knowledge of Greek numerals hopelessly muddled? And could I be putting hundreds for twenties? Or what could the explanation of these extraordinary stories be? Were my hosts playing with me? Were they the credulous victims of unscientific travellers' tales?

None of these seemed a fair way of accounting for their statements. Besides, there was the river itself to be accounted for; not to speak of the city, which was a trifling circumstance compared with the other matters, but nevertheless, in its high civilisation and its artistic refinement, would have appeared a sufficiently surprising discovery to me two days ago.

Reduced to fruitless conjecture, I determined to leave the puzzle alone, and to try to obtain camels and make my way across the desert northwards, by sheer persistence, when I had no doubt I should sooner or later arrive in Turkish or Persian territory.

It was obviously desirable to make the best use of my time meanwhile in becoming fully acquainted with the customs of the strange race among whom I was so unexpectedly a visitant.

"Have you many poor?" I asked; "and are they contented?"

Ilex looked at Brytas and smiled a little enigmatically.

"Is it permitted to ask," said the latter, "whether the poor are numerous, and how they are dealt with, in the honourable stranger's country?"

"In theory," I said (and I am sure I don't know how far I was speaking the truth), "no one need starve—actually starve—in England. If you are very badly off, you first of all try to raise money from your friends; then you live in a smaller and meaner house, you wear old rags, you eat dry bread and tea. . . finally—"

"And all this while," said Ilex, "your friends come and talk to you and bring you presents—do they?"

"I am putting the case," said I, "that you have exhausted your friends as a source of revenue. I think the next thing is the minister or district visitor. They will bring you round tea occasionally, and help you to buy rugs, which they call 'blankets.' (Tea is a warm drink, slightly stimulating; you haven't it here?)."

"No—not by that name," said Brytas. "The minister—is he paid for this service?"

"Well, no; he isn't, exactly. At least, he is paid, but not to do this— that is, he needn't do it. . . and yet he is supposed to do *something* in that way. . . then, after that—or if you don't behave—for in that case the minister will not have much to do with you unless you are so bad as to arouse his professional interest; for his real business is to cure badness— after that there is nothing for it but to go to the Relieving Officer and the Guardians."

Ilex and Brytas both sat up, with sparkling eyes. "A special officer who can cure badness! What a wonderful country yours is! We thought you were just an atom patronising, and really we were so absurd as to laugh at that; but if in your England you have physicians who know how to treat the soul, it is certainly we who are foolish! Here we have only the old empirical methods—the judge, the prison, the kûrbash. . ."

"I wouldn't distress myself, in your place," I returned. "The persons I speak of generally regard this mission of theirs as secondary to the inculcation of particular theories about religion, and they have not yet worked out any system of therapeutics which they can get put into practice."

"Not even an approach to a system?" said Ilex, with disappointment.

"Not even an approach to a system."

"Tell us, then, of those noble officials you have—the Relieving Officers and the Guardians of the Poor! I suppose they relieve and guard you, as their name indicates."

"I'm not sure, when I come to think of it, that Poor Law Guardians isn't the right name; and in that case it must be the Poor Laws, and not the poor, that the Guardians are supposed to protect. At all events, you may safely discard the idea, which I am sorry I have misled you into entertaining, that their main object—they are excellent people—is a sympathetic apportionment of relief to the victims of poverty. No; the Relieving Officer is merely a name for the servant of the Guardians; and the Guardians have to consider the ratepayers' pockets. If they decide to afford you two shillings a week, well and good; if not, you go into a kind of gaol, which it is not so easy to get out of."

"Without having done any wrong?" said Brytas.

"Good and bad alike?" said Ilex.

"'They don't *call* it a gaol," I said hurriedly; "and many Guardians will give the two shillings, as often as the Inspectors will let them. I don't understand the theory of it. The idea is, if you can work, you ought to go to something like gaol if you don't."

"But if you can't?" said Ilex.

I gave up the Poor Laws in disgust. How little one knows about things so commonplace as workhouses and rates!

Rates and taxes were a great bother to my new friends. So they are to most people; but I mean that it was impossible to make these see the theory of them. Every explanation ended in some such observation as:

"But I should have thought plenty of people would have *liked* to pick out the decent poor people, and keep them in their train"; or—

"But why should I take Chloe's money to keep Doris with?"

We did not go very deeply into the problems of government.

"Are the countries round about much like this land of Armeria?" I went on.

"Hardly. I think you will find marked differences in outward appearance and in character," said Brytas. "But in civilisation and progress we are all on about the same level, I suppose. Well for instance, you go to Bruna, in Cranthé: you find you must take your red dress off, because you are not a literate in the seven classics; you find all the inhabitants assembling—every night, that is—and performing military evolutions in phalanges of separate castes; you find everybody speaking in a voice that sounds like a knife-edge. *Quid ergo est*? What does it matter? They think no worse of you because you do not know the seven classics, and parade in proper costume with a spear in the evenings."

In conversing thus, my attention was struck by the metal coffee pot, which was beautifully worked, and would have done no discredit to Birmingham.

"What a fine design you have there!" I said; "is it old, or are such things made here nowadays?"

"I will introduce you tomorrow to the maker of it," said Ilex quickly. "And as you admire it, I have no doubt one like it will be forthcoming for you."

It occurred to me unpleasantly that I had not a sixpence, my letters of credit being with my lost effects. I felt this ought to be explained at once.

"I couldn't pay for it," I said. "You see, unfortunately—most unfortunately—my party have gone off with my money. That is, whatever their reason for leaving me, they have taken my goods and all I have with them. So I must be indebted—"

"Oh, but," said Brytas, "the metal-worker will ask you to take it as a present. It is not everybody who appreciates good work."

"It strikes me," I said, "that a good many people simulate appreciation very assiduously, if that is the principle on which he does business."

Brytas looked blank. "Why should they? To be given things they don't want and don't care for?"

"No," I said. "To be given a serviceable coffee pot."

"Nobody need be without a coffee pot; you can get them for next to nothing."

"Not such handsome ones?"

"Oh, well! But isn't it far pleasanter to have your own eightpenny pot, that you made or chose yourself, than play on a person's confidence in that style? I don't see quite how it would work. Anyhow, your admiration is genuine, and you needn't scruple to take the thing—provided it is not in your way.

Here Ilex insisted that I must be getting tired, and conveyed me across lofty saloons of varied and size—some traversed by colonnades of pillars, some fitted with a raised daïs, others with latticed galleries-to a tiny courtyard of fairy-like delicacy. It was not more than twenty feet square: in the centre a fountain's sparkling jet threw drops of crystal over dim sprays of green; at the sides an arcade of graceful Arabian arches formed a covered way. We went along the cloister to the left, and, halfway to the end, we came to an opening in the wall, where a flight of easy stone steps admitted us to the roof. Above us towered a huge mass of masonry, but on the city side there seemed nothing to impede the prospect. A few steps farther on a low escarpment of the lofty towers stopped our further progress. Ilex opened a door. A faint scent of cedarwood met me as the air of the chamber mingled with the night breeze.

"This is where I think you will sleep best," said my companion, entering, and motioning me to follow. "This door on the right leads into another room, which is also for you. In the morning I will be here early, because my own room is next—just here."

With an elaborate salutation, half inclination, half wave, my strange conductor departed into the semi-obscurity of the starlight.

I was standing at the door of my new quarters. But I could not for a few minutes settle indoors. I remained outside, glancing down at the half-visible silver of the fountain. Then I turned my eyes upwards to the stars.

They were totally unfamiliar to me!

With the stars of both hemispheres I am as well acquainted as with the alphabet. In Brazilian forests I have lain and watched the Southern Cross. I have steered my course by Orion in Arabian deserts, and marked the southing of Arcturus in California. At a glance, I knew that these were no stars of mine. No one who has not used the stars as familiar and unfailing guide—perhaps a professed astronomer or a child may have the same feeling—can picture what it is to such a one to see the heavens spangled with strange, unknown constellations.

Where was I? Who was I? What was this place? I half expected to see the strange stars start from their orbits and dance like meteors in a sudden delirious whirl on the palace.

For a few moments I suppose I half fainted, for I remember thinking that this had actually happened, or begun to happen. My nerves had been shaken by the accident and the startling events which succeeded it. The relaxation of the past few hours had been followed, now that I was alone, by a reaction. I quickly stepped into the room and closed the door, which was fastened by a flat staple of bronze. The furniture was scanty, but I had no inclination for examining it. In the centre of the floor was a bed, covered with rugs. Its four posts were of the slenderest bronze, and attached to them were curtains of thin gauze. Throwing my things off, I lay down, but without much hope of rest. I thought it better to leave the lamps unextinguished. As I lay, all was quiet, except for the fountain, scarcely audible, and for a soft but penetrating musical note, which sounded at long—or what seemed long—intervals.

The rafters of the ceiling were coloured a dull red, with a few gilded bosses. In some odd way they recalled to me the dark beams which ran across a farm-kitchen's open roof that I knew well as a child: memories of thirty years ago floated back to me, and, thinking of them, I fell asleep.

Morning came, and with it the sounds of loud music close by. I dressed and looked about me, the strains still proceeding and growing louder. Small windows, high up, and a break in the ceiling, admitted light. The lamps burned dimly in the brightness. By the bed stood an immense earthenware basin, very shallow—in fact, saucer-shaped—supported by a low column spreading out at the foot. This was filled, with clear water. A little table carried a dish of the same dull earthenware, in which was some fruit. On the panelled walls hung a few musical instruments and weapons, which I promised myself to examine more closely. I ventured to peep into the adjoining room, which I found to be still smaller. A kind of couch occupied most of the space, but there was also a cabinet, filling one end of the apartment, and full of cupboards, somewhat after the Japanese fashion. Writing materials were set out here, and there was a plain seat of cedar placed conveniently. A large palm was the only other thing that I noticed.

The music was culminating in an intense crash. I half opened my door. Immediately outside Ilex was waiting for me. As we met, the sound became quieter, and gradually stopped. The players vanished down the stone steps.

"I didn't know," said Ilex, "whether you wanted to be disturbed. But I thought you had better be awakened whilst I was still here. Do you mind?"

I explained that I had been awake for sometime, and we passed into one of the largest of the saloons we had traversed the preceding night. In the centre, an island in that immense room, was a small oblong table. Near it stood Brytas and a younger officer.

As they greeted us with the polished salutation, which I did my best to imitate—though I saw the newcomer had some difficulty in keeping from laughing-servants in short kirtles began to move towards us from the sides of the room, where, in pillared recesses, were tables covered with the materials of our morning meal. As we sat down in the seats of citron-wood, Ilex explained that the stranger was, as I understood, a supernumerary official, waiting in readiness to take the place of either of them, if need be.

"And this morning Cydonia, will have the distinguished honour of taking you through the city. You ought especially to thank us, Cydonia, for giving you this privilege! I wanted particularly to go with the stranger myself, and hear what she says of our ways."

"I know well enough," said Cydonia, "that so you would, if you had the chance." At which laughing reply Brytas refused to smile, but said to me at once, as though the matter were of the first importance:

"I hope you will not forget to consult the physician. That is the thing you must do before anything else. The royal physicians will be at the Council; but Athroës, in the next street, is an excellent authority, though too careless of Court favour to be celebrated. Go to Athroës. Then you will know what to do."

I observed that I had some knowledge of medicine, and was a fully qualified practitioner, but they still insisted on the visit. Of course, I knew the value of an independent diagnosis, but I had no idea of placing myself in the hands of an empirical Syrian. Nevertheless, it was a good chance of securing some drugs. Mine had gone the way (whatever way that might have been) of all my other belongings.

Brytas finished breakfast quickly, and departed. Ilex stayed a few moments longer, and left me in charge of Cydonia.

"Wouldn't you like," said that functionary to me, "to change your dress for one of ours? If you will take my advice, it would really be better. We shall get along so much more easily so."

I had no objection, and was accordingly provided with a tunic and outer robe, and duly instructed as to the mode of wearing them. A servant carried them into a latticed balcony, and left me to my own devices for getting them on. The tunic was easy; it was already fastened by clasps at the shoulders, and all that was needed was to slip it over one's head. But the voluminous folds of the robe gave me endless trouble. In the midst of struggling with it, however, I had to stop to admire the lattice-work. Its tracery was admirable, and the invention displayed in varying the forms little short of marvellous. Through the long gallery each square panel of latticed wall was a fresh delight.

I could not manage the robe. When I tried, having got into it, to fasten and arrange it, its folds caught me, and twisted me, and tripped me up, and enveloped me, and altogether took charge of me, in a disconcerting fashion. I got it fastened somehow, the zone tied on somewhere, and the long skirt, by dint of hard effort, raised to my ankles. All that remained was to replace shoes and stockings by sandals.

Cydonia met me with a smile of pleasure. My inextricable folds were speedily reduced to order by a practised hand, and I saw that I was dressed precisely as a Greek of two thousand years ago. It was then that it came back to me with a rush how I had found the stars strayed from their places the night before. *Could* it be true? A small matter distracted my attention; a servant was presenting me a rich, ample mantle of brocaded velvet, which I took instinctively and clasped round my neck. By no means Greek, this; and whilst I tried to reason out the hybrid costume, we passed, by the old tortuous way, to the gateway at the end of the bridge.

The inner gates, of ponderous bronze and oak, were swung open at our approach, and I was in the streets of Alzôna.

Not in the streets, either, for, strictly speaking, we were in a little square, not much bigger than the great gateway, earth-paved, and with a very narrow pathway leading to the right and left. But before us rose a fine flight of steps—rather a street of stairs than a stairway—and on either hand foliage grew, and met over the terraced path. Among the green leaves and the gorgeous gold and purple blossoms moved the people. Not many were to be seen, but most of those who were about were dressed similarly to myself, or else in the short tunic which I found to be the mark of servants—or slaves, as they turned out, in fact, to be more properly called. As we ascended the way, we passed between buildings on either hand, which recalled at the same time Greece and Egypt. More plain and massive, on the whole, than the perfect models of Greek temples which are the crowning delight of the architect, they yet had a character of lightness and freshness which is absent from the grand but overpowering structures of the Nile Valley. Fringed, too, as they were by their curtain of living green, and pulsating with the life of a busy town, they looked pleasant and familiar. We reached the summit of the short ascent, and saw its alignment extend before us as a long narrow street, foliage-arched to its farthest end. We turned sharply to the left, into a much broader street, where the rows of palms and tamerisks gave way to a central bank of green, where aloes, cactus, and caladiums grew. At a house here Cydonia stopped, and would have spoken to a slave who was standing at the doorway, but that the much-recommended doctor, Athroës, appeared in person. Negligent in toilet, tall, loose-limbed, or full of a caustic tolerance, the wiry doctor who now stood before us did not in the least carry out my preconceived ideas of the venerable *hakim*, dead to all but his preposterous science; and, while I wondered, Cydonia had discussed my symptoms with him on the threshold. I knew that since the after- noon I wrote of above, when I slept properly for the first time since my accident, no ill-consequences were to be apprehended from the effects of the camel's ill-conditioned stroke, beyond a certain amount of nervous excitement, which would before long pass off. But it was perfectly clear to me that these people had serious suspicions of my sanity. Their limited knowledge of geography led them to regard all I said about countries of which they knew nothing as raving. It occurred to me, too, that they might suspect that I was feigning madness, in order to gain opportunities of acting as a spy.

And the suspicion was confirmed when the doctor laid a kindly hand on my shoulder and ushered me through a hall, in the marble pavement of which a great tank for goldfish was hollowed out, to a tiny cabinet, where I was motion ed to a seat.

"You have had a bad accident, I think," he began, the brusquerie of the voice studiously kept under.

"Only a camel-kick," I responded, laughing. "A night's rest and pleasant company have put it right."

"Well, I'm glad of that," said Athroës; "these things are very awkward sometimes, especially when you lie for hours exposed to the sun."

"I'm certainly thankful it's no worse," I said. "And I don't see why I should trouble you and take up your time. I am pretty well acquainted with medicine, and I assure you I am quite satisfied with myself."

"My good friend," said the physician, "my time is not of the least account, so long as I am spending it as suits myself. Now, let us talk as one doctor to another. You can hear well? Your eyesight is not affected by the accident?"

"Neither my eyes nor my ears in the least," I returned, "nor my brain."

Athroës did not move a muscle. But it was not for a minute or two that he began, in a lighter strain:

"And so you come from far off, and did not know of Armeria nor any of the countries round about?"

"I come from England—perhaps you know it as Anglia, Britannia?— And I never had heard of Armeria. I regard it as a most remarkable and interesting discovery, which I don't pretend to understand, but which will certainly create the greatest excitement amongst savants at home."

The doctor did not seem overwhelmed at once by the grandeur of the prospect.

"And Zûnaris—what did you think of that?"

"Zûnaris?" I said, with a laugh; "That I can't tell you, never having been there. As I say, I have come from England, and have been travelling in Arabia. I was at present crossing the desert from Nejd to Wady Keirân, when I happened so fortunately to light upon your city."

He put a sheet of parchment and a reed-pen before me.

"Could you draw a rough map of these parts of the world?"

Map-drawing is not my forte. Still, I made out some kind of rough outline, while Athroës' keen eye watched my hand with studiously governed interest.

The work grew on me, and I did not stop until I had not only laid down the Persian Gulf and the Red Sea, but had filled in India and China and a bit of the East Mediterranean to boot.

"Which is water?" said the doctor, and I explained.

"What are these marks—short, straight lines in regular order?"

These were the words which I had printed in the orthodox fashion. They were, it seemed, quite unintelligible, and I had to say where the places were, and how far they extended. A schoolchild could have set a good many of my distances right; but they were enough for my physician.

"Now, you and I are doctors," he said, "and you know that one may have ideas—delusions—without there being anything serious the matter with one. So you'll let me ask you straight—have you any delusions?"

I was going to burst out laughing at their persistent attempt to fasten upon me the absurd consequences of the dense ignorance of the world under which they laboured, when, for the second time that day, there came flashing inexorably on my mind the vision of the unknown constellations.

You have noticed often, I suppose, how the last impressions of the evening have a certain difficulty in making themselves chime in with one's thoughts the next morning. Things we have had pressing upon our mind with insistent force at night, and which we think we shall never let go from our thoughts, occur to us through the forenoon like quite new ideas. We remember with a start our reflections of the night before, but it is two to one that our present mood is so far out of tune with that of the past evening that, important as the matter may be, it will have to demand attention more than once.

So I had, odd as it may seem, practically dismissed the affair of the stars again from my thoughts until that moment.

I started, I suppose. Athroës saw his chance, and, in short, it came out. So did the matter of the river.

Athroës listened attentively and silently. Nothing was said for two or three minutes. Then he got up and said briskly:

"Well, you will stay with us for a few days before pushing on. There is plenty to occupy your attention here—a political crisis, an economic difficulty, a new chrysanthemum, besides our habits and customs, which I dare say are novel to you. In fact, I think you'll treat us shabbily with less than a three months' visit."

At this moment a face peered in at the door. "Is it permitted to come in?" said Cydonia.

"We're coming out," said the doctor. "Stop: take this bottle and drink it tonight. I will send another tomorrow—you are staying at the Warder's Palace? That's right. And go about—see plenty; try the royal receptions. That's a prescription I don't take myself,—but no reason why you shouldn't!"

Cydonia and I passed out into the sunny street, but in my head was darkness and a whirl of unrest.

On the other side of the street was a cool covered well, or rather cistern. The shade of its roof drew me with an irresistible attraction.

"May we look into the well-house?" I said.

Cydonia readily assented, and I soon breathed more freely in its dark, noiseless recesses. The quiet and the magic glassiness of the water gradually made me a little less disturbed. I joined Cydonia, who was stretched on the pavement, idly looking into the liquid mirror, and was at once met with the remonstrance.

"Don't think I am with you! I am sure you have a headache, and I will wait quietly here until it passes off. Or, if you like, we will go in, and you shall lie down."

"I will just ask you to wait a few minutes," I replied. "The coolness here is doing me good. Perhaps the sun was too strong for me. Let me bend down to the water."

In the clear surface I could see my reflection, and I was not displeased with the appearance of the national costume. But it occurred to me that my hair was dreadfully untidy. In fact, the headdress of none of the Alzônans was remarkable for neatness, and nobody had suggested to me what an unkempt appearance I presented. The vague horrors that oppressed my imagination, the uncertainty and unrest, fled before this trivial worry. In its turn it disappeared, and I felt more inclined to take a common sense view of my adventure.

"I took my life in my hands when I plunged into the desert," I said to myself. "Any day I might have been killed or died of fever, or a dozen uncomfortable things might have happened. After all, the worst of it is simply that I can't account for things, and can't satisfy myself as to why that should be so. Mightn't I have plagued myself by the very same worrying every day of my life since I was six years old? Why not simply take things as they are, and put the best face on them? Someday an end will come, somehow. Let me stand the consequences of what I have deliberately done, and make no more fuss about it."

Announcing my readiness to proceed, I rose. We moved up the pathway, which was now considerably more thronged with passersby. At once I noticed a movement in the crowd. Heads were turned, highly-pitched voices sank, long steps contracted. And, looking for the cause of this, I saw coming up the street a handsomely saddled horse, on which sat an oldish man, erect and thin, with sharp, bright eyes, pronounced features, and a commanding mien. Some among the populace took less notice of his presence than the bulk of them appeared to. Of these one was Cydonia, who offered the careless remark:

"That is the Grand Steward—Galêsa. Horrible old wretch! Look at his thin, hooked nose; and if you were to speak to him, most likely he would never look at you! He has no more manners than a centipede!"

Indeed, the distrustful glances which the crowd gave as they eyed him were plain enough proof that Galêsa was not popular, though that evidence was scarcely necessary. The masterful contempt with which he pursued his way, coolly regardless of anyone who for the moment stood in his path, was enough to provoke resentment in any but a very spiritless or a very philosophic mind.

"You would think, from his ascetic face," pursued Cydonia, "that he thought of nothing but State intrigue and policy. Well, as to that, he is wily enough in such matters. But he is as fond of amusing himself as any of us. And his principal amusements are not what I care to tell you about. One, which I think is really particularly characteristic of him, is to call a few of his slaves together, and to insult them elaborately and with every variety of ingenious degradation for two hours at a time. He can't actually ill-use them—at least"—(this was said in a somewhat sarcastic tone)—"not without being very careful, and putting himself in the power of more people than it is quite safe for him to trust. But nobody can object to your having a quiet conversation with your slaves. And that is what he does."

"Surely," I said, "they might find themselves worse off if he had greater power over them?"

"Felix tells me," answered Cydonia, "his chief weaver, that is—that if a slave comes into the household it is not a month before there is another broken and degraded spirit there, or else they die. There are some who seem to be able to laugh at him in their sleeves, but not very many—perhaps—well, I know of one just now, not more."

"Tell me about your slave system," I said.

"Slavery is so little known to the continent I come from, and I rather—excuse my bluntness—I rather feel surprised that it exists in such a civilized place."

Cydonia laughed: "Tonight, please! It is such a large subject, and very complicated. And there is the Council Hall."

Across the road towered a large and handsome edifice, which we entered. Nearly all the houses were of one story—a fact which made the important public building very conspicuous. A long, narrow hall of entry, richly carpeted, led to the meeting place of the Council, which I was told was the civic, and not the royal, authority.

"You catch the Royal Council meeting in public and having a set debate like this!" observed my guide.

"Does yours?"

"Well, no," I was able to answer. "But we have a kind of Council which registers their edicts and talks them over, and sometimes induces them to alter them a little, and very often delays them a good deal."

I hope I was not unjust to the Houses of Parliament.

Cydonia told me that the City Senate was considering the question of offering a crown to a conspicuously successful diplomatist.

"Is the opposition on the score of expense?" I asked, "or is the diplomatist not quite eminent enough?"

"Expense? I don't quite see where expense comes in," said my invaluable Cydonia. "No, there is not, strictly speaking, any opposition to the idea at all. Only everybody with any pretensions to taste feels bound to give an opinion as to whether a crown is quite the proper thing, and what sort of crown it should be."

"Do you know," said I, "how we should arrange such a matter in Britain?"

"No," said Cydonia, turning an innocent and inquiring eye on me. "A respectable townsman would get up and propose that a gilt box be procured at a cost not exceeding fifty-two pounds ten; and the Mayor or the Provost, as the case might be, would go and order it from the jeweller's."

My friend really gasped.

"And do you call that a gift from the city?"

"Certainly. They pay for it."

"And would you like it if I sent you a ring, and did not take anymore trouble about it than to send a note to the jeweller to choose a nice one, and send me the bill? It doesn't strike me that it would be a very graceful present."

"Well, you see," I said, amused, "municipal councillors are not necessarily persons of much taste, and they know if they place the order in the proper quarter they will get an orthodox thing. Goodness knows what they would design if they were left to themselves."

"Oh, but I can scarcely believe you," said Cydonia. "Not persons of much taste! However can you trust them to manage the city if they can't even give an opinion on a little point of art criticism? Besides, I would much rather have a less perfect thing that the givers took a personal interest in than something with which they had nothing to do at all."

"But, then, they pay for it. And really, Cydonia, that is their business,—finding money, and spending it, and trying to save it."

"Not to lead and rule the city, but to finance it, and supply it with what you call gas—is that it?" was my cross-examiner's final summary of the duties of a Mayor and Corporation, after further inquiry.

"Well, yes."

"Then I think we are not quite agreed in our vocabulary. Your City Council is really a kind of public slave, with a recognised power of dipping into its master's purse!"

The accuracy of the comparison was disputable, but we were missing the debate, to which I listened for a while without being much struck by the oratory displayed.

There was a good deal that, was interesting, nevertheless, in the proceedings—notably two stately birds of paradise, which were, for some reason which I was unable to understand from what Cydonia told me, admitted to walk freely about the hall. Then, the arrangement of the place was curious. The Council sat, not round a table, nor in rows, but anyhow, on exquisite curule chairs in a kind of well, sunk four feet or so below the level of the floor, but coming within a few yards of each wall, so that there was a broad strip of standing room for spectators all round. This was skirted at the edge of the well by a metal balustrade, and columns at regular intervals of the latter supported the roof. Wrought bronze lamps swung from the ceiling. The central one was the finest I had ever seen, and, indeed, I never saw it surpassed in Alzôna. On a raised daïs sat the analogue of the. Mayor—a stiff, quiet figure, with a curious fixed expression in the eyes, firm-set lips, and a slight frown. Two pages behind the Mayor carried oblong plates bearing quaint, and probably heraldic, devices. Flowers in considerable profusion were scattered about here and there in tall vases, some of bronze, some of porcelain. The listeners were quiet and well-behaved, though very numerous.

"How is it that so many of you can find time to come and listen to the disputations of the Council?" I inquired.

"What should we do? Isn't it most important that the city should be well governed? Must it not be interesting to see the process of government, so to speak, shaping itself before one?"

"Yes, if it is so, I don't doubt it. But how can you all spare the time? If it were in the evening, and instead of any other entertainment—"

"*Do* forgive me," said Cydonia, "if I seem very stupid. But it does seem such a curious idea to me that entertainment should be reserved for the evening. Do you mean it?"

"It is so in Britain," I said, "as a broad rule, I mean, and for the mass of people. One is fit for nothing but relaxation at night. Through the day, therefore, it is waste of time, which might be given to work."

"Goodness! You must be devoted to work. We, on the contrary, argue that at no time is enjoyment so keen as in the morning. And we think a day is wasted which is spent in unremitting labour till the evening comes—or if not wasted, regrettably monotonous. Let me take you into the theatre of the minstrels, and it may amuse you."

This theatre lay some distance off. We passed down through delightful little gardens, half hidden in *insulce* of houses; open forests (it seemed) of lemon and citron trees; broad expanse of lawn, statue-dotted; terraced avenues of stately dwellings; busy streets of warehouses and bazaars-till we came to a building with a circular or apsidal end. Inside this proved to be lined with concentric rows of stone seats, facing a platform, all open to the sky. People were constantly but noiselessly passing in and out—merchants from their business, artificers from their work, children from their lessons. And all the time the tones of an orchestra of harps echoed through the building.

No applause, no buzz of conversation, no trampling or disturbance. It was the coming from one's household work into a room in the same house, where a good performer is playing. One could have listened for hours, but Cydonia was anxious that I should see the armoury, which was in the neighbourhood. I fancy there might be a reason for this plan, which was not disclosed to me, for as we passed one of the long low houses with latticed casements above and columned porticoes below, bright little figure flew out and greeted my guide with such warmth as to make it evident that a good understanding existed between them. So, at least, I thought.

"Chloris," observed Cydonia, "this is a stranger from a long distance. We are going to the armoury and will you come?"

Chloris drew herself up demurely, and went through the established salutation with the elaborate care of one who has only recently taken upon herself the obligations of adult politeness. Then she turned, and ranged herself beside us *en route* for our destination, which was a great square building—whether enclosing a courtyard or not I could not tell—with a massive tower rising, somewhat retired, at each angle. Inside there was a grand collection of the arms of different nations and periods. They were set out with a good deal of taste, and neither labelled nor huddled together. The backgrounds were carefully chosen to produce the best effect, and from symbols which were employed Cydonia was able to tell me the place where each weapon came from. One cannot wander about the world much without acquiring a nice discrimination in daggers, and the array, so well displayed, of steel and bronze completely took up my attention, and would. have satisfied a Kashmiri or a Nepâlese. Cydonia rather neglected me, and preferred to listen, with a sardonic smile now and then, to Chloris's conversation. Judging from her manner, it was not very profound.

We had hardly traversed three rooms, divided by lofty screens of pierced ebony, hung with heavy curtains, when Cydonia decided that it must be time for a meal, dismissed Chloris, who fluttered off like a pigeon (contentedly discussing a peach), and took me to what I suppose we should call a café, for we had wandered a good distance from the Warder's Palace. It was a very pleasant room, open back and front to the street and a green, shady grove. From these it was separated by vine-entwisted pillars. Its only decoration was its extremely handsome roof; plain polished tables and seats, its only furniture.

Again I was struck by the beauty of the people who sat near. Scarcely a rough-looking face appeared amongst them, though there was certainly a great range in the degree of good looks with which they were endowed. Our light meal consisted of dates and other fruits, eaten with rice, and of some of the varied mixtures of cereals and conserves of which the Alzônans, as I afterwards found, are exceedingly fond. Small cakes flavoured with almond-paste and spices ended the meal, with which we drank the diluted juice of fruit, which they call *vinon*, being, as appears, altogether ignorant of wine. (They are acquainted with alcohol as a chemical, but seem to be ignorant of its toxic qualities; nor are any of the neighbouring tribes better informed, but are in the same state of blessed or unblessed ignorance—as you like to put it.)

"Now," said Cydonia, "we will go and rest a little in the Lotus-Garden."

Near the café an abrupt hill rose. It formed no obstacle to the spread of buildings, which clustered up its side in a steep street, fringed vi.th trees, and quite impassable for anything but passengers on foot or mules; but very picturesque, for all that, to look at, in its irregular gradients. Passing by the foot of it, we reached, through a dark grey stone archway, a quiet, dreamy spot, where ponds, covered with white and pink blossoms, stretched between grassy plots planted with patches of low trees. A terrace rose along the foot of the wall that bounded the place on one side, but Cydonia stopped at the nearest clump of trees, and settled comfortably in their shadow, inviting me to do the same. A clear channel ran past our feet, watching the fish in which I fell half asleep.

I was aroused by the pealing of a great gong, which is a sound I have an extreme dislike to. The noise of a gathering crowd came faintly to our ears.

"Oh, it is nothing. Just a notice that a criminal is going to be led round the city, or beaten, or some such cheerful thing!"

"That's the second time," I said instructively, "that your customs have given me a shock today. We have long since given up displaying criminals to the public."

Cydonia did not answer, but played with a myrtle leaf.

"Don't you find it does more harm than good?"

Thus directly appealed to, my guide answered discreetly, *more Scottico*: "In what way?"

"We found," I said, "that the public sympathy with the prisoner was dangerously inflamed, or else that, in the rarer cases in which public opinion took sides against him it was difficult to protect him from the crowd. In either case there is considerable danger of disturbance."

"You don't give your countryfolk a very good character," said Cydonia. "Why they should sympathise with crime, or allow their dislikes to run into violence, you know better than I do. But there is no fear of that here, and perhaps your population may be more reasonable nowadays, as you say it is sometime since the change was made. I can't myself understand how there can be any good in an administration of the criminal law in such a way that the people see nothing of it."

"It is true," I said, "that our laws were, and in theory still are, in many respects extremely harsh, and that popular opinion is inclined, in general, to side against the authorities. And you are right in supposing the dangers of riots to be less now than they were fifty years ago. But we move slowly, and when we have once got a reform introduced we are not quick to reform it. Besides, the sensibilities of the people would be shocked by the parade of criminal justice."

"You like to keep it nicely hidden, and pretend it isn't there? It isn't the best way, do you think, to guarantee its being pure? Nevermind; I dare say if I came to your country I should see you were right. But our way does best for us."

"Are there any courts sitting at this moment?" I asked. "If so, would it be a good way of spending the day to look in—that is, if we may?"

"Oh, we did away with courts a thousand years ago—to be precise, eight hundred and fifty. The Urasites and the Kytônians have courts—none of them carry out the criminal law as you say you do, though-but our arrondissement system is so perfect that we arc enabled to dispense with them. What is the function of a court but to sift facts? And how can you judge conflicting versions of facts without knowing intimately the character of the people who assert them? We in Alzôna—we often laugh at Uras and Kytôna, where witnesses are interrogated in open court or by an examining judge. In the one case the got-up stories they repeat! The desperate bullyings they endure, in order to confuse them! In the other what unfair fencing between the judicial examiner and the helpless defendant! And always the best case will be that put forward by the cleverest scamp. But in Alzôna the heads of the arrondissement, who know the parties intimately, are judges of the facts, and they declare them quite informally, without any ceremony."

"That is exactly what our laws try to avoid," I said. "The less an English judge or jury knows of the parties to a case, the better."

"It is certainly better to know nothing than to know a little," said Cydonia. "A little knowledge may only prejudice you."

"And then," I pursued, "what security is there for the honour and uprightness of the arrondissement heads—nomarchs do you call them? May they not gratify private revenge; levy blackmail—all that kind of thing?"

"They would be removed long before they had the chance," was the reassuring answer. "And, then, their administration is being constantly watched by the heads of larger districts, who know them as well and as intimately as they themselves know the families of their own little sections. Besides, it is always possible to appeal."

"And who is at the head of all this hierarchy? A Prefect, Chief Justiciary, Prætor, Dicast?"

"The queen!"

As we left the Lotus-Garden we passed a building whose great open door disclosed a lofty, barn-like chamber of very large extent, in and out of which people were passing, and from whose roof hung specimens of handsome silks and woven fabrics. Evidently it was a kind of native bazaar, and I expressed a wish to go in.

It was very dark inside in comparison with the brilliant sunshine. As one's eyes got accustomed to the half-light, the scene was lively and interesting. I thought at first that the bazaar consisted of several shops, but I learnt that all the commercial establishments were on a large scale in Alzôna and that the whole of this was one concern. There did not seem to be much of the Oriental procedure of bargaining: customers got what they wanted, and paid for it, much as they do (upon occasion) in the West. The goods were lovely, and the room itself handsomely panelled, with a moulded cornice, and an arched and timbered roof, in the dim haze of which were a few small windows. There were comfortable seats, too. People came in and rested for a few minutes, and went out again, without anyone seeming to think it unusual; so my impecunious condition did not trouble me, and I stayed with great enjoyment for a long time. Then I begged Cydonia to take me to other bazaars. We visited in quick succession shops for fruit, for jewels—carefully guarded, these—for porcelain, for metalwork, for confectionery, until we were tired and glad to turn our steps homeward.

"I don't see any shop for the sale of flesh," I remarked.

"My good friend, we are not cannibals! You surely don't expect to see us grinding each other's bones and sucking each other's blood?"

"Do you not eat animals' flesh, then?"

Cydonia made a grimace, the more deliciously ludicrous as it was entirely spasmodic.

"Surely you don't think us so desperately uncivilised as all that! I dare say we are behindhand in many ways—even the Paranlians are always telling us that—and very likely our customs here are rather antiquated.

I don't dispute it. And the country you come from, though I had never heard of it, may be miles ahead of us. Still, we are not quite savages!"

My apologies were amply forthcoming, and smoothed the ruffled waters. Certainly, I said, I would not dream of calling them savages. What I had seen that day was quite enough to convince me of their refinement and civilisation. But it seemed to me so natural a thing to consume the flesh of animals that I never dreamt of causing offence. The apology was accepted in good part.

"Foreign nations have strange customs," said Cydonia, "and you get used to most things. Are your young children fond of flesh? And do you eat it raw?"

But here another matter struck me, and I asked to have it explained.

"You have shown me no temples," I declared. "Everywhere in Europe the temples are the first things, generally, that are worth showing to a stranger—especially the old ones. In London—which is our capital city—they would take one to see St. Paul's and Westminster, or in Paris to Notre Dame."

As I brought up the subject, I expected to gather some information as to the matter of the Alzônan religion, which would help greatly to settle their ethnical relationships; for I still clung to the vanishing hope that, in spite of so much that was unintelligible, I might be able to piece Armeria in with the rest of the earth.

"Temples? What is the use of them?" said Cydonia.

"Public worship," I suggested.

"Your country is certainly strange," was the reply. "I cannot get used to it at all. You will not mind my saying so? Say what you like about us, you know! But you are so susceptible that it shocks you to parade criminals in public, whilst at the same time you do not shrink from parading in concert your deepest spiritual emotions. Am I right about this, or have I not understood?"

"Partly right," I said, "but our services are at set times and in set terms—or at least in conventional phraseology—and participation in them is largely a matter of form."

Cydonia looked thoughtful. "I am not sure that I would be able to get on in your cities," was the next comment. "It must be so difficult to know how to behave—we think so differently."

"I am sure you would get on very well indeed," I said heartily, for the lithe, amiable figure beside me could not have been disliked or thought disagreeable in any society worthy the name. And I began to talk about English cities and cathedrals, and afternoon teas, and Deans, and express trains, and telephones, to all of which items of interest my friend listened attentively. We were now rapidly making our way home, and I began to recognise some of the sparse, tall buildings as landmarks that I had noted in the morning.

A little distance off, as we neared the gates, lay an extensive building, which had rather the appearance of a fortress, but which Cydonia informed me was the Royal Palace. At last we reached the entrance to my temporary abode.

I felt as if I had lived years since the previous night.

Inexpressibly pleasant it was to have Ilex rush to meet us and lead me to my quarters, with an unaffected delight at having a visitor to entertain. I am given to analysing my sensations, and I satisfied myself, as I bathed my face in the cool, deep water, that the pleasure arose from Ilex being connected with the life from which I had been so strangely cut off.

It did not occur to me, that so was Brytas.

III

THE PALACE

In the morning I seriously expostulated with Ilex on the score of the lavish hospitality of which I was the object. My idea had been to raise the trifling sums necessary for simple subsistence, together with enough to hire a guide and a camel or two, by treating cases of ophthalmia and other ailments which yield to European prescriptions after defying the local practitioners. But there did not seem much prospect of putting this scheme into effect. Meanwhile I was handsomely lodged and sumptuously entertained at no cost to myself.

"You are not tired of us?" said Ilex.

And when I said I was not, a brilliant smile made me feel that I could not in fairness pursue the subject.

"My turn on guard ends today," went on my companion, "and I want to take you to the palace tomorrow myself. The queen is away; still, there will be people there you may care to see."

"Is the palace itself handsome—finer than this?"

"Oh, decidedly finer. Yes, this is plain, rather. You notice there is a little emptiness about these rooms. The Royal Palace is more 'lived in.'"

"Athroës told me yesterday," I said, "that I should find a political crisis in progress. Is it an easy one to understand, and has it an admitted existence?"

"Well"—Ilex looked rather uncomfortable—"Brytas can tell you more about that than I."

Brytas muttered something about there being really nothing of any consequence in the matter. Some people fancied the general safety was in danger if three ambassadors were seen talking together. There were always rumours, if one listened—and so forth, giving me the strong impression that something of a distinctly unpleasant character was within the range of practical politics.

I saw it was useless to follow up the matter, and when I was left alone with Cydonia (who was busily engaged in drawing up a kind of official report), I contented myself with watching the process, until I had some notion of the characters used. The writing was syllabic— that is, the letters represented syllables, like those of the Japanese. As

Cydonia wrote and read the report at the same time, I began to acquire a working knowledge of the hieroglyphics. One great help in making oneself understood was the stately, unhurried rate at which everyone spoke, delivering the sonorous syllables *ore rotundo*. Otherwise it would not have been easy. The final *m*, for instance, was universally replaced by *n*; *g* was thickened into a harsh guttural like the Gaelic *loch*. The writing was purely phonetic; every accented syllable was indicated, and every sliding vowel accurately expressed. Occasionally the short vowels were so very short that I have thought it best to omit them in writing proper names.

When I had copied a good many words, I lay back in a chair to study them.

After a while Cydonia, tired of writing, turned from the table, gave a comfortable stretch, and looked hard with both eyes at nothing.

"If you have a minute to spare," I hinted, "I should be very glad to see the library—if there is such a thing about, that is!"

"By all means. Not a very big one. Come and look!"

We made our way to a room near the top of the building. Outside the warm sun flooded a little stone court with its brightness. Cydonia brought me a seat, and found a shaded corner for it. Then we went into the library and hunted amongst rolls of parchment for something interesting, exactly as if one had been at a seaside resort, and in that want of mental sustenance which is at once sudden and chronic in such circumstances.

"I don't like to keep you," I said.

"Well, I must go," said Cydonia. "Try these."

I took the four or five lacquered boxes. In each of them lay a set of rolls ready for use. I mounted to my seat, and from it I found that I overlooked the battlements.

There foamed and glittered the tantalising river, so real, so mysterious. I counted the ripples on it, as though it might be possible to detect that they were elaborate make-believes. Beyond it, the wide plain and its belt of verdure. Just visible over the trees, with a start was recognised the Index Maxima. A small band of wayfarers was proceeding across the foreground towards the forest. I turned my eyes away again, and attacked the books.

It was not very easy to read them. During the morning they served mainly as exercises for translation. But later in the day I began to make headway with a volume of geography. It was in the middle that I began it, but I soon saw that it was full, clear, and careful. And I had to recognise that for thousands of miles this extraordinary system of States extended. The only alternative was that the hugest delusion was somehow being played upon me, for no purpose whatever that it was possible to imagine. I took refuge from all perplexities in another talk with Cydonia, who came up with a bunch of grapes for a rest.

"You spoke yesterday about religion," I said. "What divinity do you worship?"

"The Eternal cannot be mentioned. It is one, and it is many. But generally the people here recognise it under twelve forms—Athené and Artemis and—shall I go through the other ten?"

The system of mythology which was explained to me was very curious. Zeus had evidently dropped out of worship altogether; so had Poseidon, and Hephrestus, and Apollo. Dionysos had become a kind of subordinate demi-god, and had entirely lost—or, perhaps, had never been invested with-the attribute of patronage of the bowl. Hêrê had become identified with one of her minor at tributes, and figured in an equally subordinate capacity. It was very strange to hear Cydonia talk; so modern a personage in many respects, and yet absolutely believing in Athene as a living and real power. Not only that, but the innocent, artless stories of the gods on earth were related to me with a certain respect.

"And do you really believe Artemis did that?" I would say.

"She might! It is not my business to inquire. It was a beautiful thing to do; therefore, as she embodies every beauty, she did it."

"But that is to ignore space and time."

"What have space and time in common with morals?"

"What have morals in common with beauty?"

"Everything. When Ilex looks most beautiful—which is when you come into the room—has sweetness nothing to do with it?"

"I think," I said, "Cydonia, your work will be suffering."

The hint was taken, and I was left alone.

I did not wish my casual stay in Armeria to be the occasion of a complication of this kind.

Until nearly the time for the evening meal I read. Cydonia came for me, bearing no malice, and as the faint flames flickered on the silver chains of the tall, thin candelabra, with a fragrant smell of spices burning in the oil, I learnt that only Brytas would be our companion that evening, Ilex having to wait on an important errand, which I could see gave Brytas some uneasiness.

The meal was a quiet one; and afterwards we had music. Brytas seemed unable to do anything but wander from one tune to another, without five minutes' rest. Cydonia and I were restless, too, except when the either was playing; and we did not talk, except for snatches of comment on the airs. We called in a servant who played remarkably well on the hautbois. But none of us could listen to it. Brytas began to play again, and kept us quiet, until, in the abrupt way which was usual, the music stopped, which we took as a signal to seek our own apartments.

At breakfast Ilex (evidently just come in) and Brytas were both in radiant spirits. No sooner was it over, than the former announced that the expedition to the palace would take place at once. For a second time I traversed those fresh, wonderful streets. A striking feature in the topography of the place was the constant occurrence of broad, clear canals, crossed by innumerable bridges of varying construction, and skirted by gardens; or by the waterfronts of buildings, marble or dark grey stone, as the case might be, but always massive and dignified. Past one of these waterways our road led to the palace.

As we approached it, the vast extent of it grew on one. A good part of it consisted of one story only; but, then, the proportions were so magnificent that it seemed rather a cluster of halls and temples than a mere dwelling. Partly these components of the pile were isolated, partly joined side by side, and partly connected by colonnades, towers, and lower ranges of buildings. The fort-like mass which I had before seen we passed by; farther on the grey stone changed to marble, and a rather heavy portico of colossal size appeared. At the back was a panelled wall of cedar. In its upper part the panels were profusely carved and pierced, and in the lower portion were five lofty entrances, the doors open, and guarded by silent white-robed figures. Ilex walked in, without ceremony, by the central portal. We found ourselves in a large square hall, dimly illuminated, and traversed by a corridor at the back, while a staircase of unpolished wood led, in ample breadth, up one side.

Ilex turned to the right, and entered a comparatively small room, saying:

"I will leave you here while I get my official work done. It will not take many minutes, and in the meantime—"

A page had followed us in, and received instructions to bring Opanthë, who, Ilex assured me, was in the intimate *entourage* of the queen, and would do the honours of the palace. In a moment, almost, and altogether before I had time to inspect as I should have liked to do the matchless ebony carving with which the walls were enriched, or the curiously wrought metal caskets, with openwork sides, standing in the room, a door opened—the partitions seemed everywhere to be full of doors, leading one could not tell where—and there came in the most beautiful girl I had ever seen. Clad in robes of white silk, fair and regal, she might have been herself the queen of the country. Her beauty did not lie in her expression, which was impassive, but in the uncommon regularity of her features and in her perfect carriage. To complete the picture, she was not very tall, and far from thin. Certainly I had seen no one in English ballrooms who would, on the whole, have been pronounced her equal in the conventional elements of beauty.

She advanced towards me, unaffectedly enough.

"Ilex says you are a stranger here, and to be looked after. Well, I'm very glad it has fallen to me to meet you the first in the palace. Now, what can I show you? Do you like to see jewellery, or statesmen, or architecture?"

"I almost lose myself," I said. "This place is so enormous and so complicated that I can't yet grasp the ground-plan of it, nor understand quite who occupy it."

She tried to explain, but had not proceeded very far when she caught sight of someone passing in the outer hall, and, with a word of apology, got up, and returned in the company of the Grand Steward, Galêsa.

This was an unexpected honour, which I had not bargained for. Galêsa's cold, contemptuous eyes glanced with something of haughty suspicion round the apartment. Opanthë told him who I was, and I was entirely overwhelmed by the polite grin with which he unexpectedly favoured me. He sat on the divan by us, and showed a flattering interest in my adventures and experiences, over which I took care to throw a discreet veil of mystery, not wishing to be generally accepted as a more or less insane wanderer.

But we had not got very far when Ilex returned, and Galêsa thereupon strode out, brushing down an ivory toy pagoda on the way, and proceeding without taking the least notice.

But Ilex did not remain with us. It was explained that a meeting of officials had been hurriedly arranged, and would make us stay sometime longer than we had expected. Meanwhile Opanthë offered to show me parts of the palace. She called to accompany us two of her subordinates, among whom I recognised with pleasure my acquaintance Chloris.

Opanthë shot a sudden gleam from her impassive eye as she noted that Chloris was known to me. The latter, however, welcomed me with cordial freedom, and by no means so stiffly as on our first introduction. I began to feel at home in the vast series of saloons and galleries, enriched with carving and glowing with colour, through whose mazes I was led: halls where stately banners hung over the thrones of the chief of the realm; treasuries of beautiful and rare objects; chambers furnished with silks and tapestry; rooms of state, worthy of a queen, in their ample breadth and magnificent walls and ceilings; arcaded galleries and carved pillars; and everywhere the royal cognisance of a golden sphinx, uniting the whole into compact loveliness. There were rooms for the principal personages among the queen's relations, for the officers of state, and for the band of attendants who here, as elsewhere, seemed to be indispensable satellites of royalty, from the menials to the minstrels and Court ladies.

Among them was numbered Chloris, and I asked her how it, vas that she was not at the palace when Cydonia and I had met her.

"I am a good deal at home," she explained. "Opanthë and I have a suite of rooms here—you must come and see them—and Etela: she has just been introduced to you, you know—the tall girl in green. But I find it's dull sometimes, and I like to get back and see my little cats, and feed my crocodile, and talk to the people at home. To tell you the truth, they are rather a stupid lot here! They think so much about dress, and politics, and promotion, I get tired of them."

A funny combination, I thought—dress, and politics, and Court gossip—and not inconceivably a fatiguing one.

"Besides," pursued Chloris, "Etela is so very—well, feeble; and as for Opanthë, she is no good to me. Then the rest, living apart from us as they do—you see, they have their own private interests, which makes one rather isolated. Of course, I am constantly meeting them; but it is different when one's own particular rooms are all together, isn't it? We three are just a little bit of a clique apart. Very nice if *we* were all charming. None of us are!"

Opanthë, with the dignitary who accompanied her, stopped, and slowly turned towards us.

"If you are not tired," she said, "I will take you across to the Slave Emporium. It is part of the palace, because the distribution of slaves is so vital a matter to the kingdom's interests."

This proposal excited Chloris immensely. Plainly it was not an everyday opportunity.

"Oh, Opanthë! Are we really going to see that? Think of it! I *am* in luck's way! May I—"

But she broke off, as Opanthë led on without vouchsafing any attention to her outburst. She consoled herself by explaining to me that the barbarian children destined to become slaves were brought, on attaining a certain age, to the palace, where they were lodged for a longer or shorter time, until disposed of to suitable applicants. It all seemed a very strange system. Chloris declared that no price was paid for the slaves; and yet it seemed that the owners had more or less power of selection. But a rather remarkable thing was that, during their custody at the palace, no one except their immediate guardians and intending allottees was admitted to see them. There was no actual bar, but it was considered improper, and no facilities for it were given.

It was, in fact, for a palace official to visit the slave quarters much as it would be for a Belgravian lady to invade the kitchen. Consequently, Chloris, with a youthful love of mysteries, was full of lively anticipation.

As Opanthë unlocked a heavy old timbered door, the girl held her breath with suppressed interest, and positively shook. But to me, who had no associations of mysterious concealment connected with the place, it was not impressive, however interesting. A tall and venerable person wearing a scarlet headdress came up to us at once, and demanded what we wanted.

"This lady is a foreigner, and the queen wishes her to inspect all that there is of interest in the palace," answered Opanthë. "In her country, Zenoris, there are no slaves; and, naturally, this is of the greatest importance for her to see, that she may not go home with wrong impressions about us. I hope you have everything in very good condition."

"It's not usual for anyone to come here unless her majesty herself is with them," remarked the custodian. "But if your ladyship assures me that all is in order, of course I can't say anything."

"You may be quite easy," said Opanthë carelessly and haughtily.

We had crossed a wide terraced garden, and traversed a stone corridor to get to the place where we now were, which was a very quiet grassy enclosure, with high walls behind us, and a low building in front, at the side of which was an orchard. Nobody but two or three of the scarlet-capped officials was visible: they were seemingly pottering about, attending in a desultory fashion to the flowers. We had to enter the building to see the slaves. Apparently, no restriction was put upon them or their movements. Chloris viewed them and their abode with an interest which she did not disguise, and I began to consider that the sentiment which excluded palace officials from the precincts was not misplaced. What pleased me was the sympathetic and kindly way in which Opanthë moved amongst those unfortunate creatures. As I watched her, it seemed like a vision of Eurydice in Hades. as I had seen it on the stage in Glück's *Orpheus*. And they seemed to appreciate and reciprocate her cordiality towards them. The faces of most of them grew brighter at her approach, as though some spell united them in a real and an unequal friendship. Otherwise it was a melancholy spectacle. Forty human beings, of like capacities with ourselves, were here secluded in readiness to be told off to a life of servitude and contempt. The vaulted stone chamber which was their principal room, spacious and lofty as it was, seemed like a prison to me; and their general attitude was, so far as one could make out, one of dull apathy. There were no jokes, no songs, no knots of lively gossipers. One could not say that they appeared unhappy or sunk in despondent wretchedness. But there seemed to be a depressed spiritlessness about them, whether due to the barrack-like system of their education or to the uncertainty of their future portion I could not judge. Perhaps it might be owing to both causes. So far as I could see they were well treated. But I thought Etela, who accompanied us, betrayed some uneasiness when I began to talk to some of them, so I desisted.

From the central hall great arches in the stone wall led on each side to smaller rooms, and at the farther end came a kitchen. Crossing this, we reached a chamber formed by the double gates of the street entrance. The porters admitted us through the inner pair, and carefully locked them before opening the outer ones. Opanthë then took me into a handsome set of rooms opening off this chamber, which she observed were used for the purpose of giving applicants for slaves an opportunity of seeing those available for disposal. Passing out into the free air of the street, we entered the palace by a small marble doorway and a little flight of stairs, and found ourselves, after some careful piloting through the intricacies of the buildings, in the hall I originally entered.

We went into a different reception room, where a dozen or so of the palace ladies were found. The usual quaint and polite greetings were gone through; coffee, sweets, and so on—though it was not midday— were sent for; and I was soon on excellent terms with the unsophisticated, pleasant company, who hardly seemed to me to deserve the strictures of Chloris. Perhaps I had expected them to be particularly vapid and narrow-minded, and was unprepared for the fresh candour which they certainly showed me. They neither quitted their own occupations in embarrassed silence nor ignored the presence of a visitor, but went on naturally with their work or talk, leaving it to those nearest me to do what entertaining was necessary.

As I sat on a low seat beside Opanthë, I talked to her and a fair, low-voiced friend of hers, whilst in reality my attention was taken up by a little group near us. The centre of this was a plain-looking cousin of the queen's (as I afterwards found)—the Princess Iôtris—whose grey cloth dress contrasted oddly with the delicate shimmering robes of most of the others.

It was long weeks—and it seemed long years—since I had heard the sound of irrepressible, civilised laughter, and the spontaneous explosions of merriment which reached me from the little group attracted my attention in spite of myself.

It was not that she said anything so very amusing, but her playful and friendly manner infused a spirit of readiness to be amused into her hearer, of which they took full advantage. She did not laugh much herself, though she smiled continually. To say that she was the centre of the group was to use an Irishism, for she actually stood, erect and firmly set, facing her companions, and rallying them in turn, while they retorted in kind.

"My friend Valthis, it is no earthly use trying to persuade me; you cannot get a genuine work of art painted nowadays—not like Lychthis, or Vitra, or Œnoné!"

"It may be no earthly use my trying to persuade you; but you can get as good artists, nevertheless—plenty of them!"

"Plenty! Well, we *are* well off! Did Lychthis, and Vitra, and Œnoné all live at the same time?"

"Surely," said another voice, "Thekla is worth comparing with any of them?"

"Ah! Thekla!" answered the Princess. "But we can't go to Thekla and say—'Paint me a picture—here are five hundred crowns.'"

The whole assembly burst into tumultuous laughter. But the lady addressed as Valthis took up the thread of the argument again.

"Could you have said that to Œnoné?"

"No, because fifty crowns would have been enough for her, in her days. Five hundred crowns for a picture would have seemed frantic. She would simply have laughed at you as a lunatic," responded the Princess quickly.

"But I always understood," went on Valthis, "that Œnoné worked for the Governor of Thorosa, and refused to do anything for anybody else."

"Your historical knowledge is correct, my child. But my point is, that one couldn't engage an Œnoné now, on those or any terms, even if one were Governor of Thorosa."

"And a good thing too," struck in a fourth. "Free trade in Art! That's my idea. Why should an artist be monopolised by one respectable Governor?"

"See what your idea has brought us to," observed the Princess. "Not an artist left in the place! Except Thekla, and that's as good as nobody. For she will only paint to please herself."

"Don't say 'not an artist,'" remonstrated a young person, who was, in the calm obscurity of the floor, at that moment engaged in washing in some colour into a parchment scroll. "I'll take the five hundred crowns—or the fifty—with pleasure And Irmathé, you're wrong if you implied that the Governor who employed Œnoné was respectable. He wasn't—not if raiding your neighbours is improper."

"I accept the correction. And I presume it is the purple of Cassius that you put into your painting that brings the price up?"

To cheap remarks of this nature the artist soul pays no attention— and the painter simply addressed some candid and helpful remarks to her brush which had got stiff.

"When a painter worked for a patron —" commenced the Princess instructively.

"The Lady Thekla is present," was announced by a herald. I looked up curiously. The Princess bit her lip, her eyes twinkling. The girl who was painting rolled up her parchment coolly and silently.

Thekla was small and short, and bent forward. She had large, restless eyes, that roamed incessantly from one point to another, and, for the rest, had pale, thin features—almost European-looking. Her movements suggested the rapid dives of a waterbird from sedge to sedge. She was evidently a frequent visitor, if not a member of the palace company, for no formal salutations were given. The Princess engaged her in conversation, and good-naturedly introduced her to me after some minutes.

"I understand you are a great painter," I said to her, and I was half sorry. Her face flushed, her fingers crushed each other, and she coughed, and scarcely could speak.

"Some people like my things. I never can do my best—it is very difficult." Her tone was abjectly apologetic. Had I made a frightful mistake? I remembered, with a gust of annoyance, the outburst of laughter with which Thekla's name had just been greeted. Was all they had said sarcastic, perhaps?

It was safest to go on. Evidently she took herself seriously.

"Do you paint the figure or landscape?" I asked.

Thekla recovered herself a little.

"Oh, nobody eyer paints the figure," she explained. "You can only, at the best, make a kind of caricature of it. Yes, I paint scenery and trees, and I am very fond of painting water. People say I can paint water—I don't know, myself I But I think there is nothing so lovely as splashing streams, coming down between green leaves—all kinds of green leaves! I like to fix them. At least, I would if I could. Do you care for such things? If you do, I will show you what I mean."

She opened a case that was by her side, and showed me a coloured drawing. I do not pretend to have the least critical taste in Art, but this struck me as Japanese work has often struck me, though it was more elaborate and not so dashing as Japanese paintings. It had a vividness and directness which seem absent from our Western galleries—a pith and point which evidenced a thorough love for and sympathy with Nature. Every crystal drop seemed to quiver with life.

She saw I was pleased, and let me see another.

It was a brown, arid mountainside. The jagged peak rose clear and distinct into the blue sky, without a cloud or a waft of mist. But the torrent's source was here, and its trickling stream was gathering out of the marshy pools, its infant course marked by the change in the character of the vegetation. There was not a solitary bird or any living creature in the landscape. Its solemn beauty and its suggestiveness of the silent forces at the root of things were produced by the simplest means, though the dexterity of hand with which the painting was done was remarkable. I am not an art critic. Nothing that pleased me more had ever come to my notice, nevertheless.

I admired it duly, to Thekla's evident relief. I should have thought her modesty affected, only that it would, in that case, have been so violently overdone as to be ridiculous.

"Come to my house the day after tomorrow," she said. "You will meet better painters than I, a great deal, there."

People were rising, and Opanthë invited me warmly to accompany the party to the midday meal.

"Now that Thekla is here," she said, "we will have a regular feast. Come on, both of you!"

Thekla and I got separated as we entered the banqueting hall. There were many more officials of various kinds there, but the younger artist—

she of the floor—took me under her wing, and made me sit beside her. At a cross-table, slightly raised, sat the Princess Iôtris, among a galaxy of other ladies of the blood-royal and high officials,—most of them much more splendidly costumed; many not so pleasant-looking. Between the two long tables the service was carried on. Opposite the daïs a high platform served as a vantage-ground for a band of harps and clarinets. My neighbour was a caustic conversationalist, and Opanthë was not far away.

"Will Ilex be able to find me if the meeting should break up now?" I asked the latter. She satisfied me on this point, and turned to speak to the nearest person to her on the daïs. To my vexation, it was the Grand Steward, Galêsa, and between him and Opanthë sat two sullen-browed men, who were evidently well acquainted with him.

"Kisêna," said one of them to my artist friend, "have you washed the colour off your face yet?" He did not wait for a reply, and received none, but guffawed insolently. I felt intensely uncomfortable. Kisêna did not in the least. She coolly helped herself to salt, and asked me in a perfectly unmoved voice what I thought of the state of public affairs.

"I have arrived so recently," I said, "I know nothing about them."

"Oh!" said Kisêna. "Then I must tell you things are pretty critical."

"In what way?"

"Mainly with regard to Uras. The long and short of it is they want a complaisant monarch here, who will do as they tell her. Beatrice, of course, won't, and there are incessant quarrels. They haven't much hope of overcoming us, but they do flatter themselves they can change the dynasty."

"Ah!" I said, "and who is their candidate?"

Here I caught sight of Opanthë's face, as a servant lifted away a huge silver drinking bowl from between us. The eager attention which she seemed to be giving to our commonplace conversation half frightened me. She was listening with tense muscles and strained eyes. I pretended not to see her, and the next time I looked she had resumed her attitude of impassive hauteur.

Kisêna did not know of any definite person being suggested as the Urassic candidate for the crown. But as we left the hall, she proceeded to say in a lower voice that the most serious feature of the situation was that strange ferments seemed to be developing among the slaves—a thing unheard of, as she explained to me, in that or any other country.

I told her I was surprised.

"Are the slaves so reconciled to their lot," I said, "as never to make an attempt for freedom?"

"People have to be pretty wretched," she answered, "before they revolt. And I do not think our slaves are badly treated, nor those of Cranthé, or Agdalis, or Kytôna. Naturally, they have their grievances."

Suddenly the columned portico where we stood grew warmer and brighter. Ilex was at my side, and carried me off to a pretty isolated house, not many streets away, where the fortunate owner had succeeded in producing a chrysanthemum of what I was told was an entirely new tint. The plant which had so obligingly taken the trouble to allow itself to come into existence was enthroned like an imperial favourite among a wilderness of mosses and ferns, a high folding screen forming a background. Open house seemed to be kept for its admiring worshippers, and the scene was laughably like some odd shrine. resorted to by devotee, whose hushed enthusiasm might show itself only in murmured exclamation of ecstasy. The smoking incense, whose vapour rose from jars set before the screen, completed the illusion. We did not stay long here. Ilex returned with me to the Warder' Palace, and I found myself once more in the little room where my first meal in Armeria had been taken. It brought back a flood of recollections, and seemed to throw me back again to my first evening in the city. The old restless desire returned to know what was the real explanation of the extraordinary experience which had befallen me.

Brytas and Ilex did their utmost to rouse me from the uncomfortable state which they could see I was in. The latter talked of the suite of rooms that was being prepared for me at the family residence, three miles away, and was very anxious that I should accept the offer of it.

"Much pleasanter than having you here! Besides, I have made all the arrangements, and we expect you."

"I can't choose!" I said. "I am endlessly indebted to you, however it is settled. And I must say it would be very interesting to me, as a foreigner, to be admitted to a private house here. Still, it does seem an infliction on your family."

"If you can't invite a stranger there, what is a house good for?" sagely reflected my host.

"May I ask who compose your household?" I inquired, rather languidly, and by way of being civil, for at the moment I felt, in spite of all the kindness I received, as dull as the proverbial ditchwater—in cloudy weather, you may add.

"Well, there is Parisôn—"

"Is that a lady?"

"Yes!—Cat, did you think?"

"No; but I thought it might have been a man's name."

"So it is. Where is the difference? I am afraid I don't quite make myself understood—"

This comes, I said to myself, of thinking one knows a language when one hasn't been taught it properly. Evidently *kyné* and *anra* both mean "person" in this tongue. I tried another line.

"It is my ignorance of the language that is at fault," I remarked. "I don't know the right pair of words. Do you say *femina* and *vir*? Or *mulier*, *homo*?"

"*Homo* is a word we have," interposed Brytas. "It is the same thing as *kynë* or *anra*."

"Not *femina— nias—vir—wir—bir—mir*?"

They looked blank.

"No, none of them. *Mara*—'the sea' (*chals*)—that can't be what you mean?"

"You said *bir*," said Ilex. "We have *persona*—that can't be it, can it?"

Philology could not go that length.

"How *do* you distinguish," I observed, in despair, "between the people who—who fight and wear whiskers and moustaches?"

But it suddenly occurred to me that none of them did wear them.

My companions, evidently thinking I had got beyond my depth in some recondite speculation, charitably—as people will do in such circumstances—began to talk very seriously about something else. I thought, and thought. Finally, I broke in upon their gentle ripple of conversation.

"Do you mean to say, then, that you do not recognise any division of people into two classes?"

"Free and slave, do you mean?" said Brytas hopelessly.

"No; in every rank, in every class. Two complementary divisions, each finding its perfection in the other."

"I never heard of such a thing," Brytas answered coolly.

"Nor I," returned Ilex.

After a pause, the former observed:

"For my part, I cannot see how perfection is to be attained, except in one's own spirit."

Upon which followed an awkward silence, during which I candidly confess I was incapable of speech.

"Well," Ilex said, with sudden brightness, "we must move off now; we have an hour's walk before us!"

It had grown dark; the streets twinkled with tiny coloured lights, and there shone fitful gleams of lamps through the latticed casements. You could not see the trees, but only a kind of feathery motion I the sky, were their fronds waved before the light airs of the night. Even the stars had veiled the splendour of their tormenting brilliance. And it was pleasant to forget them, and to lean one's perplexed head on Ilex's shoulder as the arm passed round one's waist invited one. He or she, it was consolatory, all the same!

IV

THE HOUSE

As I walked along, with odd reminiscences of the time when I was an atom of eight, and the beautiful head of the school, who was my object of hero-worship, met me in a storm, and for even blissful minutes enveloped me, together with herself, in her own cloak, I tried to argue things out. Of course, as I came to see, there was no second declension in the language, and, consequently, no distinctively masculine adjectives (I am not alluding to strong expressions, of which the vocabulary contained a moderately picturesque assortment). So there was really no means of making or inferring any distinction of the kind.

"But you mentioned marriage a day or two ago," I remarked. "How do you name the two parties to that?"

Ilex's voice was not quite steady in answering:

"*Conjux.*"

"Is the night air giving you cold?" I said. "It is my fault, in making you talk. I am so sorry!"

"No! Indeed, no," said Ilex. "Ask me all you want to know. I like to tell you."

"Well," I said, after some demur, "how do you distinguish between the parties to a marriage? Is your word *uxor*, or *posis*, or what?"

"I do not know either of those words. Just *conjux*, or sometimes *synzycë*. Quite enough, do you not think? Both of them mean 'a joined person.' That is the definition of marriage, 'the community between two persons of all human circumstances.' They are appropriate names, I think. At all events, they are all we have—oh, except *consors*; but that is only used in rather poetical language."

"And is this relation limited to two persons?" I inquired.

"There *is* a kind of movement, I believe," said my informant, "in favour of extending it to three. Only it is considered very heretical, and hardly proper to talk about. Do they have triple unions in your country? I don't want to insult you, and I know you have such very different ideas in many respects."

"Not at all," I said. "Such a relation is never thought of, and the two people who marry pride themselves on their devotion to one another."

Ilex took a deep breath and said nothing.

We were walking on in a broad road, new to me, fringed, it seemed, with gardens, and lighted by numerous, though far from powerful, swinging lanterns, and less frequent lamps on bronze pedestals. The tinkle of a cithara sounded from more than one house where lights gleamed through the tree; the clear sound of laughter came pleasant floating on the air. It had a good-natured, open ring about it that I liked. We met the watch going its rounds—a picturesque group in the dark marron figured silks, with curious maces and cymbals, and under the leadership of an officer who nodded familiarly to Ilex.

"Who are these?" I wanted to know; and on being told they were the watch, I pointed out that it could not be very difficult for criminals to evade their imposing array.

"But they are not detectives," said Ilex. "Their business is just to see that the streets are quiet and safe."

"They would supervise them much better, it strikes me," I returned, "if they were scattered singly all over the quarter. Then there would be one on the spot nearly everywhere."

"Oh, but think how extremely lonely and stupid they would get! Nobody would undertake the work."

"Pay them!"

"You would get an undesirable class, I am afraid. Some of these, as it is, are rather a scratch lot, but they are supervised by their superiors who accompany them."

"Does it matter very much what class of people you employ for this kind of police work?"

"Emphatically, yes. Perhaps you don't appreciate the fact that they have powers of arresting people, locking them up, practically ruining them—or at least causing an infinity of trouble and annoyance. It is of the very first importance that they should be thoroughly well-bred, full of tact and consideration, and absolutely worth of every confidence. You can't get that for a crown a week."

No, I agreed that it did not seem likely.

We met few people on our way—a litter or palanquin escorted by a crowd of attendants, with torches and palm-leaf fans; knots of quiet, orderly citizens; a party of flute-players *en route* to a festival of some kind; but nothing worthy of particular mention. By the time we reached the house of Ilex the moon had risen and the mists had scattered. At the open door of the long, low house a lady, dressed in dark red, stood in the light that streamed from the interior. She met Ilex with a warm kiss, and performed the national salutation in my regard. Then she took me by the hand, and led me, followed by two young slaves in white, across the big hall or saloon into which we passed on entering, to a corridor giving access to several small rooms, and finally to a lesser, but handsomely decorated, hall, quite devoid of furniture. Doors opened on its on three sides.

"Will you have these rooms?" said the lady. "That door on the left leads to the garden; facing you there are a sleeping room and a bath. The two doors to the right,"—and she opened one—"are fitted up for your use during the day. But I hope you will only retire them occasionally, and have your meals with the rest of us, at all events. These—Nîa and Lyx—will wait on you. And we have supper ready now. May I take you with me?"

I was hardly prepared for the scene that met me in the supper room. Not less than twenty people were assembled round a long table. As usual, they sat, instead of reclining. On my arrival, accompanied by the lady in red, and joined by Ilex, they all courteously rose. There were no introductions. We three passed to vacant places at the board, and placed between Ilex and a tall, thin creature, who had some difficult in understanding me, I had leisure to look round and study the appearance of the apartment. There seemed to be corridors opposite me, concealed by pale golden hangings, which relieved the plainness of the walls. From the panelled ceiling swung a profusion of lanterns. A cabinet at one end of the room was flanked by two sentries carrying banners.

The walls, as I were plain. The only relief to their dark panelling consisted in small square plates of exquisite porcelain, let into the wood in sparing numbers, and mostly of blue and gold colouring. As to the table, it was minus any cloth, and decorated merely with the silver and other utensils of the meal.

After supper we adjourned to the great entrance hall, from the side of which led the street door. There were plenty of usual soft mats and sets, and opposite the door a huge fire blazed. Near the fireplace sat on a low stool a minstrel, and by her was a harp, not very much unlike our harps in shape. The rest of us formed a wide and irregular circle round her while she played. Whilst her fingers were on the strings her expression was hard and set, but as each movement concluded, she relaxed into a confidential *moue*, with a downward sweep of her eyelashes.

"That's very nice, Ilôna," said Ilex, after she had played a long time. "But you must be getting tired. And I have something to do that I can't attend to while you are playing such good tunes—I have to listen to you instead."

Evidently my first was mistress here! Who, then, were all the other inmates of the house—not all young, not many younger than himself? I inquired of her.

"Sit down by me," she said, "that's the way, with your arm on my knee—and I'll tell you. First, there are my two sisters, older than myself, both of them, but they prefer living with me to staying in their old home. They have not been so fortunate as I have in the way of worldly prosperity, so it is quite right they should come to me, and leave the old house less crowded. There is one of them, Mira, standing laughing beside that big vase. She is immensely useful in looking after the housekeeping for me. I don't see Duruna."

"Then there comes Darûna's *conjux*, Amphôr, over there by the woodpile, telling dragon-stories, I expect, to those three children, who'll dream of green scaly tails tonight, poor atoms! Two of them are Darûna's—such a bright little thing the eldest is!—And the other (that one in grey) is the child of a friend of mine who died last year in the service of the country, as I shall possibly do this year," she added, half to herself.

"Why?" I said, startled.

"Perhaps I was taking a shady view of a things," she admitted. "But the Uras people are determined to force a quarrel on us; and the contest will be to a bitter end."

"Will they not be satisfied with changing the occupant of the throne?"

Ilex looked at me half-comprehendingly.

"Let our queen be ejected!" she said. "There is not a soul in Armeria who would not think herself a slave to allow it. And do you fancy Beatrice would live dethroned?"

"Forgive me," I replied. "It is so customary in my part of my world for sovereigns to retire from business that I thought—"

"I see," said Ilex. "You have not monarchs, but head officials, who can honourably accept dismissal into private life. No; they must crush us, or fail."

"But," I said, "have they any hope of doing that?"

"They don't give us credit for honour. They think we will let them set up a ruler of theirs over us. And there a few of us, perhaps, who would—" Her hand moved with long, impetuous strokes through the thick fringe of a rug, the capable fingers dividing it in momentarily changing groups, as if she were already in her mind parcelling out realms and empires.

"And is the outbreak likely to be long delayed?"

"One can't tell. From little things I notice I don't think it can. It isn't that I have anything very definite to go upon—trifles that, perhaps, may mean nothing."

"I won't believe," I said, "that it is likely that this beautiful city, with all its treasures, may before long be in the hands of an enemy—a vindictive one, maybe."

She stopped playing with the fringe.

"More likely than you think," she said quietly. "And the Uras people—we know what to expect from them. They took Masa eight years ago, in Lybris. The house were razed, the trees cut down, the valuables carried off, and the ancestral records burnt before the eyes of the survivors. The cattle and living things were killed, the people left to shift for themselves."

"Surely that could not be here—here," I repeated. I could not fancy the bright, peaceful streets blazing with the glare of burning houses— the marvellous carving and decoration thrown to the rubbish-heap— and of the courteous population a terrorised remnant watching the stiffening bodies of the slain. It could not be possible.

"You are a stranger and I tell you this," she resumed, "But you need not frighten anyone else by talking about it. You won't? And it may quite likely never happen; one hopes always it may not. And, then, we are not like the Masa people; we may abandoned Alzôna to them, but we will not stay to watch them work their will. After all, what are homes and chattels? Unspeakably precious; but if they are so, what can take them from us? They are ours always, whether we can handle them and see them or not. . . I love this house of mind like a friend. What does it matter to me whether it is here for me to look at or not? It lives in my heart—it is part of me. Only," she added, in a lower and sadder voice, "I am sorry for the children if harm should come."

And then, as if she were anxious not to be too gloomy, she began to resume the thread of her description of the inhabitants of the house.

"That pleasant-looking creature in a blue robe over there is good enough to supervise my slaves for me. And Kâra—oh, Kâra, will you see whether I have a history of the Ten Years' War?—*She* keeps my library in order. Then you see two rather elderly people, eating—what is it?—Nutmeg cakes—one is a second cousin of mine, whom I am very glad to have with me. She lends a sort of air of sedateness and balance to the place, don't you think? The other is her *conjux*; and let me see if I can pick out their four children."

She began to look round, and I interposed: "Who is the lady in red who met me?"

At her inquiring look I repeated: "The lady who met us at the door, and took me to the rooms you have been so kind as to let me have—your *conjux*?"

Ilex coloured.

"I have no *conjux*, my good Anglian. And"—more quietly—"that is my eldest sister, Darûna. Now, let me see, who else is there? I showed you Mira. Playng chess to our left are Vera and Arix. The one is a royal treasurer, and the other, facing us, is busy writing an account of her travels in the Far West."

"Are they relations?"

"Oh no! But we like to have them, and they like to be here. Of course, they pay their share of the expense. So does my cousin. But I think Calêna does not—she is to your right, talking to Pathis. Calêna's *conjux*, Cyasterix, is crossing in front of the fire now. She is rather clever, but doesn't get on somehow."

"Who is the tall, thin person who sat next me at the table?"

"That is Amyctalis. Poor thing! She is never able to do much beyond making her clothes. And then there are two elderly personages who have settled themselves, I observe, near the harp—Enschîna, the dark one, and Plotar, the fair one. You will like Enschîna—any amount of information about things past, present, and to come! No; for new about things to come you must go to Plotar."

"Is Plotar gifted with prophecy?"

"Oh, not personally. But all the astrologers in the place—well, what is it, Lôtz?" she demanded of a slave who approached us.

"The Lady Darûna would like to see you in the Violet Hall."

Ilex rose at once and said *sotto voce* to me:

"I ought to tell you that, of course, those two I mentioned last—in fact, everyone but the chess players and my cousin's family—are here on the understanding that I provide their entertainment, and they give me the pleasure of their presence."

"It's very good of you," I said, glancing up at here.

"Oh, we don't put it that way," she said. "Fancy how dull I should be without an interesting set of people to be about me! And we couldn't comfortably see people like Cyastreix or Calenda badly off, just because they are not appreciated. Where would my position be if my circle of friends deserted me? I should be nowhere! But, from something you said the other night, I thought I had better say so much to you. I don't want you to think the relation between myself and them is one-sided. You will soon understand."

And, with a shy smile, she was gone.

Immediately a person who had not been pointed out came to me, and amused me by relating folk-stories of the country by the square foot. She seemed a perfect encyclopedia of tales, and they interested me very much. One by one the other people went away to their own quarters, coming punctiliously to me, and wishing me a pleasant rest before they each left, to which I responded to the best of my ability. At last there were only two or three beside myself and my entertainer. Ilex returned, and we in our turn saluted the company and retired to my set of rooms, where I was finally left to my own devices and the company (the slaves having been dismissed to bed) of a decanter of sherbet, a pile of almond cakes and two cats.

But not to sleep. The room was small and a lantern with ruby glass sides scattered a light which sufficed to illuminate it in part. I had not been long lying awake when a door at the side of the chamber opened, and as I started in surprise, a being clad in loose whit muslin came in. On her head was an ornament of gold, and her arms were clasped with golden bracelets. I lay perfectly still and motionless. The strange creature moved noiselessly to a part of the room behind me, and I heard a cabinet open.

Every little creaking that I heard fancied was the mysterious visitant approaching my couch. Should I start up and rouse the slaves, or should I lie quietly and wait? With a sudden thrill I saw her come in sight again. She had a palm-leaf fan in her hand now. Her face was beautiful, but vacant, and she seemed quite unconscious of my presence. Suddenly her eyes fell upon me, and—to my perturbation—she advanced at once towards the bed.

I am not ashamed to say that I slipped out and fled to the empty courtyard with moonlight; but I was at my wits' end where to find the slaves or how to reach the rest of the house. Looking back, I saw the strange figure at the door of the room I had left. There was a stone staircase just by me in the masonry of the wall, and I shrank into it and reached the roof. There, as I looked over, was the figure below. She was, indeed, addressing me.

"Does your ladyship wish to spend the night on the roof? I will bring the cushions up, if so. But I would remind your ladyship that the night is cool, and will grow colder."

"Who are you, please?" I asked.

"Nîa, your ladyship."

"In that dress!"

"It is the evening costume of the slaves of Lady Ilex."

"I too you for a—a burglar, Nîa! How magnificent you are in all that gold!"

"It is brass," said Nîa solemnly.

"Well, I know better than to sleep on the roof in this season. I will come back to my room. What brought you into it, Nîa?"

"If your ladyship had been awake it would have been my service to fan you or do your bidding."

"Wait, then, till I come down to you." My descent was as hurried as my going up had been, and I twice succeeded in striking against uncomfortably hard stones. On reaching Nîa, I reflected that a slave's lot could not be a very cheerful one, and I determined to treat her in as friendly a way as possible. To begin with, I leant confidentially on her arm, and inquired, when she rested herself, if she was always ready to attend on her mistress.

"Lyx and I," she explained, "arrange it between us, so that we can always have sleep enough. Was that a bird, your ladyship?"

For a rustle of some kind sounded not far away. We stood, but could near nothing more.

"Nightbirds are generally silent," I said.

"At any rate," she added, "your ladyship may rest comfortably. I shall be watching."

"Nonsense Nîa!" I told her. "Go to Lyx and get to sleep. I am not accustomed to be waited on so."

We stood for a minute in the soft moonlight. Over the walls of the court a slender, pale tower rose some little distance away. A perfumed cactus made the air heavy with its fragrance. There was no sound but our own breathing.

I went in, but could not sleep.

Another look at the pearl and ivory night I must have. I opened the door, and, for another fright, there was a figure muffled up and half asleep, seated on the pavement. It was Nîa.

I insisted on her going to bed, and accompanied her to the tiny recess where Lyx and she passed the night. Her fellow servant was awake and received strict injunctions to make her behave like a reasonable being, and take a night's rest when she had the chance.

After this I gradually felt myself more inclined to sleep, and in due time I lost consciousness.

It was not long before I got acquainted with the ways of the house. None of the inmates of it seems to take life very seriously. Their time was not economised as it might have been, and they seemed to mix up work and pleasure in an unbusinesslike fashion. Their division of labour, too, was by no means systematic, and I am sure they could have got a great deal more accomplished by a judicious attention to organisation. However, it was not my business to suggest alternations in their mode of life. Mira, in a general, vague way, had the housekeeping arrangement in her hands. Lapris supervised the slaves and that meant a good deal, for the spinning and weaving, as well as many other pieces of work, were done by them; Kâra, the library, and the music. Arix and Vera had their own occupations. One could not expect the two old ladies Enschîna and Plotar to do very much. But it did strike me as very odd that Durna, Amphôr, Cyasterix, Calêna, and Amyctalis had no definite work. True, they were always ready to do anything they were asked, and they were never tired of designing, and painting, and writing, and so forth.

Indeed, Amphôr's patterns for weaving were excellent. But they seemed to have no idea of obtaining regular employment on the one hand or of enjoying a life of mere pleasure on the other. They were simply devoted to pleasing one another.

As for the children, I never saw that they differed in any respect from the grown up people in this.

They had no lessons, and went to no school. The elder ones learnt a good deal from the adults of the family, but in quite an informal way. They also read for their own information, and their plays, in which their older friends constantly joined them—were very elaborate and serious imitations of real life. I do not refer to their athletic amusements, which were mostly carried on out of doors.

But their grand occupation seemed to be simply to be allowed to take some small part in whatever was going on, or even just to be present and watch. I have heard a child crossly spoken to in Armeria, but never slightingly. The children were uniformly treated as reasonable beings, and, to my surprise, I was told that they attained their majority at twelve. They were certainly precocious and self-possessed. But I cannot say that they were either conceited or affected, as a class. It is possible that the ample share which was given them in the conduct of the affairs of the house stimulated their memory and acuteness as much as the set training of our English school do; or it may be that these faculties are best developed by natural growth, for I certainly found these children no inferior to European children of their own age.

The roomy house in which I was now quartered was built round a central courtyard. But there were in the blocks of buildings surrounding this oblong garden other smaller courts, such as the one out of which my own rooms opened. In one or two places, the single story gave place to a two, or ever three, storied broad tower. A varied and picturesque effect was given by this means to the appearance of the building. One of the small courts, too, was almost entirely filled by a square pool of water in which fish darted about, to the endless delight of Appthis, the four-year-old baby of the house. Her enthusiasm was not even damped, though her dress was, when, at regular intervals, she slid in from the slippery marble edge. Somebody was generally at hand to step in and hand her out, a convenient point about the costume of the country being that you could kilt it up in a moment through your zone.

The slaves numbered nearly twenty. Besides those employed in the ordinary domestic duties, there were several whose work was spinning, weaving, plumbing, and so on. As to the more delicate operations of embroidery and sewing, the inmates of the house undertook these themselves; and the cooking was invariably under their own supervision. Not the slightest obstacle was put in the way of my going amongst the slaves, between whom and their owners the best relations appeared to subsist.

"What would happen," I said to Mira one day, "if a slave refused to do what you told her?"

"I should get uncommonly cross," laughed the good-humored lady in question.

"But if she persisted, or was always doing it?"

"Hm! I should get Ilex to talk to her?"

"And then?"

"Well, we might try stopping her sugar, or not letting her go out, or even, perhaps, shutting her up."

She said this rather dubiously, as if such a thing would be an unheard-of-sensation.

"And in the last resort?—For I suppose it would not pay to keep a slave locked up always."

"We would apply to the Government to transfer her to someother house."

"And so she might circulate—round the entire city?"

"No," smiled Mira. "After failing to give satisfaction in three households, the authorities conclude that there is something to blame in her, and transfer her to the State *ergastula*."

"Suppose she is simply lazy or careless?"

"Much the same would happen."

"And if she breaks things, or is—impolite?"

"Much the same. Of course, wilful damage is criminal, so is jeering, in anybody, slave or free."

"Then, can an owner keep a slave shut up for life, or how long?"

"The chief of the district inquires periodically into the treatment of the slaves, and they would be transferred to another family if they were ill-treated."

"Have they any remedy if they are spoken to harshly and brutally?" I asked, remembering what Cydonia said of Galêsa.

"You don't want to try it, do you?" Mira observed. "I expect you would be safe if you did. It is theoretically possible to criminally insult a slave—practically it scarcely is."

"Then if you struck them?"

"In that case, you see, proof is easier. And a slave has always a right to demand a transfer to another household, subject to the risk of finding herself in the *ergastula* at last."

Mira did not seem to care to pursue the topic, which, she told me, was rather academic. I could hardly believe her; however, she assured me that it was extremely rare to find a slave sent to the *egrastula*, and not common to hear of a transfer.

My promised visit to the coffee pot maker's was paid in the company of one of the younger members of the family. Accompanied by one or other of the household, I daily went about the city and visited the principal places of interest—concert halls, fencing schools, markets, theatres, baths, libraries. As in the towns of Greece and ancient Italy, the baths were the most expensive and elaborate and were constantly resorted to by the populace.

Sometimes we went beyond the walls of the city and visited the neighbouring villages and a country estate which belong to Ilex, and of which the produce suppled our table. Our favourite occasion of going out into the country was to exercise the children in the conduct of military operations, such as scouting, foraging, and so on. For this purpose, the youth of the community was organised into bands, which opposed one another, and were led by their elder and acuter members. The grown up people would accompany these expeditions and advise and criticise the operations. No pressure was put upon anyone to take part in such field-days, nor was any needed.

Games with balls were immensely popular, as they are everywhere. Going out with Calêna one morning—I think we were going to the market—we passed a gate which led into a grassy enclosure.

"Oh, come in here for a few minutes," said my conductor; "I think I may show you something you have not seen before."

The centre of the enclosure was sunk two or three feet below the level of the surrounding ground, and in the wide space so formed—it was *very* wide—frantically rushing about there were forty or fifty people. I could not help laughing, the scene was so ridiculous, for there seemed to no object in all this activity.

Suddenly a tiny object shot out of the scrambling heap and struck the rampart of earth.

"There!" said Calêna; "now you'll see them start again."

It dawned upon me that the object of the rushing crowds was to force with their feet a small ball, the size of a croquet ball, to one or other end of the enclosure. It was, in short, a sort of compound of billiards and football. The sides were distinguished by a spray of ivy in the hair of the one and gilt cobra on the headdress of the other.

We stayed and watched the game for a long time. The extremely small size of the ball prevented rough play, and it was not permissible to pick it up with the hands, or to push a player. Consequently, it could be played by pretty nearly anybody, old or young, and was, according to Calêna, very popular.

More restricted to the younger people was wresting (of a kind of which neither Japan nor Cumberland would have recognised); and racing was also a favourite exercise of theirs. Gymnastics I never saw practised. I do not think the artistic genius of the race would have submitted to the strain and the ugliness of parallel bars and the trapeze.

Acrobatic and juggling feats, I found had a great fascination for these people. But it was a half-illicit joy; there was a sort of feeling that it was, on the whole, an undignified use of life to acquire a painful dexterity in balancing a ladder. And such entertainments were attended in a rather furtive fashion. It was not a thing one could with safety to one's reputation repeat too often, to patronise them.

Every day I learnt more about the ideas and customs of the country. Thekla I often saw. Since I took advantage of the invitation she gave me to inspect her pictures, we grew good friends, and she even called for me at Ilex's house one day, which was a most unconventional proceeding. An Armerian's house is his castle, in this sense, that it extremely unusual to ask to be admitted to it, however well one may know the owner. Nor is it at all common to be invited in, except for a formal entertainment. The Armerians meet one another for the ordinary interchange of conversation and civility at public places—such as the baths, the gardens, the chiefs' palaces, and so forth.

But Thekla called one morning and asked to see me. The porter brought me the message, as I was the inner recesses of the establishment, being initiated by Darûna and Mira into the art—which was not much of an art, after all—of Armerian *pâtisserie*.

"When you have finished with Thekla," said Ilex, who was playing at sewing in the corner of the stone hearth, and interchanging a volley of critical remarks with Mira, "you might ask her if she will have some coffee. I will meet you in the entrance hall."

So I did, and Thekla stayed, and was made acquainted with the population of the house, who were decidedly impressed—so I gathered—by the visit of so extremely celebrated and unassuming a person. She took me home with her, and we had a solitary meal in a long, light gallery, open on one side to a hall of majestic proportions. In the house of which this formed part she lived, quite by herself, except for two or three free servants and her slaves. An army of pet animals made it less lonely; chief of these an antelope.

Visits like these and hospitality on the part of all Ilex's friends I owed to my foreign and mysterious origin. But that had other consequences as well.

One evening, a few days after I had settled down in my new abode, a loud knocking disturbed us as we listened to an account by Arix of perils by waters in the Western Ocean. The street gates opened, and through the waving muslin curtains one say the glare of torches. A letter was brought in on a cushion to Ilex, with great reverence, and she opened and read it with a troubled expression. The interruption spoilt the story, and we all went early to our own apartments.

The next morning Ilex said to me: "The queen wants to see you."

V

THE QUEEN

I instinctively looked at the dress I was wearing.

Ilex laughed slightly. "Oh, we are not particular here; it is not like Kytôna, where you must invest in a Court costume all beetles' wings before your approach the Golden Palace. No; any decent dress will do; don't trouble about that. But what I want to tell you is, in short, you will see that it is very unusual that anyone should come here from places we don't even know the names of. And there are people who are suspicious everywhere, and just now, when things are in a rather critical condition, they are especially likely to take fancies into their hands. So that if anyone who does not know you properly has suggested to the queen that you are really from Uras, you will see it can't be helped."

"Is that the general idea about me?" I said, in some surprise.

"No; by no means. I cannot imagine why the queen has sent for you so suddenly, though, unless it is to be satisfied on that head."

"Would you like me to leave here?" I asked. "Because it must be disagreeable for you to have a suspicious character about."

"Now, have I really deserved that? Do you think I would let you go if the envoy from Uras himself said you were his spy? Do you think I would believe him, or care whether other people did?"

"Why, what should make you believe in me so? You have only known me a week! Suppose I tell you I *am* a Uras spy!"

"Nevermind why! And you won't tell me so! . . . Still, I want you to make a good impression on the queen. That is why I tell you plainly what she may want."

"Is she old or young? What is the Court etiquette? Don't let me damage my country's reputation for civilised behaviour."

"Just be natural, and remember that she has a line of a thousand years behind her, and the responsibility for millions of people on her mind. That's all. She is the most unaffected person. Oh, she is quite ten years or more older than myself. Will you come now?"

It seemed laughably summary, this process of slipping out after breakfast to interview royalty. The sooner it was over, the better, however; and Ilex and I sallied forth to walk to the palace. No carriages were to be seen in the streets, and though the aristocratic method of conveyance ·was to be carried in a palanquin, with a train of attendants, for some reason Ilex preferred to go quietly on foot. Nor did we go to the great entrance, but we were admitted by a small private way into a long corridor, and ushered into a cabinet to await her majesty's convenience.

Almost immediately an officer of the household, with the golden sphinx emblazoned on his breast, took me into the adjacent room-a tiny chamber, all brown wood and flowers. In the centre stood a narrow oblong table; seated at it, facing the light, was a rather small figure. She motioned me to the other side of the table, and I was face to face with Beatrice the Sixteenth.

She half rose, and I saw she was not so small as I thought. But I had hardly attention for anything but her face. It was serious and delicate, with searching eyes that pierced whatever they lighted on, and firm and noble mouth. I never saw anyone whose face seemed such a transparent index of her mind. The complexion was dark, the features small, but not particularly finely chiselled.

I forgot all about the proper salutation, and simply bowed. She smiled very pleasantly, but rather mechanically, and insisted on my sitting sideways towards her, on a low divan.

As I did so, I glanced through the window. A sheer descent led down to the river a hundred feet below.

"You have been some days in this city?" remarked the queen.

"Over ten, your majesty."

"And you come from far away? It will be interesting to hear all about your country, and it must be written down in our archives. Nobody had any conception there were civilised races beyond the deserts, except the few we know well."

She talked to me in this strain, inquiring about the climate, productions, and cities of Britain for a few minutes, and then observed:

"It seems so unaccountable to us that, coming across the desert as you were, you should know nothing of Zunaris,—nothing of Lathene. Surely you must have passed through these countries?"

"Unless your majesty knows them by different names, they are places I never heard of. Can your majesty tell me how they dress in Lathene?"

"In Lathene," said the queen, "the general dress is much the same as ours. They are not like the Kytôna people. But it is very hot there, and the materials are very thin and gauzy."

Her majesty's lip curled as she spoke.

"I can't in the least give a satisfactory explanation," I pursued recklessly. "For one thing, your climate is far too temperate for the latitude. For another, the stars are all different; and, according to my notions of the world, there ought not to be any big river here."

"And you cannot tell me how you crossed the Further Desert, nor what is on the other side?"

I was silent. How could I confess my absolute ignorance of the existence of the Further Desert?

Then suddenly she spoke: "Do you know the position of affairs with Uras?"

I know I changed colour. And I stammered as I said: "Partly; from conversation, and Ilex has told me something; but I don't understand well, or, indeed, at all."

The queen laid her hands on the table, and bent towards me.

"Eight hundred years ago," she said, "Uras gave Armeria a sovereign. Is it fair, foreigner, for that alone to claim to control our actions, and to have a share in our legislation? Yet that is the demand I and my Council have received from Uras. Armeria is powerful, its people more refined, its arts more polished, its independence unquestioned for eight centuries. Excellency, I should be unfit to rule a country estate if I did not resist pretensions so absurd."

I bowed and was still silent, uncertain as to whether cordial concurrence or diplomatic reserve would best remove the suspicions which now too plainly existed. My pulse quickened, and it was an effort to listen quietly.

"Uras thinks itself our match and more," she proceeded. "Oh, I know they think us an effete community! Their blatant chivalry will ride over our levies like a horse in a flower field. That is their idea. But it may be— otherwise. Have they forgotten their war with the Quôsa barbarians?"

She looked interrogatively at me, but, of course, never having heard of the Quos a barbarians, my expression was convincingly vacant.

"Well," she resumed, after a moment's pause, "Uras has five soldiers to our four. I don't deny that. Stronger, too, I admit. And they are not too scrupulous. On the other hand, we are better armed, we have (let me say in confidence) better leaders, and we are right!"

"Do your troops believe the same, your majesty? And what do the Uras rank and file think?" I said, as she seemed to wait for me to say something.

"Everyone in Armeria—nearly everyone—is convinced of it. And the Uras people—they will fight when the Queen of Uras tells them: not out of any affection for her, but for sheer love of fighting. Love of the hammer-and-tongs fighting itself, that is, for they take no interest in strategy," she observed, with a quiet smile, "and particularly love of it against submissive opponents. Oh, it is very fine to see a Urassite give a lesson to a cringing bit of a Gôlam!"

"They have a strong position at a town called Lêtis," she proceeded, "where their forces are known to be concentrating, and not even myself knows more. There is no chance of assistance from outside. Our troops are not yet in the field, but our mobilisation system is such that it is not necessary. Whatever happens—this is the last thing I want to say to you—if there is war, Armeria will experience a vast amount of harm. Alzôna may be occupied by the Urassites—and we know what that means—and that is only one contingency.

"I want your advice. You are an entire stranger, and you can see things with an unbiassed eye. Three days ago we received a message from the Court of Uras. It was this: 'That they would abandon all pretensions to control our laws on condition Armeria hands over to them its five frontier towns.' The minor stipulations are unobjectionable—liberty for Uras to maintain that its claim was well grounded, and only given up in exchange for solid advantage; maintenance of the established laws and customs of the five towns, and so forth. Now weigh well all I have said: think of the certain loss and possible ruin war will bring, and tell me what you think."

"Your majesty," I answered, "if the policy of Uras is what you say, it would be wiser to hand them your crown at once, than to accept that offer."

"If it is—" she returned dreamily. "But if they are sincere!"

"The trend of their diplomacy is best known to your majesty's advisers. Can you—"

Here my speech broke off. A flash of light appeared on the queen's arm, and I saw that the silken sleeve of her robe had caught fire. In a moment I had sprung to her, and enveloped her arm in my dress. She treated the matter rather lightly, and smiled gravely, examining the blackened edges with attentive interest.

"I sincerely hope your majesty has not got burnt," I hastened to say.

"Oh no!" she said deliberately. "I think not."

"Well, may I be permitted to look? Sometimes one does not feel the bum in the excitement. I am a physician, or I should not presume."

"I am obliged. But it is not necessary. You have my thanks—my warm thanks—for what you did. Your sleeve is ruined, isn't it? You, will permit me to make amends for my awkwardness, some day. You are not hurt, are you?"

"I think not, your majesty. In any case, it would be little matter."

"Let me see," she commanded; so we discovered two small blisters on my wrist, and her eyes grew soft, and her voice more natural. She blew out the taper that had occasioned the damage with uncalled—for vehemence.

An officer entered. "Tell the Chief Physician to attend! Or stay," said the queen, "take this lady to the compounding-room. Let her be treated by the physicians there. When you have taken her, send the Lady Ilex to me. Not before, do you understand?"

She held out her hand for me to kiss, and swiftly laid both hands on my shoulders.

"I trust you," she said, after a second or two. "Say nothing about what I have told you."

Rather elated at the unexpected success of the interview, I followed the retainer to a large square room fragrant with aromatic odours, and lighted by long, narrow windows, high up the walls. It was the sort of room in which one might expect to see stuffed crocodiles depending from the ceiling, and black cats acting as familiar imps, such was its air of medieval pharmacy. It was, after all, in medical things that the classical traditions were most unchanged in the Middle Ages.

Here my wrist was made considerably more comfortable. I sat on a heap of rugs, and chatted with the superintending surgeon, watching meanwhile the preparation of mysterious mixtures and potions by the staff of subordinates. Before long Ilex came. She did not know anything of what had occurred, and wanted to know what the bandage meant. I explained I had managed to injure my hand a little, and she was very much concerned, and wanted to go home at once. The presiding genius of the place, however, made me take a concoction composed then and there with her own hands, assuring me that there was no better remedy for the effects of excitement and shock.

"Have you been much excited? And is there much shock?" asked Ilex, perturbed.

The surgeon gravely murmured something about shock being never entirely absent in such cases; and for my part I laughed rather impolitely at the notion. The medical authority, however, insisted that shock was shock, and should always be treated with the due remedies and precautions. "In fact, the mere sight of your injuries produces in me a certain amount—small, it is true, but appreciable—of genuine shock; consequently, I shall have to break through a rule which I constantly observe, to drink no liquid between just after breakfast and my next meal. I will take a properly proportioned dose-three-fourths of a beaker—of this Syrilis cordial."

"What! Are you so badly hurt?" said Ilex anxiously. "And how did it happen?"

"My constitution (of which I take every care)," said the doctor, "is very easily disturbed by mental impressions, and—"

"I didn't mean you, Rôthôr," interrupted Ilex. "Excuse me. I know how easily affected you are. But what is the matter here?"

"It's nothing, Ilex," I said. "I'll tell you all about it as we go." So saying, I got up, and with warm thanks to the surgeon, who was, in spite of a few harmless weaknesses, no novice at the work of an Æsculapiad, we made our way to the grand entrance. I told Ilex exactly how my accident happened, and she listened thoughtfully.

"It's strange," she said. "Beatrice is not the person to make a slip of that kind. That little taper is always burning on her table, and she ought to be used to it by this time."

"Did you see her?" I asked.

"I was sent for," she replied. "But the Kytôna ambassador had to see her on urgent business, with the Arch-Marshal; and she sent word that I need not wait."

"Then we can go where we like?"

"Quite. But wouldn't you like to go home? You must! We will have palanquins, and you shall lie down and be comfortable."

But I would not hear of it, and I asked Ilex to take me to the Bronze Walk Square. This was a useful place for a private talk—a paved space of moderate size, enclosed by a low terrace on which grew patches of sweet herbs, and quite free from any cover for eavesdroppers. "Listening outside houses," used to be a criminal offence in England once, I understand, and was penalized by indictment at the assizes. Whether the mere listening at keyholes by a person already within the street door was equally strictly regarded, I do not know. But I doubt whether, anywhere, it has ever been held illegal to pick up scraps of conversation from behind trees, and under the shelter of shrubs or garden seats. It irritates one to think of being so easily and innocently overheard, and so I chose the Square.

We talked about indifferent things till we reached the place. Once Ilex began to speak in a cautious voice, when the street was empty but for ourselves. As a stranger turned the corner she had stopped abruptly. Arrived at the square, however, she turned to me quickly.

"Well?"

"Well?" I replied mischievously.

"You know what I mean! How did the queen receive you?"

"Very affably. She asked for and received a good deal of valuable information about my remote country, and the Arch-Registrar is to take it all down—I hope in golden ink. And on purple parchment. Purple would flatter me extremely."

"But was she pleased that you should remain here?"

"How can I tell? It is to be presumed that she will allow me to remain until the Arch-Registrar is finished with me."

Ilex beat the long folds of her dress impatiently with her strong, delicate fingers.

"It isn't *that* I want to know, Mêrê"—which was the way they pronounced my name. "Did she say anything to you about Uras?"

"We will keep moving about a little, Ilex," I observed. "Isn't it as well? It looks suspicious to come into the middle of the square and stand."

"Well?" said Ilex again, as we slowly moved on.

"Oh, about Uras. Yes, she did mention it—told me some interesting facts about its army, government, and so on."

"And what led up to that?"

"Let me see. I hardly remember, I am afraid."

"Surely you can." She struck a pebble lightly with her foot as she spoke.

"I fancy," I said, "that she just said it all abruptly, without its being led up to by anything."

"And nothing was led up to by it?"

"What should be?"

"Very well, you ridiculous Mêrê!" said Ilex. "I see you will only tell me at your own time. I will wait!"

I relented, and made the position as clear as I could to her.

"I think we may be satisfied with what has passed," I said. "The queen began by inquiring about my country, and expressing the surprise which you all feel at the way I have come here—a surprise which, I needn't tell you, is particularly keenly felt by my own self. While I was saying something more or less incoherent about this point, she suddenly mentioned Uras, so I am quite certain your surmise was correct. Then she summed up the pros and cons as to war and asked my advice."

"Your advice!" said my friend. "I don't understand that move, quite. Your judgment may be extremely sound, and I am sure it is. Beatrice doesn't know that! Why did she ask you?"

"She said I was a stranger, and unbiassed. Then she told me one or two State secrets—ah! Perhaps I should not have mentioned that—and that was all."

Ilex seemed lost in study. Her next remark considerably staggered me.

"You must tell me these secrets, Mêrê!"

It was not said dictatorially, nor imploringly, but in a quiet, matter-of-fact manner, with a note of confidential appeal that was extremely puzzling.

"Ilex! . . ."

I had come insensibly to depend so entirely on her for guidance in the strange city that it took my breath away to hear her calmly demand the impossible

She flushed a little, but bent a steady pair of eyes on me, and I saw there was trouble ahead.

"You must!" she repeated, with that reassuring persuasion still in her voice. It was fascinating. I felt almost as if any act would have seemed right, if someone were with those tones to take the blame of it off one's conscience.

But it could not be—of course, it could not be. Ilex would see that in a moment. I had only to explain.

"Every word she said I would repeat with pleasure," I began; "but do you know the last words she said to me? 'Don't tell anyone what I have said. I trust you.'"

"Nevertheless," said Ilex, with placid audacity, "you must tell *me*."

"Surely it isn't fair of you to ask me! The queen trusts me; how can I do what you are wanting?"

"Does the queen not trust *me*, then?"

"Of course she does."

"Then why object to pass her confidences on?"

"Because they *are* confidences. She may have any quantity of reasons for—"

"For not wanting me to know?"

"Well, if you put it so."

We walked on in silence for a little.

The next thing she said was:

"If I tell you, Mêrê, sincerely and plainly—'water and flame,' as the children say—that the queen has no secrets from me; that I will stop you the moment you begin (which is very unlikely) to say anything I ought not to know; that I take on myself the whole responsibility of assuring you that you ought to tell me; that my life will be ruined, probably, if you don't—wouldn't you do the one thing I ask you? I never have asked you much!"

"Can't you see it's impossible?" I replied.

"Why impossible?"

"Because I practically promised I would not."

"And do you keep literally every promise you make?"

She said it rather condescendingly, and I answered, tartly enough:

"Your notions of honour—perhaps you don't use the word in the sense I mean—must be very remarkable here. They are not those of my race!"

"What is the use of getting vexed?"

"Because you seem to think I would be mean enough to think little of a solemn promise," I said hotly.

"Was this solemn?"

"Well, it comes to the same thing."

We turned and walked away from the terrace. The grey slate flags of the pavement succeeded one another with monotonous regularity.

"Would you," she said quietly, "give a lunatic a knife because you had promised it to the same person when sane?"

I made no reply.

"Or if you knew that to keep a promise would harm the person it was given to, would you keep it?"

Still I said nothing.

"Suppose, Mêrê, someone confided to you her intention of doing a thing that seemed right, but which you afterwards learnt she would regret all her life having done; that you saw no way to warn her; that there was no chance of preventing the evil consequences if the act were done—would you not break the seal of literal secrecy?"

"I am not going to enter into a discussion of casuistry," I said. "Of course, there are cases in which literal obedience is virtual defiance. But this is not one—"

Ilex faced round on me, tall, commanding, with a set purpose gleaming in her eyes.

"This *is* one!" she said, half smiling, but serious in spite of it. "Mêrê, don't you trust me when I say it is one?"

"And do you say it affects you?" I said doubtfully.

"That doesn't matter. Certainly it affects me. But, directly, it affects yourself."

"Me?"

"Tell me, and I will show you."

"Really, it comes to very little, and how it can affect me I cannot see. The queen told me of a proposal that has just come from the enemy—from Uras—and she asked me whether it was worth accepting."

"The proposal being that we should give up to them Dioce, Hymlas, Ionitz, Kraga, and Myalia?"

"Yes; or perhaps—where are those places?"

"On the Uras frontier."

"Then you are right."

"Now I see," said Ilex. "And what did you say?" she went on, anxiously.

"Say?" I replied. "It was an absurd proposal, and I told her so."

My companion's face brightened.

"That was well!" Then she relapsed into silence, while we strolled towards the streets.

"Now you will tell me," I ventured, "why this information was so tremendously important. You knew it before."

"Indeed, I don't know that I will. I'm vexed. . . it seemed to me once that you would have taken my word without so much pressing."

"I never doubted your word, Ilex!"

"No; but you did the same thing. You assumed I was asking you to break the queen's confidence, that there was really nothing to justify repeating what she said, though you could see I implied there was."

Her regal calm had given place, all at once, to an irritable vexation, which contracted her brows and quickened her footsteps. I felt a difficulty in knowing what to say. I could not admit that I had behaved otherwise than the strictest code of ethics dictated—unless in giving way to her—and yet I felt, somehow, that I had not treated her as I should.

"I wish you could see things in my light," I told her. "I only did my duty—what I considered to be my duty. . . We are brought up in England to fulfil our pledged word to the letter, and—"

"And in presence of that mechanical duty you forget the prior pledge that is in the keeping of those you know. . . and love!"

IRENE CLYDE

She was too impetuous to argue with. We passed through an archway in a blank yellow stone wall, and found ourselves in a rich garden of tall flowers, colonnaded by a gilded series of slender pillars, above which soared a vision of cream and gold fresco. Ilex plunged into the midst of the yielding grasses, and lay down with her face on the dry moss.

"Do you mind," she said, "waiting here a little? I should like to rest."

"Of course I shall be very glad to do just as you like," I told her.

I could not quite lie down, so I stood with my arm round a strong reed that grew near. Before long she started up, and proposed to me that we should go. But before I could answer the most extraordinary sight I had yet seen came before my notice.

Two and two there came a white-robed procession, the first twelve or twenty playing instruments—flutes, some of them, and others harps and viols—and the rest singing with a rapt, unconscious air. The music was weird and sweet, going off into halftones and enharmonics more than any I had heard. It was not Oriental, either: there was too much definite purpose in it. The words I could not make out. After these came two torch-bearers, dressed in yellow brocade, and carrying links of burning wood, which sent forth a powerful and scented vapour. The most peculiar figure in the whole line followed immediately—a tall, bent form in black silk robes enveloping the wearer far more completely than was usual, and embroidered with fantastic devices, which somehow seemed familiar. A cap, furnished with two brazen wings, increased the strange figure's height. Behind, there was borne by an attendant a silver staff. I saw with a thrill—I don't know why—that this was in the form of a serpent. Other attendants followed, each with some object in charge—it might be a golden stiletto or an ivory box filled with sand.

"It is the Grand Astrologer," said Ilex, as the seven small children who brought up the rear passed. "Apparently the queen has requested the geomantic experiment to be made."

"Do you believe in magic, then?"

"I can hardly say we do. But these ceremonies are very ancient, and they satisfy some minds."

The Astrologer's procession, chanting, wound its way up exterior staircases, until it reached the summit of the building surrounding the garden. Then the musicians and torchbearers descended a little distance, and the attendants, depositing their magic implements, did likewise. The silver staff was delivered into the Astrologer's own hands, and he was left alone on the highest level.

"Well, let us go," said Ilex. "They may be hours before they are finished."

"Who are they?"

"The players and singers are the College of Minstrels. They live in common—I must show you where—on a very grand scale. The others are the Court Magicians."

As we passed, a burst of penetrating pathos reached us from above, and died away after a few bars. So we left the rites of magic in progress, and walked mutely through the streets until suddenly we met the genial and blunt presence of the Princess Iôtris.

"Where are you two off to? Ilex, I have a piece of news for you: the Lady Phanaras is coming back to Alzôna. Then you can resume the attentions that were broken off so suddenly last year. There is an opportunity for you!"

Phanaras! Somehow I felt an uncomfortable *gauche* sensation, and a kind of fear of this being of whose existence, two minutes before, I was not aware. Fear? It seemed ridiculous. What was there to be afraid of?

I glanced at Ilex. Her colour was heightened, and she seemed embarrassed and did not speak. I broke the silence.

"Is she so very attractive, then—this lady?"

"Well, not to most of us. Ilex is the lucky person who sees the beauty none of the rest of us can discover. It is like mashed dates and cheese, or the seven epics of Tathylis—a sealed glory to all but the elect."

Ilex struck quickly in:

"Have you heard whether the Constable of Uras is visiting Cylos, as they said last night in the Forum? And—oh, I had nearly forgotten—could you, some day, lend Darûna your sceptre? She wants to make a drawing of it for her collection. I dare say you know she has a whole gallery of them—sceptres and maces and such things—and she would be immensely obliged. And another thing I want to say: do you know that Sethys' chief cook has got to go? Sethys could do no longer with never being allowed to have what she ordered for meals. She put her foot down yesterday, and told her precious cook that it wouldn't do—said that the law did not actually compel a city senator to take braised chestnuts when she wanted stuffed cucumber. The cook, bless you! Did not think it necessary to pay any attention, so, when barley soup was called for, lentil porridge was produced. Sethys, in that dry, apologetic way of hers, sent for the despot.

"'I am so very sorry, Mil,' Lyx tells me she said; 'it is most unfortunate.

It is impossible to get what I want. In my busy life I cannot stand vexations like these.'

"Mil was most profuse, Lyx says, in assurances that all would be well from that day thenceforth, and that bygones would be past, never to return. Sethys listened a long time, until the end of the discourse. Then she very deprecatingly observed:

"'I am afraid I am letting you waste your time, Mil. You may have a good many things to do, and—I have applied to the supervisors to transfer you!'

"Mil, struck dumb, found, when capable at length of utterance, that Sethys had discreetly withdrawn, and, as discreetly, she declined any further interviews. So you can have Mil for the asking—and there isn't a better cook in Alzôna."

Iôtris laughed with undisguised enjoyment.

"I will try and get an invitation from Sethys," she declared. "She used to be so proud of her festival-dinners. I wonder how she will evade me."

We smiled sedately. A Princess might take a licence in angling for invitations which in anybody else would be highly indecorous.

Pleased with the joke, Iôtris left us, with a chuckling nod.

"Don't forget Phanaras, Ilex! What is more to the purpose, remember—she certainly won't forget *you!* You lucky individual!"

Ilex shook her slender frame as a swan shakes its wing-feathers. However, she said nothing until we had traversed a street or two. She suddenly observed:

"Mêrê, I dare say you were right. . . I shouldn't have expected you to have such confidence in me. I am a stupid thing—always was!"

"I am so sorry," I said, "that you should have been vexed with me. I owe you—"

"Vexed with you! No; I was—but I stopped you?"

"No."

"I was just like a child that has come against a door in the dark—shaken and feeling injured, with nobody to blame. It feels inclined to tear about and break things, and I am afraid I tried to break your respect for me—if you have any."

I felt remorseful at once. But what could I say? Except to link my arm in hers, there seemed nothing to be done to mend matters. Her proud carriage softened instantly into a gratified acceptance of the caress, and we went on, regardless of the fact that occasional worthy citizens found it remarkably interesting that Ilex should be on such terms with her ultra-barbarian visitor.

She talked more freely now, and listened with great attention to my minute account of the interview with the royal Beatrice.

"She asked your views on the point of politics—you can see why?—It is plain enough to me, or anyone who knows her. If you were an emissary from Uras, don't you see what a splendid chance it would have been of giving fatal advice in the innocent garb of an unprejudiced stranger! No spy in his senses would have hesitated to give a delicate and duly modest push to the royal mind in the right direction—unless he were playing a very deep game indeed."

"Do you think so?" I said doubtfully.

"I quite think so. And," she added abruptly,

"I should not be surprised—don't start—if the incident with the candle was deliberate on her part."

"To see if I would let the palace be destroyed? That seems rather like firing a house to roast the pig, as a writer of ours says."

Ilex knit her brows.

"No. I hardly meant that. I can scarcely express what is in my mind. Still, I do think that in all probability Beatrice lit that sleeve on purpose."

"Considering the danger she personally ran," I objected.

"She is not accustomed to stick at trifles," said Ilex inconsequently.

After this day I spent more and more time at the palace. On the next occasion I happened to be there four or five of us were indolently seated in the shade of the beeches which grew by the side of an extensive lawn, reminiscent of England and tennis, when the queen, with two of her ladies, appeared near us.

We did not rise; it was not expected or liked. But the wonderful eyes of the queen fell on my strange face, and with great friendliness she smiled and talked to me, about flowers—which she loved like myself—and of poetry and war. I told her of Virgil and Spenser, the innocent worldliness of Horace, and the clang of the "Iliad," of the formless melancholy of Ossian, and of Elizabeth Browning's clinging melodies. And she told me a great deal, too, though she listened more than she spoke. A concourse of her ladies gathered round us, and among them was the Arch-Minstrel, a poet and (what does not follow) a judge of verse.

"Achla," said the queen to her, when I had recited—vilely—a bit of the "Æneid" (which, after all, I maintain is better work than the equally artificial Idylls and Bucolics)—"isn't that fine? But why is Thekla not here to listen? Everytime I have sent for her lately, the messenger has brought back word that she is not at her house. Is she studying the crags of the Piraethal Mountains, or steeping herself in the lakes and brooks of Lasen?"

"Literally, your majesty?" inquired Cydonia, who was present.

"Literally or artistically—it makes no difference," returned the queen, who made no practice of descending to an encounter of repartee.

"Nobody has seen Thekla," declared Iôtris, "for a fortnight."

"I haven't," said Chloris.

"I haven't," added another courtier.

The queen turned sharply on her heel.

"Why didn't I know?" she demanded.

We looked at one another with raised eyebrows.

"Really, it never occurred to us to compare notes," said the Arch-Minstrel. The Palace Warden and the Signet-Bearer had strolled off.

"We thought Thekla had something on hand to keep her away," remarked Chloris.

"But what *can* be the reason?" again demanded the queen. "Did none of you inquire whether she was away, or ill, or what?"

We looked at each other again.

"Well, one inquired of the porter, and all that was said was just that she wasn't in."

"Somebody must go round and see," said she, with what I thought unnecessary anxiety. She would have despatched an attendant, but Achla volunteered to go.

A light breeze was blowing, and driving up clouds from over the palace turrets. Someone discovered it was likely to rain, and we turned towards the building in a long, brightly tinted procession.

Chloris determined to escort me home, and we settled to call at Thekla's house on our way.

The stately, cold facade looked gloomy to me for the first time. Chloris went boldly up to the porter and inquired for the mistress. She was "not within."

"Then she was away?"

The porter shifted his glance, and observed that he rather thought she must be.

"Her intendant must know," said Chloris. "Will you ask Trysë?"

"Her ladyship's intendant, secretary, and warder have all been at her country house for ten days or more."

"And she is not there?"

"I believe not. Her ladyship frequently goes into the country, painting, without leaving word with her slaves where she is."

"Yes, I know," said Chloris; but, turning to me as we went, she added: "All the same, ten days!—That's a long time, Mêrê, to make an impromptu dash into the country without leaving any message for anybody. A day or two's different, isn't it?"

"I didn't much like the porter's look," I confessed.

"They can't have killed Thekla, and be waiting a chance of getting away abroad?" suggested Chloris, with plaintiveness in her voice.

"Of course not. That's entirely absurd," I assured her, from my intimate knowledge of the customs of the place.

"Why is it absurd?"—rather hopefully.

"Well, wouldn't the intendant, or—what do they call her?—The warden, come back from the country, and inquire into things before very long? Wouldn't they have cleared out at the earliest chance long before this—before ever Thekla's affectionate friends (like us) came round interfering?"

She yielded promptly to the pleadings of optimism.

"Of course they would," she said. "Mêrê, I wish you would stay here always and clear up mysteries: you do it so beautifully."

"I haven't the least objection, if the city will only pay me a good salary," I returned.

"But you seem so clever at it," said she, quite seriously, "that surely you would like to do it, whether you were paid or not?"

"It hadn't occurred to me to look at it in that light," I admitted; "and you will agree that, if I must exercise my talents somewhere, I might as well do so amongst my own people at home."

"I am sure you *do* come from a very long-way-off foreign country, as you say you do," interposed Chloris, eagerly and with conviction. "Because, either that or else you are a great poet. Oh, I am a girl of sixteen, I dare say, but I know decent writing when I see it. And those bits of Virgil (Virgil, isn't it?), they're very fair indeed! If you made them up, you must be a celebrated poet; if you didn't, you must come from unheard-of places."

"Isn't there a third alternative? That I am out of my senses?"

"Now, I put it to you," said Chloris, with indignation, "if any insane person could write like that! *I* don't believe it. *You* know, it is all so strong, and calm, and measured—I can't find the proper expressions. Eminently sane, *I* should call it. And, besides, I know you."

"And know me incapable of writing anything so good!"

"Now, I didn't mean that. But, if it is any satisfaction to you, I am perfectly convinced that it would be malignant cruelty only that would doubt your sanity."

Since our interview with Iôtris, a few days before, I had heard nothing of the Phanaras she mentioned. I refrained, with a foreboding which I could not well account for, from speaking on the subject to Ilex or any of her household. But it now occurred to me to ask Chloris. I did so cautiously.

"Have you many visitors to the city, Chloris?"

"Oh, plenty, Mêrê! They come from all parts; and I think," with shy pride, "they like to come. There are plenty of things going on here, and we try to make them enjoy themselves. And, Mêrê, I'll tell you one thing *you* can do. I've never told you yet, but I'm sure you would like it."

"Thank you; I shall be glad to know about it," I said. "But, Chloris, tell me this. Do strangers form part of the society of the place, then?"

"Oh, yes, always. They, many of them, have family ties with us, and then they generally stay in our homes. Or they may stay at inns; or occasionally they hire houses. If they do not know anyone here, they generally apply to the queen for recognition."

"I see. Such a visitor as Phanaras, for instance, where would she stay?"

"Phanaras? Oh, now I remember who it is! She isn't a visitor. No, she's native, and has her own house. But she is constantly abroad. Alzôna is too respectable for her; she pretends it is too dry. She goes to the sea-coast towns, the hills, the sacred wells, everywhere but here. Anywhere, so long as she can make an old idiot of herself, with trains of people surrounding her, whom she thinks her devoted admirers. Really, they are all making fun of her. And the airs she gives herself! As if she were a—a camel!

"Last year," Chloris resumed, being fond of a spice of gossip, "she came here for a month or two. Nobody is quite so ill-natured or frivolous in Alzôna—at least, of course, they *may* be, but they daren't show it—as to make a joke of the poor thing; and therefore she considered us an appreciative lot. She singled out Ilex, and pretended—indeed, I think she believed it," said the girl, with a hearty burst of laughter—"that Ilex was dreadfully fond of her, and too shy to say so. And, after a fortnight, Ilex simply had to give in and go to Norene—for change of air, which means peace and quietness. It is a very dry climate, so Phanaras could not consistently go there, too, and left the city soon after."

"And is she nice-looking?"

"She's not bad-looking. But her nose and lips are hard, and she is painted and powdered and wigged. Ugh! Keep me from her!" said Chloris.

"Perhaps Ilex was really impressed, and felt it hopeless to admire too much natural and artificial charm."

"That's one of Phanaras's faults. She is as proud as a hill. Nobody is her equal in rank and accomplishments! And, really, Ilex is twice as rich, twenty times as cultured, and two hundred times as good."

"But has nobody a prior prescriptive right to Ilex's attentions?"

"Nobody. Surely you can see that for yourself."

She eyed me more curiously than I cared for, and I changed the topic of conversation.

"That pleasure you promised me just now—what is it, Chloris, please?"

"It's a splendid thing!" said Chloris enthusiastically.

"You shall consult the Royal Astrologer! And we'll do it today."

"About what?"

"About your country, and where it is, and how to reach it. Would you go at once, though, if you knew the road?"

"I don't think I would," I answered. "Not until I saw how you manage the Uras difficulty."

"Oh, we'll soon give a good account of *them*," said Chloris comfortably. "Very well, then, so long as it doesn't mean our losing you, you may see the Astrologer anytime. Only let me go with you; because I proposed it, didn't I?"

"Certainly you did. But do you fancy the magicians are any good? Can they really tell?"

"Some things they can; not everything. And the more extraordinary a thing is, the better explanation they can give of it. I could tell you lots of remarkable things."

Here she launched out into a long recital of occasions on which the magicians had proved their powers, and hardly ended until we were back at the house of Ilex.

She left me with a wave of her little brown hand, whilst I passed indoors and sought my rooms. Both Lyx and Nîa stood at the entrance to the courtyard with drawn swords. I felt puzzled, and passed rapidly between them, when I saw, to my utter astonishment, the queen and Ilex talking together. It seemed such a little time since I had left the palace, that for a while I could not understand how the queen could be before me; and her presence, in any case, was quite unaccountable.

"Here she is!" said Ilex.

For the moment I felt that surely this was someother lady, resembling her majesty; but she spoke.

"You used to see a good deal of my Thekla! The week or two before last, did you see her?"

I thought for a second or two, and I remembered that, altogether, I had not been long in the town.

"Yes, several times."

"And did she ever mention the idea of going into the country or away?"

"No; not to me."

"Or seem ill or unhinged in mind?"

"Not the least, my queen. She was always very kind and rational."

The queen's face wore a set, yearning look, as she turned to Ilex, with a wan smile.

"There's nothing for it but—the worst," she said.

"Your majesty—no, not that!"

"You do not know what I know! All last week there have been rumours brought to my cabinet of underhand work going on. I expected some *coup*, but it was all too vague to do anything against. I strengthened the arsenal, I put an extra guard at the treasury. We replaced the sentinels at the inner gates by officers of the Prime Watch.

"But I never thought of this! She knows all our plans and counsels, and she is shy and timid, so the wretches have secured her, somehow—somewhere."

Then she began to speak in quicker tones.

"Understand, they will do themselves no benefit. She will tell them nothing. But they may do all sorts of things to her. One does not know—hardly kill her! But she was so easily frightened, and those—"

Here the queen's voice was more broken and agitated. She stopped speaking, and we also stood silent. The night had sunk, and a thin crescent moon shed a fitful light on us. Beatrice's breath came heavily once or twice.

"Oh, my Thekla! My Thekla!" That was all she said, but the words seemed to tear her heart with them as they left her lips. Then her placid dignity came back, in appearance, at least, and, summoning her palanquin bearers, she returned to the palace, escorted by a dozen slaves of Ilex's with torches. Chloris had called for me and gone again.

The confusion and stir of a royal visit, instead of masking, heightened the tragic impress which the events of the evening had left on my mind. The courtyard seemed haunted, and sleep was long in coming, though it came at last, as one gets to learn it will come, like other blessings, to those who do not seek it.

VI

The Latticed Door

Nothing could be heard of Thekla. That was always the tale day after day, until one forgot to ask any longer. The free servants produced to the royal inquisitors a note unmistakably in the vanished artist's handwriting, enjoining them to leave for her country house, and prepare it for a visit from her, with two friends, within a week or so. They had been daily expecting to hear from her, but, finding themselves in comfortable quarters and their own mistresses, they had not troubled themselves to communicate with her.

Her slaves were closely questioned, but nothing could be made of them beyond the statement that she had gone out early in the day with her colours and brushes, saying she might be away for sometime, which they at first thought meant for a few hours, but they afterwards concluded that she must have gone to her country estate when she did not return. Not being sure, they could not give a definite answer to callers, and thought it best simply to say their mistress was not in.

"It was none of our business," said the porter, "to go explaining to visitors where we thought she was, or to chatter to callers about our mistress's affairs," which was a just observation, though entitled to less weight than it received, for it was the authenticated custom of slaves to impart such particulars pretty freely to outsiders.

For some days, when I went to the palace, Queen Beatrice was invisible. At the time Ilex used to have to attend daily as a kind of secretary to a military council which met there, and I used to accompany her, and remain left in the company of the ladies of the Court during the sitting.

We missed the queen's presence: it focused the interest of affairs. Without it, our company of courtiers was aimless and disorganised. We fell to lounging idly about in twos and threes, and no one seemed to care to begin anything. In these rather demoralising circumstances I found myself one day occupying a divan with the beautiful favourite Opanthë. We were alone, and in the next room a lively party had, for once, started a noisy piece of merriment, to which they were giving themselves up with *abandon* and much laughter.

Opanthë yawned slowly and delicately, and, slowly turning, she took notice of me. Her sinuous silken form lay indolently on the cushions. With a start like a spring uncoiled, she looked cautiously round, bent towards me, and said, hurriedly and swiftly:

"You are playing your part well. You don't know, perhaps, that I am on your side. Or have they told you? You see, I know who you are, so you may trust me."

"Really," I said, for I was at first too much astonished to see what she meant, "I don't know what you mean. Do you mind explaining?"

"Excellent! Now not another word! Don't speak—there is no need. You and I and Uras understand each other; that's enough!"

Here some of the revellers burst in, panting and flushed, and I had time to grasp the meaning of her words and to fix on a line of action. There seemed only one explanation. She held the theory that I was from Uras, and so strongly as to run the risk of declaring herself on the same side. The horror of the position overcame me. Here, in the heart of the queen's advisers, there was—to put it bluntly—a traitor! Should I unmask her? I felt my hands clench.

My caution, the outcome of years of desert travelling, suggested that the better plan was to wait.

To make an open, or even a secret, accusation against one of the most trusted officers of the royal household, and one of the most intimate councillors of the queen, was more than I was prepared to do without consideration. My own position was not of the securest; even a hint to the authorities to suspect Opanthë would raise an immediate doubt of my own good faith. They would think at once that I was trying to bolster up my own insecure credit by impugning hers. Moreover, it would not, I reflected, be easy to make people believe that she, as an agent of Uras, would confide with such readiness as I thought the matter over, it appeared to me so incredible that anyone would believe that the unimpulsive Opanthë should make such damaging revelations to me without very good reason, that I decided not even to tell Ilex what had happened.

"Suppose," I thought, "that this is all a blind, a 'put-up job,' that Opanthë is testing my credibility for her own or the Court's better information? She has said nothing that I am bound to bring to the Government's knowledge. Least said, soonest mended. I tell Ilex, suppose? And Ilex may insist on the queen's being told; may even tell her, in spite of any promise she gives me, if she thinks it her duty.

And then, if that, or anything like it, happens, I shall have accused a powerful Court lady of the blackest treason on the strength of a few words which she can deny or explain away."

My reasoning may or may not have been satisfactory—it scarcely was, to myself—but away at the back of it was the feeling that the direction of delicate affairs is, like trumps at whist, better in one hand than two. And, in short, I preferred to keep the shock I had just received to myself, until a favourable opportunity should arrive of making use of the information I had so unexpectedly acquired. It was not necessary at present to inform Ilex or anybody. Being useless, it was an irresistible inference that, in the particular circumstances, it would be dangerous.

I did not doubt that Opanthë would be very well assured that no evidence could be procurable against her to corroborate any charge I might make. And, without formulating a charge, how could I obtain her removal from the queen's counsels? It was best to let her plot, and to make my own counterplots. Ilex was a dear creature, but I did not know her capacity for diplomacy, and our recent discussion had made me uncertain as to her code of morals. It is no good using a drug unless you know its nature.

"Mërê, you're very dull. Is something the matter?" said Cydonia. Her voice was kind and half subdued, but I saw Opanthë's eyes fixed on us with a fiery sparkle in them, accompanied by an unaccustomed darkening of the fair forehead.

"Now, why is this?" I mentally inquired. "Is she vexed at having gone so far? Does she bear some grudge against Cydonia? Or, perhaps, it is all just fancy on my part?"

She did her best, at least, to prove it so, for she came to us immediately with her most gracious smile—which, I am bound to say, Cydonia received in exclusive measure—and engaged us in animated conversation. Usually calm and contemptuous, her lapses into cordiality, real or simulated, were very impressive. She sustained the burden of a lively talk without much assistance from her companion, who scarcely spoke and seldom smiled in answer. I soon withdrew, and watched them from a distance.

Puzzling over the possible meanings of every trivial occurrence (for I saw treason in a gesture and innuendoes in a smile) brought on a headache. I grew duller and duller, and welcomed the advent of Ilex with relief.

The next day it was that Chloris arrived, in a high state of excitement, to take me to the redoubtable Astrologer. She had carefully selected a lucky hour from the almanac, and had dressed herself in the appropriate colour for the time of day. It will be obvious, therefore, that she was rather disturbed when I informed her that my own dress, which was not of that tint, was the only one I possessed.

"Couldn't you borrow one?" she anxiously suggested.

"Everybody's away," I said. "Iris blossom or something to look at in the country. And I should have been with them, only my headache yesterday prevented arrangements."

She looked so distressed that I began:

"I might borrow from Lyx—"

"Fancy you in a *slave's* dress!" she said indignantly.

"No, come along. It doesn't really so very much matter, perhaps. And the Second Magician may have them to lend—I'm not sure."

We passed between the silent porters at the door into the sun. It was an experience of exhilarating freshness. The house our own for the day, an interesting and curious interview in prospect—a little uncanny, maybe, but pleasantly exciting on that very account—a brilliant sky, flowers, and a perfect atmosphere. We went a long way off, into a part of the city strange to me, where a great tower of grey stone reared its head above all the surrounding buildings. As we approached it I thought the streets grew stiller and the people less frequent, whilst here and there could be seen a curious headdress of yellow, veil-like, that I had nowhere noticed before.

At last we reached the base of the tower. It stood in the midst of a colonnade, about which yellow-crowned figures sat and flitted in a stealthy way. Adjoining it was a low block of buildings of the same grey stone.

The entrance was a plain, round-headed arch. At either side was a statue of a dragon-like thing in green porphyry. Everything in the city was in such delicate taste that these grotesque effigies gave one an uncomfortable feeling. And there was something eerie, too, in the portly smoothness of the living guardians who stood behind them. They stared with a rapt, vacuous smile, not at us, but as though they saw sights which were hidden from our gaze—and not elevating sights, either. It was with an approach to a shudder that I passed these motionless, white-robed warders. Chloris did not mind them, however, and stepped briskly in, motioning me to follow. Through the arch, we reached a tiny courtyard with a stone stair, by which we gained the first floor of the tower. In a narrow and short passage here, screened off from the interior by a handsome wooden partition, sat a thin, brown person in yellow, before whom was a low barrier of a similar kind, crowned with a sort of desk. She was not weird at all, and nodded pleasantly and with a bright flash of her eyes above her sunken cheek to Chloris.

"Is the Royal Astrologer at liberty to receive visitors?" my conductor asked.

"When they come from such distant countries, it would be inhospitable to deny them audience," was the answer. "Let my friends go into the Hall of Offering, and so soon as the Honourable Astrologer is free, they shall doubtless see her." She pointed to a curtain in the woodwork.

"That's fine!" said Chloris to me, after thanking the acolyte. "We don't go into the place where most of the people wait, so we won't have to wait our turn; but we can see the Astrologer as soon as there's a chance."

A tall, thin, dull pink figure thrust aside the curtain for us from the inside with rather a startling movement, and we were in an oblong room of moderate size, unlighted, except for the piercing of the panels and the flame of a single wrought-silver lamp—enough light to see that the other walls were of polished ebony, or some such wood, and that the furniture was even scantier than usual. A shelf projected near me, and I offered to use it as a seat, when Chloris interposed.

"Please don't, if you don't mind. Not that I care, really, myself; but it is just a kind of prejudice. Come over here and sit in this little recess."

"And why not here?" I said, crossing over.

"Oh, well, nobody does," she returned. "Long ago, quite ages since, this used to be the principal antechamber to the Astrologer's rooms, and on that shelf stood a statue of—you know—the Twelve Deities, under the form of a Lerasiote vinedresser, which they once jointly assumed. Everyone who came to consult the Astrologer made an offering before that place, and it was thought by everybody the most sacred place in Alzôna or the world."

Her voice fell involuntarily, and we looked towards the vacant altar, half as if some emanation from its vanished tenants were still about it.

"Where is the statue now?" I asked, with a rather hushed voice.

"In the museum of the Theslyic quarter. It got to be too troublesome for the magicians to clean and repair it when it needed it. So it was sent out to be renovated, and as the offerings had dwindled down to a quarter drachma (that's two pence three-farthings of your money)," she added, being proud of her arithmetic, "they were abolished altogether, and the statue never brought back!"

A sudden, strange sight then came before us.

At the far corner of the room a bright object began to appear, like a long streak of sunset cloud. How far distant to call it, I cannot say, but it grew rounder, and rose, until it floated in our view, a great globe of fire-red light. Slowly it ascended before us, not dazzling, but self-luminous, and shedding no particle of reflection on the chamber or its furnishings. I looked round. Chloris had gone; I was alone.

In an instant and without feeling any hand upon me, I was removed from the place, and found myself in a comfortable brown room, with a triple window, admitting the welcome daylight from the north. Chloris stood near a divan opposite.

"I forgot!" she panted, laughing. "When we come from the Hall of Offerings, they keep up the absurd old custom of doing it in that style. I should have told you! Are you nervous?"

I certainly felt rather unnerved and inclined to be disagreeable. But I had no time to exhibit any annoyance, or to give Chloris instruction in tact and consideration.

A tall and queenly personage wearing multitudinous folds of some soft, thin white stuff, and a winged helm of beaten gold, smiled gravely upon us, and held open a door.

Another voice from within pronounced our names.

"Stop a minute!" said Chloris in perturbation, to our introducer. "Can't you lend us a bright-coloured dress? Don't you keep them? Very well, then, you should! It really is altogether behind the times, this establishment. I do wonder at you, Perizon! You *used* to have sense enough!"

And she led me in, with her youthful chin very much in the air. The hall we entered was of a very fair size, occupying nearly the whole area of the tower, for twenty feet or more of its height. A raised dais ran along the wall at one end, with a high partition at its edge, over which one or two figures seated on the dais itself appeared. There was plenty of light, and round the room, in deep silence, were seated persons whom I knew to be magicians. They were on gilded curule chairs, though some had slipped off them on to the rugs at their feet; and each was flanked on either hand by a rich cabinet of black oak, in which reposed the instruments of her art, and which also screened her from interruption. Between the bays formed by these high cabinets, which projected into the room, there were, on two sides of the apartment, windows. At the back of the great dais were seven colossal statues, appearing to sustain the roof, which was studded with stars. The statues were veiled thinly with gauze, and seven golden altars rose before them. As to the centre of the room, it was plain and empty, but for a few waiting aspirants, and an incense dish or two. We walked to the dais and ascended it close to the wall. I noticed that behind the statues the wall seemed to be full of stained glass, like jewellery. At one end of the dais, a plainly attired figure was seated, writing on her lap. In the centre, surrounded by parchments and papers, spread out on the long shelf above the partition, scattered on the floor, stuck in the perforations of her curiously wrought throne, sat the Royal Astrologer.

For a moment she took no notice of us. Then she stood up and rose to her full height. Turning silence. She advanced to me, pressed my hand (an unusual act, which somehow affected me strangely), and kissed Chloris.

"Come with me," she invited, in a low voice.

We passed up a stairway, through a corridor, and into a small room, occupied by a single person only, who was seated on the only available bench—a fixture it was, making a break in the cupboards and shelves that lined the walls. Chloris and I sat by her. She did not stir. The Astrologer stood before a small table, and looked inquiringly at us.

"Can you tell us—we want to know," said Chloris—"where my friend comes from?"

"Why, she knows best!" said the magician, laughing in a good-natured way.

"Well, then, how to reach it, and how she came here. We are all absolutely puzzled!"

"Come!" the Astrologer said, "that is not so difficult. Don't you want to know, Chloris, what kept Cydonia from taking you home from the festival at Ochthrys three nights ago?"

"I have had all that cleared up at first hand, thank you," returned Chloris. "And I wouldn't bother your Excellency with my private affairs. I couldn't think of it," she continued, with raised eyebrows.

"Well, I dare say I should dismiss you to Zolaris if you did," the Astrologer replied. "But about this! I needn't keep you while I make any experiments, because, for my own curiosity, I worked out the question some little time ago, and I'm ready to give you an answer to most points you care to put to me.

"Now, what do you say?"

The figure on the bench quitted its statuesque silence, and observed abruptly:

"Why not tell them straight out what you know?"

"Because," said the Astrologer, "this method is the most convincing. Haven't you any questions?" she went on, turning to me. Her eyebrows contracted as she bent a searching gaze on me—a look I have seen in the eyes of a caged hawk.

"Where is Arabia?" I asked, under this compulsion.

"Here."

"Which is the road to Aleppo, then?"

"There is none."

"No means of getting there?"

"I did not say that."

"By camels?"

"No!"

"Then how?"

"In this way. Let me explain at full length, otherwise it will be unintelligible to you. Can you follow a difficult line of argument? You are a professional person; you can. Forgive me for asking you.

"When you say, 'Where is Arabia? Where is Aleppo?' There is only one answer possible for me to make: 'Here.' That is, you might float through all space, from star to star; and beyond the bounds of this star-system you can see, from one universe to another, and never find them. You might pass the limits of matter and search fresh universes, of which these of ours are the atomic dust, and never find them. You might shrink to the sphere of the ultimate atoms which create matter, and explore infinite new universes within each of these, and never find them. So far as space reaches, they are nowhere!

"But observe me. Space is penetrated through and through by spirit. In the nature of things there are more realms of space than one, and these realms penetrate and coexist with one another, though remaining perfectly independent. Let me illustrate by an example. Suppose two straight lines a and b. they intersect at a point AB. At the point AB, which is common to the two lines, the line b penetrates the line a. A denizen of the line a, if we can suppose such a thing—perhaps you have amused yourself with imagining the conditions of a being limited to one dimension, when you were learning geometry?—such a denizen of the line a incapable of imagining existence outside that line, wall be entirely unconscious, on arriving in its travels at the point AB, that it is in the line b as well!

"Now, suppose it begins to move along the line *b:* it is evident that it will be a good deal at a loss to account for itself. And it will meet with many extremely novel facts. Can you apply the parable?

"Think how different the same scenes appear to us at different times in ordinary life! It is just because we have got into a new realm of space—have got into a 'new line,' as we call it—only, in these cases, the line we have got on to is at such a very little angle from our old line that we are not puzzled or disturbed. But you have got considerably more of a jerk. What is the last thing you can remember about your travels in Arabia?"

"A camel-kick," I said, half dubiously, half incredulously.

"I was trying to unfasten my instrument case when the beast lifted his hoof, and—"

"Precisely so," said the Astrologer loftily—"precisely so! The shock to the brain has sent you clean out of one plane of existence, so to speak—or line of existence, to keep to our old illustration—and set you down in another. In which," she added, politely inclining her head, "we are very pleased to see you."

"But no such thing has ever happened? Surely no such case is recorded?"

"It is not for me," said she, "to divulge the secrets of my profession. It is sufficient that it is the only possible explanation."

"Then is this my body?" I inquired helplessly.

"Has it been turned over with me from my old scheme of things? Or have I been provided with a new one for use here?"

"That I really am not sure about," said she apologetically.

"It's her own," remarked the statuesque figure.

"The transit was on the axis of the intersection."

"Now, really," plaintively remonstrated the Astrologer, "you never seem able to get it out of your head, Apheloë, that that was a purely imaginary case. We *assumed* last night that the transit was on the axis, and worked out the results—"

"Oh yes, you're right. I remember," said the statue, with some asperity and without the least relaxation of her rigidity.

"Then," I said, "my body is probably lying about loose in the Arabian desert somewhere?"

The Astrologer bowed.

"Most likely it is," she said.

"Eaten, I should say," said her companion.

"Anything that eats my remains will have had an unpleasant time with the contents of my pocket medicine case," I observed. "It contained some highly uncomfortable poisons."

"Ah, they wouldn't come with you," said the Astrologer wisely. "You may consider yourself lucky—but no doubt your strength of will has something to do with it—in preserving so much of your appearance as you have."

"Perhaps unlucky," I said. "I might have improved my looks a little."

She smiled politely, and Chloris, who was making friends with a pigeon that inhabited the recesses in the stonework of the tower, rose to go, suppressing an incipient yawn.

The Astrologer addressed her with a good deal of seriousness.

"I need not enforce on you, Lady Chloris, the absolute necessity of keeping secret this consultation. It will be to your own interest not—"

Chloris interrupted the solemn address.

"To speak the candid truth, I don't understand a word you said. And I gave up trying to. Really, I thought you would have been some help."

The magician glanced at me with a quizzical look, as though she would say: "You and I can make allowance for a child's self-importance," but made no remark.

As I passed her, I said:

"One word more. Can you place me back in the old state?"

"That is quite possible. Anytime you wish to try the experiment the best efforts of the College are at your disposal. It is a most interesting case."

"And can I come back again?"

"Oh, certainly."

"My best thanks. Some day I may apply to you. Stop! I don't want to be dropped down in the middle of the desert. Can you deposit me somewhere about Hexham, in England?"

"With a little difficulty. You will have to travel, I am afraid, to the limits of the Western Ocean, until you come to a town where two colossi guard the entrance to the harbour. Beside them is a square temple whose walls are plated with bronze. In it you will find the person who can enable you to have your wish."

"Now," I added, "are journeys like these common? Do you go voyaging into strange states of existence yourselves in this style?"

She looked the least bit embarrassed, but, professionally calm, she made answer:

"We never have—there is no harm in telling you so. I will not say that we have not received visits from the inhabitants of other spheres. But we know little of them. There is a certain risk in the journey back which you will not experience, having made the transit already once. You have, so to say, established a groove, and your coming and going will be easy—even some of us who might be sufficiently attached to you, you might take with you."

"Attached by a sufficiently substantial chain?" inquired Chloris sweetly from the stairs.

We descended, and were offered almonds and sherbet by the strange old creature, for whom I had somehow almost a liking.

Then we were dismissed by a narrow outer stair, which crept round two sides of the erection in a most dizzy and exciting fashion—though safe enough in reality—for weaker heads than ours.

The unprepossessing custodians were still smiling their mirthless smile, the dragoons stood grinning at us as we passed. It was a relief to dive away into the busy haunts of the people, among the crowded magazines and the lively cafes, where the cool green gardens overflowed with streams of bright humanity. We joined in the concourse. It was still early in the day, even as they, who rose at sunrise, measured it. There was a large open square, marble-paved, the four sides of which were composed of buildings of an uncommonly splendid kind. One-storied houses being the rule, it was rare to find such an assemblage of lofty erections. Their great height was thus made more impressive still. I had only been once here before, but I had no eyes today for the gleaming white columns, nor the delicate coping of the frieze, sharply cut against the deep shade within the colonnades. In the midst of the square there was drawn up in line a company of soldiers, which attracted all my attention. For I could not get rid of the uneasy feeling that in no long time the State would have to fight for its life. Hitherto I had had no opportunity of seeing the kind of way in which it would approach the business. One is accustomed in Europe to think of the training of a soldier as a compromise between instruction which develops individual initiative and drill which suppresses it. The tendency in Alzôna seemed to be to discard drill as an artificial prop, much as modern armies have discarded the manufacture of "Dutch courage."

"It would be needful with an army of slaves," remarked Chloris. "But practice and common sense give just as good results with intelligent, free people—that's our idea; and then we preserve the power of all our soldiers to act independently upon occasion."

The evolutions of the twenty or thirty who composed the body we were watching were certainly carried out with a precision and surety which was delightful to watch.

"And are you thinking of joining our army?" said a serious voice behind me, with a tinge of humour in it.

"Athroës, how very inconsiderate of you to startle us in that fashion," said my friend.

It was indeed the eminent doctor. And the three of us spent a thoroughly unsatisfactory and charming afternoon—unsatisfactory, that is, to the harnessed modern mind. Athroës was at his or her best, and in a most gracious mood. Chloris kept quiet, and had only one or two slight passages of arms with her. Even then she seemed flattered at the serious way in which Athroës regarded her argument, instead of covertly laughing, as she often did at people. We had no less than three visits to the cafes, Athroës insisting that there was a particular kind of cake, which she was not in the end successful in obtaining anywhere. We strolled irresponsibly, into and out of concert-halls, theatres, and gymnasia. We sat beneath palms, where the scent of white flowers was heavy on the air; by the side of placid sheets of water, acacia-fringed; in the shade of terraced mounds, whose low summit blossomed with stretches of anemone, red and white.

"Come," said Chloris, when Athroës and myself had concluded a lengthy disputation on a medical question, "let us join in this ballgame that's being started here."

"Me! I can't play!" I exclaimed.

"Oh, you can!" she insisted. "You know the points to remember. Nothing is easier."

Athroës warmly concurred in the suggestion. In a town where everybody is (more or less) the social equal of everyone else, there are no scruples about joining the company of strangers.

"But will they have us?" I inquired.

"Yes, of course; they'll be only too pleased. The more the better. See, one of their sides is far too small. They will have to bring some over. Let us join it instead."

And so I found myself—a respectable practitioner—taking the field in this absurd game. There were twenty-one of us a side in the event. Some treated it pretty much as a trial of skill and as a sort of active billiards or bowls; others, mainly the younger element, were much more energetic, and shortened their robes by pulling them through the zone, so as to give their limbs freer play—a constant practice with the people of the country when engaged in any active exercise. As one often does when learning a new game—at least, such is my experience—I covered myself with credit, a distinction which, I hasten to say, I entirely failed to live up to in the future. We had four points to the other side's one when the players agreed to stop. I was surprised to know that the afternoon was over, and that a meal would be waiting our return to Ilex's. We brought Athroës home with us, and had supper *en famille.*

"I must just go and get some pistachios that came to our house from Kytôna the other night," declared Chloris. "I won't be gone ten minutes."

While she was away I took the opportunity of mentioning to Athroës where we had been in the morning. Chloris had never referred to it all day. She was obviously sore at the ill success of her idea, on which she had led me, as she thought, to build such expectations. Consequently, I did not like to say anything in her presence. But now I told the doctor.

"You would never guess where we went this morning?"

"No? Wouldn't I?"

"To the Royal Astrologer's! Chloris had an idea she could put me in the track of getting to my own country."

"Well, and did she?"

"Hardly, though she kindly offered to export me, through the medium of a foreign brother magician. Her explanation was that I had been precipitated by a mental shock into a new plane of existence altogether."

I gave a hearty laugh. After the matter-of-fact proceedings of the past few hours, there seemed a good deal of absurdity in the mysteries of the morning.

Athroës, I expected, would treat the suggestion with a still more emphatic contempt. To my surprise, however, she listened attentively, and merely exclaimed:

"Hm!"

"Well, surely it's an absurd hypothesis?" I urged.

She slowly peeled the rind from a pomegranate.

"It's the most reasonable explanation I've met with yet," she remarked.

"Surely you don't believe in such fancies?"

"Look here," said Athroës, tilting back her chair a little and balancing a section of the fruit on the point of a golden dagger-like knife, "I'm a physician. I don't deal in metaphysic, nor yet in psychology. I leave that to others. I know very well that the conditions of the body operate on the mind to a certain extent, and to that extent I am willing to deal with it. I also am aware that the mind and its emotions operate on the body, and to that extent I am likewise prepared to consider it. But I am not, on that account, going to travel outside my science, and devote myself to a course of ethics. Nor am I going to give myself up to the study of the soul and its vagaries and become a psychologist. The magicians have that in hand, and I'm inclined to accept their results."

I sat in silence awhile. Athroës did not seem disposed to enforce her views upon me—she never did—she applied herself, instead, to the dessert, and filled me a beaker of white liquid from a jar that stood near.

"Try this. Ilex gets it from the chestnut groves, and you won't find much to beat it."

Chloris was longer than ten minutes, and she had not long returned when there was a blaze of light and noise outside, and our travellers came back from their expedition. Athroës departed with Chloris, and for a short time the house was full of bustle and movement. But not for long: it was late, and Darûna gently but firmly induced us all to bed.

VII

THE FRONTIER

I lex had an expedition planned for herself and me the next day. She had instructions to proceed up the river as far as the barbarian mountains, to convoy what I understood to be goods and merchandise, which they would bring by way of tribute. As the course of the river skirted the rival realm of Uras, it was clearly advisable that we should keep our eyes open, so as to remark the condition of things there.

The sun had scarcely risen next morning when we parted. We passed out at the massive stone gate, and found a broad, flat boat waiting for us at the quay. It was poled along, not rowed, by energetic water-folk, and there sat in it quite a disproportionate number, as I thought, of armed retainers. Ilex and I came alone, without any servant, and we were accompanied on the voyage by a single State official and two young secretaries. Despite the efforts of our crew, the progress of the boat was not rapid, and we did not reach the limits of Uras until evening. But the way was not dull. The shores, certainly, were flat, but they were not monotonous, except the north bank, which bordered on the desert, and was a kind of no-man's-land. On the contrary, the south bank presented now a pleasant assemblage of houses; now a solitary and romantic tower; now a dense mass of riverside foliage; now a grove of stately trees, where stray fruit-gatherers would come to the water to see us pass; now a broad green meadow, with asphodels that would have comforted Homer's heart; now a solitary monument, with herons its only guardians.

A little shallop with two occupants pushed off to meet us as we approached rather a handsome dwelling, a mile or two from the nearest village. The two young girls who rowed it hailed Ilex familiarly.

"You're safe so far, I see," said one.

"Yes," replied Ilex, "no ambush so far."

"Well, you can go on. Opalissa reports alright."

"Of course we're all right. Even if war had broken out, they daren't interfere with our transit on the river."

"Oh, of course not. All the same, they would! Nothing easier than to engineer an upset on the quiet."

"Well, so long as you say all's clear now, that's enough. Our people are patrolling the north bank?"

The girl in the boat gave a slow nod, with a meaning look, and then they let us forge ahead. As we passed the little craft they gave us a parting flourish of paddles, and the late speaker's eyes rested on me, and grew larger as they did so.

"Take care of yourselves, too," shouted Ilex.

The rowers returned a cry that was nearly inaudible as their boat slipped swiftly down-stream.

"Shall we stop on the boat, Mêrê, or go on shore?" said Ilex, as we approached the wharf outside a grey rubble wall, which was my first glimpse of Uras.

"You know best. Is there any reason why we should do one or the other?" I answered.

"No particular reason," she said. And, indeed, unless you wish to see Achis, which is the name of this distinguished town, it will be pleasantest to sleep on board."

The crew and armed followers lay down in the capacious bottom of the boat. The rest of us found berths on a canopied platform which we had occupied during the day. One of the young secretaries, who was a handy personage and given to looking after the comfort of her fellow-creatures, mixed us warm draughts, aromatic and cordial, of which we were glad enough, as the night grew chilly on the water at this season. I fell asleep with my last glances fixed on the form of a sentinel, stationed on our raised deck; wondering, in a sleepy way, why he had no rifle, and what would happen if a party of Bedouins with firearms were to come upon us.

A sharp crackle wakened me. But it was not the firing of guns, but the result of an attempt on our friend's part to light a fire in a small brazier. Finally successful, she invited us to coffee by way of breakfast, and we went on our journey against the stream. With infinite curiosity I scanned the southern bank as we glided past it. This, then, was Uras, the home of the subtle and inveterate enemies of my hosts! Nothing appeared in the look of the place to show it, as one had an irrational but deeply-rooted idea that it should. The same panorama prevailed, of stately foliage of forest and river-grass, alternating with clearer spaces, where green pastures stretched away from the banks to low hills in the interior, or where collections of houses, walled or open, called for attention. Some of these riverfronts to the towns were very striking—

but no less so in Uras than in Armeria. By midday the company in the boat seemed, I thought, a little excited for some reason or other. The cause was soon plain. The river broadened, and grew full of moored craft. To the left of a thick belt of trees appeared a bit of grey wall, which rapidly revealed itself as an imposing riverfront, behind which rose minarets, turrets and columned balconies. It was Cantalûna, the capital of Uras. Flags flew from the towers of its great central gate, to which a wide set of steps led up from the shore. Near the summit of the wall (not a very high one) was an open gallery, with arcaded pillars; and in it I could see three or four people watching the river. At the gate, too, there were not a few townspeople congregated. And these were Urassites! I could not take my eyes off them.

Just then, our boat, with much splashing and some objurgation, suddenly stopped, and there darted past our bows a long, narrow vessel, very light and low, and heavily gilded all over. It had, I should say, twelve or twenty rowers, and in the stern, without any canopy, were two erect forms, on whose faces were unmistakably marked disdain and determination.

Our pilot, stationed at our stem, bowed till I momentarily expected to see the obsequious functionary go over the side into the stream: and I noticed that all the boats in the neighbourhood paid a similar compliment.

At the same time Ilex explained to me:

"That's the Queen of Uras, and her cousin, the Chief Treasurer."

"Which is which?" I said; but Ilex had gone forward to speak to the State officer who was with us. I turned to the invaluable young secretary, who told me the nearer to us was the queen.

"At least, she is very like her portrait, she said. "Her hair is much lighter than the Treasurer's."

She turned out to be right, and I followed the course of the elegant craft with much interest until it lay alongside the steps. A brilliant assemblage had gathered near the gate, but the queen sprang out and walked sharply past them, when they turned and accompanied her, in a confused procession.

"Has she come back from a journey?" I hazarded.

"No, your ladyship," said the sentinel of the night before, looking up from below with the same frank readiness to join in the conversation that one remarks in a north-country servant or workman; "it's her usual style. She always has a lot of attendants."

"Nice life, too, she leads them," muttered a retainer over her shoulder.

For a long time we poled past the city. Clumps of palms appeared over the wall now and then, and the various towers, gates, embrasures, and galleries afforded plenty of interest. After a while, however, the wall came to an end, and before long only a minaret's summit could be seen to remind us of Cantalûna.

A chance remark I dropped made Ilex think I would like to visit a town in Uras: so we brought up for the night at a place called Lythomais, instead of pushing on to Kytôna. We drew up to a low wharf, where one or two people were loafing about; and none of us was sorry to have the opportunity of a walk on land, after the cramped accommodation of the boat. It was arranged that we should all try and find quarters in the odd little fortified town, with the exception of the Government Agent and a few of the crew and escort, who were to stand by the ship.

"Give me the stars for a bed-curtain," observed the first-named, in an unwonted flight of eloquence.

"I can't stand being shut up in a domestic gaol all night!"

I quoted Dr. Johnson at the Agent.

"'A ship is a prison, with the additional chance of being drowned,'" I said. "*A fortiori,* a boat is—"

"Oh, but I can swim. And what's to hinder me walking ashore?"

We might have argued the matter at some length, but the rest of the party were apprehensive the gates were going to be closed. So we strolled in, between two massive round towers. Ilex inquired about sleeping facilities. The ancient custodian of the gateway informed us there existed in the place only one khan, or travellers' resting-place, and was sceptical as to its holding the whole party. Pressed as to other possibilities, she (or it might be he) admitted that strangers were sometimes known to be received at the house of the town seneschal. This was pointed out to us a little way along the wall. Ilex and I decided to make investigation there, while the rest of us occupied the khan in force.

The town seneschal did not live in a very imposing dwelling, and after the houses in Alzôna it seemed very rough and small. But this was only an out-of-the-way village, where one could not expect the luxuries of a capital. As everywhere, it was a one storied house: but it had two substantial square rooms built like towers, close together on the roof. The arched doorway was closed (a rare thing in Alzôna) by a heavy door with a good deal of metalwork on it. A knock brought up the seneschal in person, who was no more impressive than the dwelling, but who, after consultation with the rest of the family, agreed to take us in for the night. The preliminary discussion was a long one, and as we stood at the door listening to the voices within, word came from the others of our party that the khan was roomy enough for them all, and, with squeezing, would hold two more.

"Shall we just turn round and go?" said Ilex.

"Perhaps that would hurt the seneschal's feelings," I answered. "Let us wait and see what turns up."

What turned up was that we were offered one of the roof rooms, divided into two by a most elaborate and beautiful, though roughly executed, screen of acacia-wood. An apology was offered for the fact of the evening meal being over, and we were introduced into the principal apartment of the house, where the family were assembled by the firelight. A handsome, tall, cross-looking personage was presented to us as the *conjux* of our host. We excused her failing to appreciate visitors at that time of night, but she certainly did not exert herself to be agreeable. Two daughters of the house, on the contrary, were pleasant enough in their way. Others, old and young, were present, whose relations to the household I did not clearly gather. Ilex and I did not stay long downstairs, but made our way to the room we had secured, where swinging lamps had been lighted. The streets, which had been absolutely deserted before dark, were now much livelier. For a good while we watched the populace, and I was surprised to find them not very much different from the Alzôna people.

There was a certain *gaucherie* about them, which might be due to their rustic remoteness: and they seemed less intelligent and graceful, perhaps. But I had expected to find a race of fierce swashbucklers, and, except here and there, no such grisly people were observable. Yet, after a while, I did recognise that there was a spirit abroad in the crowd which was foreign to that of Alzôna. A pushful, swaggering carelessness of others showed itself pretty distinctly to the observant onlooker. And in point of physical development, there was no doubt that the town folk here were possessed of bigger frames, stronger muscles, stouter limbs, louder voices, than my shapely friends of Armeria. Only I had expected something a great deal coarser still.

At last the crowds grew noisy, and a Babel of strident repartee, not too decent, arose in the street. We left our station from which we had looked down, in the shadow of the tower, and made our way to the back of the house. Here we were alone. We did not talk much. There was a seat in the rampart which ran round the flat roof, and we mounted on it, and finally settled down in one of its corners. Ilex seemed strangely embarrassed. I could not understand it. For myself, I was thoroughly content to be where I was—if I must remain in this strange world. If I *must?* Was there any motive for my leaving it? Could I be better off, or happier, in the world I used to know? Safer?

What made Ilex so silent? Did she know of any danger of which I was ignorant? Were the raucous shouts of the passing crowds directed at us? The murmur of them rose in the distance, and I shivered a little.

"You're cold; we'll go in," said Ilex.

"No, indeed; it's so much warmer than on the river!"

"But you shook with cold this minute."

"It wasn't cold, really. I was thinking "

"Never mind. It's time we went in. I wonder what our respectable host thinks of us sitting out here in the starlight. Not a thing the Urassite is addicted to."

"Isn't it?"

"No; they much prefer a bustling causeway or a comfortable cafe. Unless, indeed, they are up to mischief."

"Then you don't think there is anything to be feared from them tonight?"

"My good Mêrê, no! They haven't the invention necessary to think of it." She and I turned slowly to the tower where our room was, she passing her arm round me in the fashion I felt so comfortable.

"We are as safe here as we could be at home."

"You remember Thekla, though?" I said hesitatingly.

"Ah, that was a *coup* of the Government's. She opened the way to the chamber as she spoke. If there were agents of the Government about in this little hole, there might be trouble. But they are too busy elsewhere."

She kissed me, and we slept the sleep of the just, undisturbed by risks, real or imaginary.

The next day we pursued our voyage, past the kingdom of Kytôna. On successive days we proceeded along the river-shores of smaller estates; all interesting to me, and containing plenty of material for observation from the boat's deck. Latterly, a thin blue chain of mountains was to be seen in the distance ahead, and the river was rapidly getting shallower and narrower. At last we came to a point where an artificial pool, filled with craft, communicated with the stream. Here we stopped, and commenced an overland journey, which lasted nearly two days. It was almost evening when we reached the base of the mountains, and we spent the night in the open air.

The vegetation had assumed a more tropical appearance; the nights, too, were much warmer,—which seemed curious, considering the comparatively short distance we had travelled. Our way the next morning led across an open plain dotted with patches of bamboo, to a magnificent gorge. Sheer precipices rose on each side to an immense height. Veils of green trailing plants with vivid flowers clung to the dark crags, and bright flashes high up the rocks indicated the streamlets that trickled from the mountain top. The climb was not a long one, nor a steep one either. The defile broadened into a wide amphitheatre of rocks, from which an abrupt descent led to an illimitable extent of country.

The view was splendid—forests, clearings, moors, stretched away to the horizon. Here and there, smoke rising proclaimed the existence of houses.

"And what is this fine country?" was my first question, when my admiration had subsided.

"This has no name. It is the country of the barbarians," said the young secretary, and, when I glanced interrogatively at Ilex, she affirmed the same.

"It seems to me," I said, "that I should feel inclined to make myself mistress of a good slice of this territory. Why, you might be the most powerful monarch in the world!"

My companions, somehow, could not be brought to see the force of this argument.

"There are the barbarians there already, you know," observed the other secretary—(not the amateur steward).

"But think what a lot of good you would do them!"

"If they would let you," interposed the State Agent.

"Let you! They would *have to* let you. Surely you are not afraid of barbarians!"

"Well, then," went on Ilex, treating the subject with extreme levity, "you would be a ruler over so many wild rangers. I personally prefer to be a citizen of a civilised town for choice; where one can have plenty of friends and interests!"

"But you could bring people with you and build your towns."

"And civilise the barbarians by squashing them down? It doesn't sound a hopeful experiment, Mêrê."

"It has been tried with the greatest success by my country-folk," I assured her—I hope not mendaciously; but I begin to think I may have been a little too positive on the subject, when I recall the civilised barbarians I know.

The Agent, who was a matter-of-fact person, took the trouble to explain that the relations of the barbarians with the civilised world constituted too delicate a matter for anyone even to think of disturbing the *status quo*.

"Where should we get our children from?" she asked.

And just then there emerged from the cover of a clump of trees a procession of dirty, unkempt denizens of the prairie, evidently the inhabitants of the land. They moved with a free and haughty air, for all their insanitary condition: but what caught my attention most was the fact that one or two infants lay in the arms of each. Tiny babies they were, to the number of a hundred or so; and they were promptly stacked, like so much merchandise, on the ground between their affectionate parents and ourselves. On our part an equally imposing pile of carpets and woven tissues of the commonest kind was erected. While the Agent and Ilex examined the one heap, the native chiefs inspected the other. Their examination was perfunctory. Each party was used to the other's dealings, and took the quality of the supply for granted. However, Ilex asked me to accompany the Agent and her in their tour.

"What is the meaning of this?" I wanted to know.

"These are the weekly supply of citizens for Armeria," she replied. "These people are glad to be relieved of them, but they squeeze a return out of us (these carpets) by threatening to cut off the supply. They have business instincts, these innocent children of Nature!"

"May you reject weakly ones?" I said.

"Oh no. Only if there is actual disease. As you are a physician, you may be able to give us some help."

I accordingly advised the Agent with great gravity and assumption of wisdom in each case. That officer, however, knew as much of pathology as I, and the net result of my assistance was that we detected a broken leg that had been badly set.

"Poor little mite!" said the Agent, with a gentleness that surprised me. We stood and looked at the atom.

"Look here!" resumed the Agent, "we'll pass her. She's had a bad time in her few months' life; and she'll have a better with us than she will here."

Of course, it was not for me to raise objections. Ilex had tired of the inspection; so had the native chiefs, and she had gone up to them, and was immersed in listening to their eloquence, and in giving directions for the feast of which we mutually partook as the next item in the day's proceedings. The barbarians behaved very well at this repast, though it was a little laughable, when one considered it, to be solemnly picnicking in a long row, *vis-à-vis* of a similar range of extremely uncleanly savages of unconventional ideas as to table etiquette, The meal ended, we retired, leaving our friends in possession of their booty. Our crew and escort, laden with our living freight, which they carried in great baskets slung on poles, buckled to for the return journey. This being downhill, there was considerable danger of an upset; and I liked the extreme care which every member of the party took to avoid injury to the precious burden.

As we entered the pass, I turned and looked at the spreading panorama. The barbarians were wending their way, in a thin line, along the plain. I felt conscious of a certain thrill of pleasure as I turned my face towards Armeria.

Emerging from the cool defile, we passed a shallow lake, the resort of several white-winged birds, like cranes, with a flamingo or two amongst them. Doubtless there were flocks of these behind the tall rushes and papyrus that grew round the lake's margin.

As one of the cranes rose and flew towards the south-west, my eye, following it, fell on an interesting monument which seemed strange in this unpeopled district. It was a small erection of pure Greek design, and was said to serve the purpose of a rest-house, in case traffickers should be overtaken by the night in bad weather.

I wondered that no cities had grown up here, for the Agent told me—and I could see—that the troops of people which gathered here from many lands was enormous. Cavalcade after cavalcade passed us. The first to go by hailed from Uras, and we took absolutely no notice of it, nor it of us. But there were others whose leaders we saluted more or less effusively. Their bizarre differences of costume, coming as they did from such widely scattered countries, was most entertaining. One set of travellers would wear helmets with great glittering crests, reminding me irresistibly of pantomime. Others would wear half-diaphanous gauzes; others carried ponderous axes. Some bands were dressed alike;

most, however, were not uniformed. Long robes, short kirtles, talkative parties, solemn processions, formally ordered hierarchies, loose crowds—each nation seemed to have its own peculiar way of bringing its children home. The most startling thing was to see a troop, which I was told came from a state far to the south, called Apracôta, attended by officers carrying genuine Roman fasces—whether as an emblem of rank or as religious symbols, I could not tell, but the resemblance was perfect, down to the cross binding of the fastenings.

Ilex told me where each party came from, so far as she was able, and when this source of conversation flagged, we talked about the children.

"These will be Star children," she observed.

"Every week has a name—Star, Eagle, Crescent, Stag, and so on. I am a Fuchsia myself, because I was brought when the *Kamprôna* (fuchsia) week was current."

"You!" I said, amazed. "You were not brought in this way? You're not the child of some—"

"Some disreputable barbarian? Certainly," she said, wonderingly. "Of course, we all are. Are you not?"

"No!" I returned, helplessly. "But you don't mean—"

"Didn't I make it clear that we came weekly for supplies of population? I thought—"

"Oh yes! But not *all*—I didn't realise that you all—"

"I see," said Ilex, not in the least discomposed by my discovery of her shady origin. "It wasn't *quite* clear. One forgets you are such a complete stranger!"

She put her arm round my neck, with a friendly pressure of her fingers on my shoulder, that made me feel a wild longing to prove her to be no scion of the degraded race beyond the mountains. I said, with a gulp and a smile:

"Don't you see that you're defying every law of heredity? How can you possibly be descendants—you especially—of those wretched savages? You who are cultured, well-balanced, kind-hearted people—fair-minded, high-principled—! It is not possible."

"I'm not acquainted," said Ilex, "with what you call the law of heredity. Has it anything to do with the law of nature? Anyhow, you may trust me for the facts. I fancy that if the law won't square with them, so much the worse for the law!"

"But I hate to think," I said angrily, "that you are descended from a savage! It can't be!"

"There is no need to think it. Why should you think about it at all? I'm certain I never do. You needn't teach me to, Mêrê!"

That remark, very quietly made, brought me to my senses. I was behaving uncommonly rudely, and much more like a savage myself than a person who prided herself on her ancestry. I calmed down, and would have dropped the subject only that Ilex took a malicious pleasure in bringing the discussion to a natural instead of a sudden termination.

"Mind you, I admit," she said, "that these tribes (we know next to nothing of them) sometimes get supplies of children from civilised states far away. You may fancy me one of them! Personally, I don't want to be other than my fellow-townsfolk, however."

After this amazing and rather disconcerting conversation, I submitted in silence to be taken down to the boat, which started on its return journey accompanied by two others, as our party was so considerably increased. The stream being with us, we reached Alzôna in much less time than it had taken us to travel up the river in going.

As we sat on the little platform and watched the broad current which bore us on, in company with bits of twigs and branches of other forest debris, the Agent told us of a curious experience.

"Nobody knows anything about these tribes, It's true: and yet I myself have spent months, off and on, over the mountains. Not many, though, can say that! I think I could find my way to the wells, and a river or two—yes, and a track that would take one to the village of the chief barbarian of them all. If anybody wanted it!

"I'll tell you, I was once next to going there—very much against my will. Lady Mêrê, this business of dealing with the savages is one which one has to be brought up to early. To get to know their ways is half the business, and you can't begin too soon. It runs in families, doesn't it, Lady Ilex?—And mine has always had one or two folks in the trade.

"Very well; I was young at the time—seventeen perhaps—and hadn't been more than a couple of years—if that—allowed to go about by myself entirely among these people. I had been with my *conjux* visiting a little village of theirs called Vangnula. Iërelîn (that's my *conjux*, Lady Mêrê)—she was sent for suddenly, to interpret for the Governor of some Western State or other, who had come to see the place in great style. It would be a week before she came back, so here was I, alone in this uncivilised place, with nothing to do but to study the habits of these creatures.

"And I might have got some very valuable ethnological information together. But, unluckily, that's just what you mustn't do if you want to get on with the barbarians. They are such close creatures. Stop in your own quarters, talk business to them, and you're all right. Take any interest in their family arrangements, though, or go near their houses, and, by the ocean! what a riot there'll be! That's the nuisance: you have to get to know these things, and what you may do and what you mayn't. Or else you get into no end of trouble.

"For instance. The tribe I was with was just as quiet and peaceable as a set of lambs. Nobody ever dreamt of danger amongst them. Yet, two years after I was there, they massacred the Syltis agent in cold blood—and worse than that—for what they chose to call insult to their gods. What it was they wouldn't explain: and we couldn't guess. Because they are not a sensitive people by any means about their religion. They don't mind discussing it—(some *do*)—and they even stand chaffing about their gods, quite calmly. So what had roused them, nobody knows. And it's no use inquiring.

"Well, for days I occupied myself as I best could. A Urassite or a Kytonian would have hunted. A Priqua would have dreamed. I could do neither, and I grew tired. The special work Iërelîn and I were sent to do—glossary-making—I couldn't do alone, because she was in charge of it, and my part was principally clerk's work. I used to take long stretches into the country in different directions, with a barbarian guide with me. I had a very distinguished guide—a daughter of the chief. A prim young affair, she was—knew her way about, though—and might be sixteen or so."

The Agent took a deep breath and shifted the rugs.

"We got pretty thick, tramping about together. And, really, she was intelligent, for a savage. I haven't your enthusiasm, Lady Ilex, for anybody and everybody, from a cat to an empress" (Ilex flushed faintly in deprecation), "and I can't pretend to see a friend in an unadulterated barbarian. But this girl I did very nearly make a kind of friend of. It's a long time ago—a long time—and I can scarcely realise it now. I suppose she wasn't really—but she seemed to me to be superior to the run of savages. And she was sharp enough—never could miss the track. And kind-hearted, I think—she would never be guide for hunters, because they killed things, and she never would watch them kill the goats for supper. So we used to go out every day, more than once. And I used to enjoy her quaint remarks—quite clever, sometimes, they were—; and I kept thinking how Iërelîn would be amused, too, when she returned.

"Well, they say it doesn't do to make intimates of savages. I don't know how that may be: I haven't repeated the experiment. And I don't know how it would have turned out if I could have brought the girl away to Armeria. But this was what happened.

"Late one night—it was the night before Ïerelîn was expected—I was sitting in my quarters in the company of a dim oil-lamp. Perhaps I had eaten something that did not agree with me:—perhaps I was impatient for the next day, but, like a senseless idiot, I could not turn in and go to sleep, but must cast about for something to keep me amused. What I thought was a very happy idea struck me—though, as I'll tell you, I altered my opinion of it next morning. That was, to hunt up Sakaluna's hut, and have a good talk with her. I started to carry out the notion on the instant. There seemed something interesting in paying a nocturnal visit to the native houses, which we always carefully kept away from. I *was* a brainless young ninny—but we all do absurd things now and again. The night was very bright. I was pleased and excited at finding something to occupy me so well, and I reached the savage village in no time. I knew the knot of huts the chief lived in, and I heard Sakaluna's voice in the nearest. I pushed aside the grass-cloth curtain, and walked in.

"But, my conscience *(Irta)!* I had reckoned without my host, very literally. There were five or six people in the hut. Some screamed, some flew to the corners—it makes me laugh always when I think of it—and Sakaluna stood like a ghost, trembling. I began to do my best to reassure them and to talk to my guide. She answered in the shortest snatches of words, and I saw in a minute or two that it was hopeless to go on.

"'Well, I *have* startled them!' I said to myself. I tried to say a word or two more—that I hadn't thought they would be so frightened, and so forth. But it was no use! Big and little, they kept up the to-do: it was laughable, but provoking. So I turned to go; but first I went up to Sakaluna, and took her by the hand, and told her exactly how it was, and how vexed I was to have caused any disturbance.

"Well, she wouldn't look at me. She stood like a statue, and kept her eyes away and shook. So I couldn't do more, but I came away. I hadn't got halfway back before I felt sure someone was following me. If you had been trained as I had to nightwork in the forests, you could have told it too. Perhaps you could scarcely say how. Anyhow, I felt quite certain of it.

"'Maybe Sakaluna wants to explain matters,' I thought to myself. 'If so, she shall catch me up, I'm not going to turn for her.' For, you see,

I didn't half relish the way I had been received by her and the rest of her lot.

"I slowed down a bit, however. Half an hour later I was lying on my back in the chief's hut, with a kind of savage council of war being held over me. Don't ask me how it happened, for I was unconscious for a few minutes. Whether I was struck with a club, or lassoed, or what, I can't tell. I know my head ached sufficiently. Well, there seemed to be seven or eight old chiefs present, leading the talking; and half the tribe appeared to be squeezed in, squatting and silent, except for a thick sort of groan now and then. I can tell you, my blood ran cold as I listened; and I called myself all the names I could think of for not having the sense to sit quietly in my quarters, and forever coming out at all. Their talk was all of taking me up the country to the great chief, with a cheerful view to my being clubbed or stabbed or poisoned—and their principal controversy was as to which of these particular modes of despatch to recommend. As I grew more and more collected, it seemed the oddest, strangest thing that these commonplace people, that I knew so well, should be consulting, in a matter-of-fact way, about putting a sudden end to me! And me there, listening to it all—!

"Then, you know how, when something very important's happening,—how you take notice of little things?"

"Your mind seems to take refuge, by a kind of irony, in trifles?" suggested Ilex.

"That's the way to put it. A lady like you knows how. I know what I mean, but I can't put it in those words. Same way, though, I've seen a prisoner, brought out to be degraded, look round as if little things caught her eye and took up all her attention—bits of matting, furniture, boxes; it doesn't matter what. Just as if the business on hand was quite a secondary affair. I've seen it, too, in troops before coming to close quarters.

"That was the feeling I had then. I can see that hut-roof to this day, with its smoky beams and the pots hanging from them, the bunches of plantain and the long spears. As I lay and stared at it, I thought of making one try for safety. I said, as impressively as I could—I was flat on the floor, remember:

"'I don't know what I've done to rouse your prejudices. But take care how you treat me. If any harm comes to me, my queen will see that you answer for it! She will do me justice!

"The old chief had the impertinence to answer:

"'We will save her that trouble.'

"I gave them some more of my mind, and finally they covered my mouth with a square of grass-cloth. So I could only reflect on my own imprudence, and the ceiling. I gave up listening to their debate, and thought feverishly whether it were possible that Iërelîn might come back early and trace me. At last, I was stupidly conscious that the assembly had broken up. The people and chiefs streamed out; the principal chief and *conjux* (I suppose) retired to a kind of porch, where the only door was. I could not wriggle out, except through there, and as I was pretty firmly fastened with tough creepers, they did not trouble to watch me. I didn't fall asleep, you may be sure. I rolled about, trying to get loose; but to very little purpose. Except to tire myself a good deal. I was lying quiet, when I started violently at hearing a low voice.

"'Hush!' it said, fast and low. 'Don't speak! Don't move, now! Hush, let me reach you. I mean well!'

"I can tell you I felt a queer sensation when a form touched me— mind, I didn't know in the least who it was—and felt to discover which was my head, and which my feet. This didn't take long, and in a moment after, I laughed convulsively to myself, feeling the fastenings cut by a quick hand.

"'The voice said, 'Stand up, and make no noise. I have left the chief sleeping in the porch. Can you walk? You had better wait a minute till you feel less stiff. The door's open, and you have just to step over the chief. I will go and lie beside him, and if you touch him, I will pretend it was me. It is too dark for him to see. You will find the opening by it's being a little lighter outside.'

"'Who are you, then?'" of course I asked.

"She told me she was the chief's *conjux,* and she said in a shaky whisper that I had done them an irreparable wrong, etcetera, and brought insult on the house and the tribe. All the same, she had determined that I should not be killed. Why? Goodness alone knows! You may be sure I didn't ask her. It might have been interesting to enter into a discussion as to motives, but the time and place weren't favourable. No; I waited for her to settle down, and then I stole to the porch—one can laugh at these things now—fixed the light patch with my eye, delicately felt for a hard footing, and skipped successfully over the sleeper. I was outside; and I strolled through the village on to the path for home: and that's all of any interest I remember. Except fainting dead, when I met Iërelîn as the sun was rising," concluded the Agent. She stared hard at the forest that was slipping rapidly past us, and then rose from her bent attitude, and took a long drink of a special compound that Ilex thoughtfully provided for the expedition."

"Did Iërelîn and you go back to the village?" I inquired.

"Not likely!" observed the active secretary.

"Did you ever see the chief's *conjux* again or Sakaluna?" asked the other.

"I never did," said the Agent, deliberately and rather stiffly.

"You gave them a wide berth, I should say!" laughed one of us.

"But then, did you never hear of them? Never knew if Sakaluna grew up: nor sent a message to your preserver?" said Ilex.

"Well, if you *must* know," replied the Agent, "the tribe deserted the village, and moved off to far inland. And when some of our people visited it next, it was empty and ruined. There was a child we got nine years ago, reminds me very much of Sakaluna. You know, Iprys," she said, jerking the words out rather awkwardly, as she addressed the secretary, "Mila's youngest; Erythre. Mila the geographer. She's a nice child. Whether she'll be like my old friend at sixteen, I can't say. Her chin and mouth remind me—" She was silent a while.

"And this was long ago?" I said.

"Eh, what?" said the Agent absently. "Oh yes. Thirty years—twenty-five by any reckoning. Ah, but no, you're *not* coming into my coffee," she concluded, addressing a lizard, which had just been carried up along with our afternoon refreshment.

By evening we had reached Alzôna, and disembarked.

Quiet as our going away had been, our return was received with great enthusiasm. At the quay at the foot of the great gate a long line of rose-coloured figures was drawn up, stretching away through the portals into the city. At their head stood the queen herself, together with several of the principal officers of state. The Agent delivered to her a written list of the cargo. She smiled pleasantly, and spoke with great kindness to Ilex and myself; but she looked terribly thin, and her eyes shone more brightly than I cared to see. As she turned to precede us into the town, however, her royal carriage was no less proud than in weeks past. Our prizes, carried by a hundred of the people, followed her, flanked by our escort, and we ourselves brought up the rear. Crowds of citizens, common as the spectacle must have been, assembled to see us go past. Flowers in profusion were thrown in our way. At the palace the queen left us, but watched us go by. She waved her arm slightly to us, and I saw Galêsa, who stood by her with his ill-looking son, look at her for a moment with an indescribable expression of cunning triumph. My mind went back to the unsettling revelations of Opanthë. I felt I could not rest until I had learnt what developments had taken place in my absence.

For the moment nothing could be done. We moved on, to the sound of flutes and lyres, to the Erythraion, a handsome building of warm red stone. In its cheerful portico were grouped a number of the officers to whose care we were to resign our charge. The head of our procession stopped, and Ilex moved forward. She took me by the hand as she started, so that, somewhat against my will, I became a prominent figure in the proceedings. The principal officer received us with solemn courtesy, and a kind of time-honoured formula was gone through, ending in our stepping aside and handing over the new small citizens to their temporary custodians. The hundred townsfolk, the escort, and we were then feasted in an open courtyard, surrounded by pillars. I sat between Ilex and one of the officials of the place. The first question one put was naturally:

"And how is the Uras business going on?"

"Very badly!"

"But war has not broken out yet?"

"War! Oh no! I hope it won't come to that!"

"It isn't generally considered inevitable, then?" Ilex quickly struck in.

"Oh no, Mêrê, that is a mistake. I don't think we most of us anticipate anything so serious, do we?"

"A good many of us are beginning to," gloomily replied the official.

"Well, don't!" said Ilex. "It's the surest way to make it come. Anticipate cramp, if you're swimming, and you are halfway to getting it. Anticipate a refusal, if you're asking a favour; and you may save yourself the trouble of talking. Anticipate a fall as you walk on a mountain-path; and over you go. Make sure of defeat—dwell on its certainty—and you *can't* win. The only way to do anything worth living for, is to believe with all your heart in impossibilities. Then they become possible."

"I don't know that I altogether agree with you," said my neighbour; but Ilex declined the discussion being engaged by the Governor of the Salîtra quarter—an important personage, who had joined in the day's ceremony—in a lively colloquy respecting the unfitness of the Arch-Surveyor. I could only hear snatches of what they said, such as:

"But the Principal Assistant—"

"That's not my point; I admit the work gets done, but—"

"You may rely on it; before long, half the roads—"

"Indeed? Then Beatrice must be very much occupied—" So that I turned to my neighbour again.

"It must be bad for the trade of the country that this uneasiness should be so prolonged. For I suppose it does amount to that; there *is* uneasiness amongst people about this?"

"Indeed there is: but it is hardly acute; it doesn't affect our daily affairs much. Still, the negotiations which are going on must be important, because the governments won't trust to despatches, but are constantly sending special emissaries. Not many people seem to notice this much; but, for myself, I think it is very significant. And so do most of my friends."

I expressed my agreement with her. It was clearly necessary to be keenly alive to every move of Opanthë's, and with that view I determined to frequent the palace as much as possible. And yet it was desirable not to be much with Opanthë alone. She might be communicative; on the other hand, I might commit myself through my ignorance, and arouse her suspicions. In reflecting on my best course, I grew *distraite*, and I am afraid I did not prove a very lively companion during the remainder of the meal.

IRENE CLYDE

VIII

THE LATTICE

A nd so I went to the palace constantly. So often, that Lyphra, one of the children of our house, informed me one day that Athroës said I had become a regular courtier—to my mild consternation, for I did not want my movements to be conspicuous. However, I felt by this time pretty sure that Opanthë would put my frequent presence down to zeal in the fulfilment of my supposed nefarious duties. And, besides, Athroës was a professed mocker at courts and courtiers.

It was interesting to watch Opanthë's behaviour towards me. Nearly invariably it was as entirely unconscious of any special relation between herself and me as could possibly be figured. I had difficulty sometimes in convincing myself that I had put the right interpretation on her enigmatic utterance. Calm, more than a shade contemptuous, carefully polite, and always strikingly beautiful, she did not seem to be in the least disturbed in mind or spirits by the anxieties of the time. Only, very occasionally, she would shoot out a glance or give a peculiar curl to her handsome mouth, which plainly showed in what light she regarded me. And, on one of my first visits after the expedition to the barbarians, she showed this more obviously than she usually allowed herself to do.

The good-humoured Princess Iôtris has been drawing me out to speak of my adventures on that occasion.

"Yes."

"And occupied your time well on that occasion?"

The look which Opanthë gave me was most comical. Her habitual impassiveness was shaken for the moment, and amusement at the *double entente*, irony at the expense of the Princess, and intriguing familiarity towards me, struggled for the mastery in her expression. It was the only time I saw her off her guard, and she immediately quenched the whole of these emotions in a factitious fit of coughing.

"My dear Opanthë," said the Princess blandly, turning round to her, "I should advise a visit to the Western Ocean for that throat of yours. That's a very bad cough."

I expected her to blush, for there was an unintentional *double entente* here also. But she did not.

"Thank you, your highness," she said coldly, "It was not anything the matter with my throat—only an accident."

Iôtris was a little obtuse—sometimes, I thought, purposely.

"Well, it certainly *sounded* as if something were the matter with your throat," she observed, laughingly, "and very uncomfortably so."

Opanthë did not answer, but she neither blushed nor moved a muscle. She went out in a few moments, nevertheless.

The Princess failed to observe her departure and took me by the arm confidentially.

"You saw nothing of Thekla on your travels?"

"Nothing your Highness."

"I'm sorry for Beatrice," she proceeded. "I really am. She is not expansive to strangers or to most of us—a queen she can't be. She has to keep up her dignity. I dare say you've noticed Beatrice does—kind and assuming as she is. But one can't live on an icy peak always—Thekla was the person she unbent to. They were such friends. It was Thekla's art that made it easy and possible. I don't know whether you think much of our art; but we consider Thekla a genius—queens of art and cities are naturally equals. And as a cousin of Beatrice's I knew more than many people what Thekla was to her."

"Did she visit Thekla much?" I asked, knowing that I never had seen her at the house.

"No, you don't understand, of course! No, she could not very well go much there. That would have raised comment. But Thekla was constantly here, and would spend hours alone with her. And she was so good; nobody could be jealous of her, or grudge the pleasure it gave Beatrice to have her."

The pleasant-faced Princess looked grave and gave a little sigh.

"Well, I hope she may come to light, no worse," she added in a lighter tone.

"Indeed, I hope she may," I said, "she was always very good to me!"

Iôtris glanced quickly at me.

"Was she? Then you will do your best to find out what has become of her, won't you? In case you are ever in Uras—you might keep your eyes open for traces of her. Sometimes children know things that might put one on the scent. And I think you would win a child's confidence."

"Do you know what I do, your highness?" I said.

"No!" She turned a half-quizzical face towards me, but listened with grave attention.

"I should capture the most easily accessible magnate of Uras, and retain him till Thekla was delivered up."

"Couldn't!" smiled Iôtris. "Far too delicate negotiations are going to make that possible. It might be an elegant method of precipitating war—otherwise your solution, I am afraid, hasn't much merit."

She laughed and began to address herself to the company generally.

"Ilex tells me our friend from Anglia doesn't approve of our barbarian descent," she remarked.

A tremor of horrified susceptibilities was distinctly apparent.

"I approve of *you*, at all events," I said boldly, glancing round the assemblage and smiling, and, I believe, blushing a little at the same time.

"Of me in particular?" said the girl whom I mentioned as having been engaged in painting on my first visit to the palace.

"Certainly. Of you and several others in particular," I replied. The Princess laughed and clapped her hands.

"She had you there, Kisêna—she had you there!"

Kisêna was accustomed to laughter and placidly watched the amused faces as though they formed a very interesting study.

As, sometime after, Iôtris was leaving the saloon or hall where we were, she said quietly to me:

"You are in no hurry to leave us, then?"

"No, my Princess."

"Perhaps not at all! Is it true what I hear—that Ilex and you are *kerôta*?"

"*Kerôta*, your highness? I do not understand."

"*Kerôta*. One is *kerôta* when one wishes to be *conjux* of anybody. But forgive me if I have spoken recklessly."

For, indeed, Ilex was so much to me that the suggestion, based as it appeared to be on common rumour, affected me curiously. I do not know how I answered the Princess, but I am sure I denied the report; and equally sure that I confirmed her suspicion that it was true.

I could not think it over calmly. The words "*conjux* of Ilex!" *would* not form themselves in my mind. A burning impulse to seek out the Astrologer, and try to escape to the familiar world by whatever occult means, overtook me. But the mere experiment was to involve a long and difficult journey, according to her pronouncement. It was impossible to think of it at present.

I slipped away from the palace. There was a place not far off, where tall white columns of soaring marble served as supports for a wealth of ivy and dark green climbing plants; their shafts held up only a frieze and cornice, across which curtains could be spread. Here I had learnt to come for quiet. At the base of a great Doric pillar I leant against its firm flutings, and followed with eyes the serene aspiration of its sisters opposite, as they raised into the very sky their crown of marble entablature. The snowy whiteness, the cool green, always worked on my mind like music. And I went home without showing any traces of perturbation.

For all that, I felt the effects of that minute's rush of wild feeling. It threw me back for a time on myself. I had insensibly ceased to feel a stranger in the city; now, for a while, the sensation of detachment returned. It was not long proof against the friendliness of the occupants of the house I stayed in—but it had the consequence, meanwhile, of directing my energies into the impersonal channel of politics and intrigue. I devoted myself assiduously to watching the development of the conspiracy on which I had so unexpectedly stumbled; and, in the process, I made frequently repeated visits to the palace, All the time there grew less and less change of a peaceful settlement.

On one of the occasions on which I ventured into Opanthë's apartments, Galêsa strolled, with his usual overbearing air, into the room as I was looking out of the window, and seated himself near her, on a couch on the opposite side, between the door and the fireplace. I should explain that the room opened onto a long corridor, which led at its farther end to a chamber specially reserved, on account of its seclusion, for important purposes.

Opnathë, with as near an approach to excitement as I had ever known her display, and without waiting for compliments—which, indeed, it was not Galêsa's practice to bestow—hurriedly exclaimed:

"Galêsa, who do you think is being lodged in the End Room tonight!"

Galêsa, who was sitting bent forward, with a knee in the capacious embrace of each palm, and a somewhat deeper scowl than usual on his features, turned a slow head half towards her inquiringly.

"No less a person than a special messenger from our ambassador in Uras, with despatches. They are playing a game with us, my friend. They—"

Galêsa made an impatient jerk in my direction.

"She's alright. She's one of us. There's no time to argue that point. Galêsa, they are bringing things to a crisis now."

"How do you know?"

"Nevermind how I know! The certain matter is that our guest must not reach the queen and that the despatches must—reach us."

"And how?"

"How? Isn't the game in our hands? Haven't I a key for the door? Is there anything so simple as to invite the messenger to a goodnight glass? I will enjoy one with her—of a different mixture! Tsuch! Then you come up the stairs, as if to see me on state business—most urgent—two or three strong retainers with you, and plenty of cord. You find our friend sleeping—you lower her gently from a window—the small courtyard just outside is dark as pitch, and there will be nobody about so late. You descend by the stairs unruffled: you and you friends take the dispatch box with you, or leave it for me to annex. Meet a confederate or two in the courtyard, who will have taken charge of her majesty's messenger, and walk coolly out with her as an opium-dosed slave. Nobody will question a person of your consequence."

"No, it seems a good scheme," he said slowly. "Are you certain the drug will work?"

"Certain! Not the first time of trial, Steward! And you have no resource. Think how much depends on appearances. An official sees you, in full official costume, superintending the hauling along of a half-dressed, half-stupid creature. Nothing in the world is easier than to pass it off with a high hand. Indeed, I would recommend you to carry her halfway round the palace before attempting to go out."

Galêsa grinned intelligently, but his face fell.

"There is one fatal flaw in your plan."

"Not one," said Opanthë confidently.

"Who is the officer of the guard in this part of the palace?"

"Cyndonia."

"Then it's no use! She is sure to be hanging about the corridor. I know this part of the building is so secluded that the duties of the officer are simply a sinecure, but that doesn't weight with her. I have met her at three in the morning pacing the passage like a tiger in a cage. Why, I can't tell. But she is sure to interrupt us."

"You may be perfectly easy about that," Opanthë said, with contemptuous triumph. "She would give her eyes for ten minutes here with me, and I shall let her have an hour."

"What!" said the Grand Steward.

"I know you never think about these things. But you should," said Opanthë. "A good many people have done me the honour to consider me worth notice. If you were not too much occupied with yourself, you would see that Cydonia is simply infatuated—self-contained as she is."

I privately doubted the accuracy of her diagnosis.

"Well," said Galêsa, "if things are so, it is quite time we took measures of some kind—your plan, if no other. As you remark, it is no time for argument. I must get my assistants picked and instructed. You will have *your* arrangements to effect, likewise. When is she expected?"

"She might come anytime after dark."

"Who's your informant?"

Opanthë smiled her superior, aggravating smile.

"Understand, you are not to know that."

"Humph! . . . Well!—You are sure there is no moon?"

"Not unless a new one is presented to this planet."

"And your drugs—yes, you say that is alright?"

"Quite."

"What are we to do with our ambassador's envoy—in the end, I mean?"

"Why do you ask me? After tomorrow she can do no harm. Apologise—say some of your servants found her lying in the palace grounds—took kindly care of her—suggest sunstroke—anything."

"After tomorrow she can do no harm—they will wait no longer, that's certain. Their forces are signalled in motion—the queen leaves for the army—and we open the gates when she's gone. Ha!"

A subdued and nervous chuckle escaped the statesman's lips.

"And—just once more—you are quite certain about Cydonia? I wish—I wish we had someother officer. Could we put her off duty and send Psydrophé round? She will sit with a lamp and a book or a map in the antechamber and hear nothing all night—short of a gong."

"My Galêsa, it's the most fortunate thing, I tell you, that we have Cydonia. She simply worships the air I breathe. You notice she is silent and abrupt. Pure shyness! It affects her so to be near me. I can engage to occupy her attention for you."

"Isn't it because you would like her to feel so about you, that you think she does?" said Galêsa bluntly. "Are you sure of your ground? Don't let us make any mistakes."

"Is she not always here? Does she not follow me about the palace? Are not things always being sent 'to improve the look of the room'?"

"But you are not often alone. Other share these rooms."

"Who, then?"

"Chloris."

"Chloris! Chloris is a baby! I suppose you will be saying that I may expect to be supplanted by Etela next. Really, Galêsa, Chloris—?"

"They are near neighbours."

"Yes, and know each other too well to be excited about one another. You do not know!"

Opanthë was getting warm. Galêsa hated anything like a scene with his equals and rose to go. As he left the room he gave me a glance of uncomfortable suspicion.

His confederate smiled.

"Silly old creature!" she said. "Mêrê, you will help us in this! You have all my secrets now—public and personal."

She indicated a darkened recess in the wall by the window, screened by a bronze lattice, and opened the latter.

"Just slip in there, Mêrê, and then, if there is any scuffle, you can burst out and help us."

I complied, with a grim smile at the thought of the kind of assistance they were likely to get: when, to my horror, I found the lattice firmly fixed by a bolt which Opanthë slide in.

"Can't you leave it a little open?" I urged.

"Not possibly!" said she. "Etela would be sure to suspect something if she saw it ajar. She is such a frightened creature!"

"There is some coffee in there," she resumed, "and some cakes, if you feel hungry. Don't rattle the cups."

She moved to the door as she said this, and was gone before I had time to remonstrate, or to feel quite sure whether she meant well or ill. I heard the key turn in the lock.

Considering it over, I thought my best policy was to make no objection to her wishes, and to wait my chance. It was long before she returned. Etela was with her.

"Etela, will you stand behind that lilac silk screen?" she said. Etela obligingly did so, and got between screen and wall.

"Stand against the wall. Thank you. . . now if you move one foot or make one sound, this poniard goes into your heart! Your heart! You understand?"

Apparently Etela did.

"I can't see you, Mêrê. Are you there? Oh, yes—you're not quite hidden. A little farther back, please. Let me see if I can touch you."

A long blade was inserted through the diamond lattice, and carefully dabbed against me.

"Yes! That is right, keep just there."

She made up the fire and lit the lamps. At that moment voices were heard in the passage, and if I had commanded a view of the doorway, which a screen hid from me, I should doubtless have seen the household procession, headed by the chamberlain, escorting the queen's messenger to her chamber.

Opanthë left the room and was absent sometime.

"Etela!" I said, "Etela! Come here and unbolt this latch! Don't be so absurdly frightened! Speak, anyway. Whisper!"

But Etela would not give a sign of her presence, and a more uncomfortable sensation than to be alone with a person whom you cannot reach, and who will not speak to you, it is hard to imagine, short of actual pain.

Later, voices were heard at the door, Opanthë's and Cydonia's.

"Come in, Cydonia, sit down and rest a while." Her voice vibrated melodiously. Usually it was hard and measured.

"Thank you. I will stay in the passage," I heard Cydonia reply.

"Nonsense! See my beautiful fire. It is so much more comfortable in here. Why should you want to stay out in the cold?"

She laughed. "It isn't very cold, Opanthë. And, somehow, I like it. I suppose I am used to it."

Opanthë went out to her.

"But, Cydonia, I want you! Don't be shy of me! It would really please me if you would come in. Don't think I say it out of civility."

"I'm sure you don't. But I think I had better keep outside."

"Cydonia," she murmured, "*Dear!* Come! I do so wish—"

"It's very kind of you. I'm intensely obliged, but at present I think I must stay out here."

Their voices were lowered for a minute or two, and I could not hear anything but the soft splashing of the fountains outside. When suddenly Opanthë's beautiful figure shone in the doorway and she exclaimed angrily:

"Very well, then! You are anxious to insult me. What have I done to you? But I cannot prevent you—affront me to your heart's content. I wonder that you don't come to the door and scoff at me. Do, if you like!" She sat by the fire, pal and erect, with dilated nostrils and flashing eyes.

As I looked at her from the lattice I could not help admiring her. Outside I heard Cydonia softly humming an air.

After about a quarter of an hour—(as I judged by the sounds of the changing guards—it seemed longer)—Opanthë got up and crept out to the corridor.

"I have such a temper, Cydonia; you won't think more about it? You are so hard to offend yourself! Say you forget it and come and sit with me—to show it."

"Of course, I forget it. What was there to forget?" responded Cydonia agreeably.

"You sweet Cydonia!"—and an amicable conversation followed, in such low tones, that I inferred (not incorrectly, as I subsequently ascertained) that the speakers' heads were in pretty close proximity. The next words I heard were: "Now take me in, dear, and put me in a seat. I feel dizzy tonight."

She came in, leaning on Cydonia's shoulder and as she sank onto the couch, she drew her hands between hers and made her sit down also.

"Well, just for a few minutes," said the officer.

Should I warn Cydonia? Better not for a little while. The look of the weapons ready to hand was not encouraging to a peaceable individual, closely cramped up in a cupboard, whose lattice was no protection against a sword-thrust. Cydonia might not stay long. If she did, then I might screw myself up to the point of declaring my presence.

And when Opanthë, a little after, complained of a draught, Cydonia, with alacrity, sprang up, and drew the heavy portiere. "I'll go back now," she said.

"No! No!" exclaimed Opanthë, "or I'll think you are vexed with me yet! I am very weak and nervous tonight. Don't leave me here all alone."

"Please, Cydonia. I am like a child, I know! I don't know what can be the matter with me, but I haven't a scrap of self-command. Don't go!"

"I'll send some of the fan-bearers at once. Where's Etela? I do hope I'm not to blame for it," said Cydonia.

"Dear, no!" she replied. "but don't if you love me, send for anybody. And do stay!"

"Well, I'll leave the door open—see!—And stand within the curtain. That will suit us both. I can see if anyone passes through the chink between the folds."

"Who do you expect might be passing?" Opanthë said quickly.

"Expect? Oh, nobody! That is, nobody who shouldn't be here. Etela will be coming, and, to tell you the truth, one is never sure what goes on. Palace slaves are like others, and they are up to mischief where one least suspects it."

"How could any of the slaves penetrate here?" said Opanthë pettishly. "I wish you would be sensible, and sit comfortably by me."

But Cydonia was obdurate, and stood, talking at intervals, with her eye on the corridor.

"Opanthë!" she said, in a low voice, "somebody's coming up the corridor! The shadows are moving on the pavement. Hush!"

For Opanthë had swiftly risen from the couch and approached the curtain. Cydonia motioned her away with her long blade, which glittered towards her in the light of the flames.

"Gods! She threatens me!" panted the palace beauty, as she crouched in a heap on the floor, trembling with passion.

"No, no that! No, dear!" Cydonia said, coming quickly to her, and gentle patting her shoulder. "Only I wanted you to keep away from the doorway, and I dared not speak. I must go and make out what it was."

She put the curtain aside and went. Opanthë, with the poniard, glided after her.

"Etela!" I said, "Etela! It's a question of life and death! Do you think so much of your own life, that nobody else's is of any account to you? For Heaven's sake come and unbolt this latch!"

To my inexpressible relief, a fluttering figure darted across the room, and, in an agony of apprehension, released me. I caught up on of the long swords which were lying on the floor and put a light one into Etela's hand. It is odd to remember what care I took to choose a light one, when every second was precious. We went out into the corridor. Cydonia and Opanthë were standing at the door of the end room, which was open. I stood in the dead silence irresolute for a moment—two or three. Then Etela's nerves gave way and she burst into a wail, imploring us not to let her be killed, and so on.

"Fly down the corridor," I said. "Alarm the palace. Let nobody pass from here, not if it was the queen herself. I will not let Opanthë pass me—don't be afraid of her."

I fear she was too much overcome to do as I told her, but she pulled herself together, and flew like the wind. This took very much less time to enact than to tell. I myself hurried up the passage in the contrary direction. Opanthë smiled joyfully when she saw me.

"That's right! Thank goodness you're come, Mêrê! I could have killed myself when I found I had forgotten you!"

My answer was to pink her sword-arm—not a heroic act, nor a straightforward one, but necessary.

"Opanthë is in league with traitors, Cydonia!" I cried. She sprang into the room. The door was forced back in my face. A moment later it yielded again and I saw the sleeping form of the envoy, calm and still, with Galêsa and two others, setting on Cydonia.

A moment later, and the lamp was extinguished. We were driven towards the door, and gradually down the corridor. I confess I trembled when I reflected how much it would be to the advantage of Galêsa and his friend if Cydonia and I—especially myself—were not left capable of telling our version of the fracas.

I had never learnt the art of fencing, but I was not unfamiliar with the feel of a sword. Galêsa, on the other hand, and Cydonia were excellent swords folk. The narrowness of the passage prevented the numbers opposed to us from telling, but we were continually being forced back towards the staircase, where we should be an easy prey.

"Come!" I said to myself, "we *must* make a stand!" As was inevitable, I felt the cold steel of my opponent's sword—and more than once.

"Splendid!" my companion found time to say. "Mêrê, I am never so pleased as when I have a good fighter beside me." Which bloodthirsty sentiment appealed to me strongly for the time being.

At last the hurrying of feet was heard through the clang of steel. Our opponents lowered their points, and turning, I saw a crowd of disturbed and excited denizens of the palace—and in advance of them, a slight and solitary figure.

It was the queen herself.

"Am I to be favoured with an explanation of this?" said her majesty.

Galêsa grinned unpleasantly as Opanthë joined us.

"I can only tell your majesty that I came to visit the state messenger from Uras, with reference to our important dispatch just received—here it is in my sleeve—when I was set on by these ladies, who have succeeded in—"

The queen abruptly stopped him.

"Why did you not ask for me? Why are these retainers of yours with you?"

"It was not necessary to disturb your majesty. More important, I considered, that you should be fresh at the audience tomorrow," said Galêsa, bowing with more grace than I could have thought him capable of. After a moment he added: "As to my retainers,—your majesty see they have been of some use!"

Again abruptly, she turned to me.

"And, Mêrê, why are you here?"

"Opanthë saw fit to lock me in her room!" I answered. "Why she did I shall be pleased to explain—only it will take sometime."

"Your majesty will not believe," said Opanthë's measured voice, tinged with its melodious deep thrill that came into it with excitement, "all the inventions of an adventurer and a spy! It's true I shut the creature up. Shall I inform your majesty—"

But the slight imperial form turned from us to her Castellan. The wondering circle of inmates of the palace, of all sorts and conditions, stood about us, none venturing to speak. The tall and simply figure of the Castellan, sleepy but attentive, bent to listen. In the distance the Arch-Sword bearer's guards passed through the central hall, coming nearer and nearer, with the precise footsteps of soldiers.

"Emoron, let these six people remain here in separate rooms. See that the palace surgeons attend to them at once." Then to the rest she observed, "no one will go through the corridor tonight. Athalis and Cronista, you will stood here, and see that that is carried out. I will send you a guard. That prohibition doesn't apply to me and I'm going through with Aelon and Vassôné. And let us have a file of guards, Emoron!" she called to the Castellan, as the officer conducted us away.

Opanthë walked near me. Her sleeve was stained and wet. I felt it more comfortable to fall back a little. Suddenly a white form flew past me and the queen appeared by Opanthë's side.

"You have had a nasty stab!" she said. "I am very sorry, Opanthë, however this has happened!"

The lady addressed nothing, but smiled sadly and with resignation at her sovereign, who again observed gently:

"I am *very* sorry. I hope you will all get put right directly—before long—" And she was gone again, with four of the guards whom we then encountered.

As we went one did one's best to tie up the hurts one had received. There hurried to us, one by one, the medical staff of the place, and four or five of the Castellan's people.

"This has better be your room, Opanthë," said the Castellan, leaving her with a surgeon and an officer, at the door of one of a series of chambers which overlooked an inner court. "And this is yours, Cydonia."

She gave Galêsa a third and myself a fourth. The two retainers were sent off to less distinguished apartments.

I expected the room to be locked. But the only precaution taken was to station an additional officer outside, as I could hear by the conversation that was carried on near the door way. The elderly and deferential surgeon who attended me was a garrulous individual.

"Yes, Lady Mêrê, it isn't many—accidents—that happen in the palace that I don't know something about. It's only two years ago that—by the way, what's your general constitution? Good? I don't like this cut on the knee, if you're delicate it will give us trouble. Hmm, a good deal of trouble. Yes, I was saying, I remember two years ago, when Ioris fell from the arched gallery close by the central hall there. No one this moment knows how it happened. What work we had to bring her to! And she only lasted a week—a day or two more than a week—after all. The queen wanted to brick up the arches, but I said to her: 'it's perfectly safe, your majesty! Perfectly safe! She must have been sitting on the balustrade, which no one ought to do.'—And so she must, though we'll never know for certain."

A stream of refreshing water was directed on to my burning flesh by the skilful hand of the surgeon, who resumed:

"No. Nobody was near, up above there, when she fell. The nearest was a son of that abominable Galêsa,"—(curious that Galêsa should be mixed up in this!)—"He was reading in a cabinet but he heard and saw nothing. A pity that he did not happen to take a turn in the arcade just then! How things come about! He might have saved her! Now! Lady Mêrê, I will put on this unguent and bandage. Allow me."

"Your memories of the palace go a good way back, do they?" I asked.

"Ten years," returned the surgeon. "I practised my art for forty years in my native town, and never was unheard of. Then the Viceroy, passing through, gets thrown out of her palanquin, and I, by good luck, am on the spot. She took me with her to the towns she had to visit—now, *she* has a spirit, Lady Mêrê, she wouldn't miss one them—and when she brought her report to the capital, she recommended me to the queen. So here I am, a Court surgeon, and honoured with employments like the present."

"And you don't like Galêsa?" I said.

"Who does?"

"His children?"

"They! They despise him! They are contemptible boors—contemptible boors!"

"How is it that they are so unlike the rest of the Court?"

"Ah!" the surgeon laughed with conscious ignorance, "there is a strain on old brutality in the city, which gets less and less, it is true, but which shows itself here and there. . . what could you expect of the people brought up by Galêsa?"

In the morning I was early awakened by the streams of gold pouring in through the open lattice. Less agreeable visitors were the Provost of the imperial palace and a couple of clerks, who made an exhaustive (and exhausting) interrogation, with regard to events of the previous evening.

"Why did you not discover the conspiracy before to the royal household?" inquired the Provost sedately.

If she had said "to the queen," it would have been a difficult question to answer. As it was, I had the response ready.

"It was impossible to be sure of them;—for a stranger like myself, at any rate!"

The thin face of the Provost coloured visible.

"Galêsa," I pursued, "was a member of the household, I may remind you. So was Opanthë."

The Provost coughed.

"Strictly speaking, Galêsa hardly is. I ought to say that messengers have been sent to the house where you are staying, to explain what took place last night. It is by the queen's order. Is there anyone else you would like to have told?"

"No one, I think," I said, "you will see that the queen has my thanks, will you? And may I send a message to Ilex?"

"I will take a suitable occasion of expressing your sentiments to her majesty," said the Provost formally. "And I think it would be best if you did not attempt to communicate with your friends at present."

"Will *you* be good enough to tell her then, or see that she is told— Ilex, I mean—that I am sincerely sorry if I have been the occasion. . . have caused her any unpleasantness."

"There is no objection to a verbal message," assented the Provost, rising with slow dignity and moving towards the door. "I will see that it is transmitted. Though I cannot promise to do so immediately; as you see, my duties this morning are arduous and protracted."

She took her leave, together with her clerks, the last of whom scattered a profusion of parchments from her arms. It was a little while before they were gathered up, during which the Provost eyed the scene disapprovingly. I felt a good deal more comfortable when they were gone and the last gold of the scribe's muslin skirts had disappeared round the door corner.

My meals were brought me by two pages, who assured me that my presence would not be needed after the next day. In the afternoon, as I was half lying on a couch of soft rugs and wondering how events would shape themselves, I saw something move at the door. It startled me, it looked so much as if the hangings were walking. The movement ceased—began again. The curtain seemed to grow; and then I saw that a fine, long-haired cat was the cause of the phenomenon. Exactly the same colour as the draperies, it advanced into the room, purring, and not too sure of its ground. With its large translucent eyes fixed on me in the manner of its race, neither confiding nor apprehensive, it presented itself as a welcome relief to the monotony of waiting. Duly encouraged, it brought its furry self to my side.

I was not very fond of these animals, and I could hardly account for the pleasure it was to me to scratch its soft coat, and to watch its clumps of paws pounce on the end of my zone. Then I suddenly recollected. It was just such another that Jeanie Mackrell used to have in Edinburgh, long ago. For half an hour I was in Scotland again. How often I had gone home with Jeanie after classes, and found a kind of home for myself there! And now she was fifteen years married; an invisible wall was between us, on the other side of which she looked down on me, from a pedestal of matronly dignity.

My thoughts instinctively turned to the hours when I made my way back to my own abode in the evening. Those mysterious light evenings of late, cold spring! When one has been sitting by warm fires in brightly-lit rooms, and, under the spell of winter habits, has vaguely fancied that darkness set in long ago—but one passes out, and it is dim, but not dark; and there is a pale green light in the northwest, against which the low factory chimneys stand out distinct and awful—not terrible, for in the light there is summer implicit, and the wayfarer knows that it will swell in the leaf buds, and in the hearts of living things, until the earth smiles back to the sun.

It was ridiculous that Jeanie should patronise me! Could I not laugh quietly at it?—Solemn, good-natured, commonplace, Jeanie! Indeed, I could not. There seemed something wrong about it. I had no notion of patronising her, because she was hopelessly incapable of passing an examination. Why should she treat me as a kind of responsible baby, because she was *Mrs. Skinner?*" And then my hurt arm shot venomous quivers along its fibres—though it was only a scratch I had, there—and there began to trouble me restless disquietude, of the resource and inventiveness of the conspirators. I grew more and more uneasy.

What if they could put a good face on the matter! Had the queen examined the wine cups before anyone in the secret could have tampered with them? Could Opanthë find any plausible reason for locking me in her room,—which Etela could prove? What proceedings would be taken the next day? Might not all that had happened be turned against, myself—myself and Cydonia?

I put my wrist round the furry neck of the cat and meditated anxiously. Was there any message I could send to anyone, that could assist in clearing up matters? Would it do to ask for an interview with the queen?—What might not Galêsa be telling her at the moment? What was being done? Gradually I lost consciousness; and only awakened when my careful attendant came to renew the dressing. The verdict was a great deal more favourable on this occasion; and my inquires as to the time the treatment would last received a satisfactory response. The good, chattering doctor rambled on at length, relating a series of more or less believable cures; and at last left me fairly comfortable.

Another figure was on the threshold;—clad in absolute white, with the royal sphinx in silver, and bearing an ivory and silver sceptre. A very young figure, which looked straight forward, avoiding my eyes with the self-consciousness of youth. Evidently a royal herald.

"I acquaint you," it said in a monotonous voice, "that tomorrow morning you will be charged, before the queen, with High Treason."

Then the worst had happened!

"Stay a moment," I said. "At whose instance?"

This seemed to be a common inquiry, for the answer was immediate.

"At that of the Most Excellent, the Grand Steward and of the Very Honourable the lady Opanthë, one of the queen's high attendants."

"And on what grounds, then?" I pursued, finding the vision thus communicative.

She dropped somewhat into the colloquial style, replying:

"That your ladyship will find out in the morning."

"Am I to meet an accusation without knowing its terms? Well, I don't know your ways. What may the penalty be?"

"Ten years in the dungeons and—"

"Yes?"

"And to be nine times beaten at the Trophy of Victory."

Decidedly a pleasant prospect!

IX

The War

I did not sleep much. The morning found me fresher, however, and it was even with some interest that I entered the Inquiry Chamber, which was the scene of the day's proceedings. I had never seen it previously: it was plain, good-sized, panelled hall, near the centre of which was placed a massive oblong table, with a dozen or so of capacious chairs round it on all sides. I had one of these, and opposite to me I found the queen, with a serious-looking personage whom I did not know on either hand. At one end of the table sat Galsa. Opanthë also was there,—separated from me by the Uras messenger. Cydonia was father to the left. Otherwise, the arrangements were much like those of a court of justice, except in the public's being frankly excluded. The Castellan and her officers kept a free space round the table, a special guard being stationed near the queen. Beyond, there was a room for an interested crowd of the privileged inhabitants of the palace. For all the awkwardness of the situation, I could not but spend a moment in admiring the group of palace guards behind the queen. Their creamy robes,—their gorgeous feather fans,—their sparing decorations of rich gold, their glittering scimitars,—impressed the eye by a *tour de force*. But I did not forget to salute the queen, who nodded agreeably in return across the table.

The Provost also leant towards me from the end seat, and whispered loudly that my message had gone to Ilex, and that she wanted me to know that she was doing what she could do to—but here everyone stood up, and a short procession could be descried making its way from the doors towards us. It proved to be the queen's eldest sister, with her train, and she took a vacant seat on her majesty's left. Cydonia caught my eye at the moment, and gave a flashing smile of recognition, which partly reassured and partly puzzled me. Evidently she did not think of Galêsa's charge. But, then, did she know of it? Perhaps it only applied to me.

The queen began to speak, playing lightly, as she did so, with the papers and parchments in front of her.

"There are a few points which must be cleared up, about this affair of the night before last. The Lady Ophantë accuses the Lady Mêrê of treason, and the Provost does the same in respect of the of the Lady Opanthë and the Grand Steward.

"Would any of those persons like to offer any remarks?"

"Your majesty knows I have been your most intimate associate for all my life," said Opanthë. "I have served you and your House—you best know how. I permitted this lady to believe what she pleased about me, in order that I might find out what sort of a creature Ilex had introduced into the palace. Knowing from herself that she meant to conceal herself in the messenger's room, I locked her in mind. Either realising her mistake, or else thinking me an untrustworthy sort of traitor, she escaped somehow, and brings Cydonia down on me, to save herself. I say nothing about my injuries. There are merged in the attack on your crown."

"As for me," said Galêsa, "I say the same. I have not had Opanthë's chances of listening to so many compromising confidences from this precious foreigner—"

"Galêsa," interposed the queen gravel, "we must be civil to each other."

Galêsa bowed.

"But I say unhesitatingly that she has listened to language, in my presence, and conversation—that prove her disloyal. And as for me, you know why I was in the corridor that night."

He sat back with a cool smile of satisfaction and I felt it was my turn to speak.

"May I know the particulars of what is alleged against me?"

An amused, subdued smile flitted around the august company. People at the edge of the auditory turned interested ear to the table, or looked round to repeat to their friends farther back what had been said.

"Not just yet," said the queen, biting her lip.

"We want you to tell us anything you like—but not to ask questions."

"May I have a moment to think, then? . . . Has your majesty read the answers I gave the Provost? I am still asking questions! I sincerely hope your majesty doesn't mind."

"On the contrary, I will answer those two. Take your time to speak; and, of course, I have read what the Provost knows."

"I don't think, then, that it is necessary for me to say anything."

"Then there are some questions that the Provost will ask you ladies," said her majesty, settling herself to write.

The Provost, rising, put a long series of interrogations to the various people at the table,—including Etela, the Foreign Secretary, and others.

The queen's serious neighbours added a few more: and the proceedings drifted into a low-voiced conversation between herself and these two. This was dull and my attention wandered. The queen seemed kind,— but, then, she was equally so to Opanthë, and it was scarcely possible that she should believe one of us without condemning the other.

Suddenly two silver trumpets gave forth a call mellow and soft indeed, but so startling in the half-silence that the blood went rushing to my head.

The silence grew complete, and the queen spoke.

"Of the two people most concerned in this matter, each admits that she has given colour to the notion, true or false, that she was in the interest of our enemies.

"On the one hand is the word of our two trusted officers. On the other is the word of one to whom we are bound by the ties of hospitality, and who is commended to us by our dear friend Thekla's affection, and that of our good subject Ilex. But we notice that the observations of Opanthë and our Grand Steward do not quite agree. According to the former, Mêrê entered into the mock treasonable conversations of the latter. But the Steward only says she listened to them, and will tell us nothing of what she said. On the other hand, Mêrê has told us a good deal about poisoned or drugged wine. And we can find no trace of drugs, nor does Her Excellency the Lady Zenoia, who has kindly given us every assistance, think that any such attempt was practised upon her. She has been so advised by her own physician.

"And it is certainly a remarkable and incredible thing that an officer of our Court should, assuming her to be an emissary of secret enemies of the State, suddenly open her mind to one whom she believes to be working in the same interest, on a mere assumption. I have called it incredible: but the peculiar facts attending Mêrê's arrival here make it just credible; when one reflects what exceedingly foolish things people will sometimes do.

"But I cannot understand why Opanthë though it necessary to frighten Etela into inactivity. She explains that she knew Etela's ways so well that she was sure she would be an embarrassment, and compromise matters somehow. It is not a satisfactory explanation, to me.

"On the whole, I cannot see that either charge is sustained. I cannot see my way to sentencing my Grand Steward and my chief personal attendant to the penalties of treason on what has been said. Accepting all the Mêrê has said, I am willing to believe that the official were merely sounding her,—though there are some curious coincidences in what she says she heard from them, which you can't help thinking show that *somebody* was in touch with enemies of this State.

"And I do not see that I should not extend the same construction to Mêrê's acts, or silences.

"But this is not a time when the crown can afford to be advised by person whose acts are subject to so much suspicion. The Grand Steward and Lady Opanthë both feel that the Council of State was acting rightly in dismissing them from their offices,—as it did this morning. I hope they will use their increased leisure in increased efforts, of this active and vigorous kind, to circumvent the enemies of the realm.

"We are obliged to all of you for your attendance. Come, Alexandra!"

She offered her hand to the Princess, her sister, and swept from the chamber.

We rose. Galêsa darted a glance of concentrated hatred at me, and began to force a passage blindly through the crowd, without waiting for the queen's final exist, like the rest of the assembly. Opanthë was less perturbed.

"Shall I be entitled to a retiring allowance?" I heard her inquiring of the Arch-Treasurer, quite seriously. But Cydonia would not let me wait.

"We must go and find Ilex, first thing," she declared. "No doubt she will be somewhere not far away."

In the great courtyard, arcaded and full of tall ferns and palms, we could not see her. We turned through one of the arches, and, to my slight consternation—for I hardly knew how I stood in her eyes—the queen was standing in the apartment we entered, surrounded by her staff, and not too propitious. The room was pierced by many wide, lofty arches, and a good many people were in it.

"Shall we turn back?" I said to Cyndonia.

"No, let us cross the room. Stop! What is she saying?"

Her majesty observed in pungently silvern tones: "Who was the officer of the guard when this affair took place that we have just disposed of?"

"Brytas," said somebody; and the queen, motioning that officer forward, observed, still with cool acidity:

"It is extremely to be regretted that the late Grand Steward was permitted to penetrate into the palace at night. An officer who can allow things like that is fit for the command of a fifth-rate town;—

exactly fit for the command of a fifth-rate town! You can take over the command of—where?—Pyramôna!—Tomorrow."

The Uras envoy, who was next the queen, visibly jumped. Brytas, I was glad to see, did not seem to mind much,—but she did not remain, but went quickly away. We tried to follow her long strides; encountering Ilex, however we gave up the chase.

Till I met Ilex I did not know what a strain the morning's work had been to me. When I saw the friendly and familiar face, and was clasped in the slender arms, and looked into the dear confiding eyes, I think I gave way, and I know I remember nothing that happened until I found myself in the room of a friend of hers, one of the Court Treasurers, who—blessing on her!—Abandoned it to us with a courtesy that was as spontaneous as it was appreciated.

It was not until late in the afternoon that we ordered palanquins and set off for home.

And it was not until we were alone in my quarters that she said:

"Mêrê, why not have told me?"

"Then you know all the story?" I said, surprised.

She nodded twice, but still kept looking at me with uplifted eyebrows, inviting explanations.

"How did you know?" I persisted, and she relaxed her gaze, saying with a laugh"

"The Provost of the palace—a most inquisitive person—called here, and asked me a good many impertinent questions yesterday morning. So I thought it was my turn to display a taste for knowledge, and I went and turned on the stream at the fountainhead. In other words, I saw Beatrice the queen."

"And you found her gracious? She was not offended with you because of me?"

"My dear, she is simply grateful to you for providing her with an excuse for getting rid of those miserable, wretched, detestable, crawling, venomous insects! But, look here, Mêrê, why could you not tell me about it?"

"Because," I said, pulling myself together, "I didn't know you always as I know you now, Ilex!"

"That is quite a good answer," said my friend, beaming. "And I will come over beside you, and make you some lemonade with coffee in it." Which she proceeded to do, with a soft pat on my dress whenever she passed in the course of the process.

"Do you know," she repeated, when we were *vis-à-vis* over the cups, "the queen thinks you have done a great service to the country. Really, yes! Because it shows that there must be a conspiracy at work, more or less widespread. And now we have a clue to detect it with—we know Opanthë's friends and Galêsa's. She wants to talk to you, but not openly; you must go to the palace disguised somehow. They would suspect a closed litter. How would you like to be got up? As an elderly, astrologer, or a bronzed sea captain from Flores, or a—what?"

"As a small lion," I suggested. "And then no one need see my face at all!"

"No," insisted Ilex, "you will never be known if you are made a good brown colour. You are so beautifully white!" At which I laughed outright.

"That's right," said Ilex, without being taken aback in any degree. "It shows you are not hurt much!"

"And, indeed, I got better very fast. My visit to the palace was duly paid, under cover of nightfall. The queen received me in an immense hall, the walls, receding to a dark distance, covered with curious black carvings of ebony: a single little table, crusted with nacre and silver, the sole furniture. She looked at me a moment in silence with knitted brows; then she advanced nearer, and put her hands on my shoulders with a gentle pressure.

"I want to talk to you a great deal, Mêrê," she said, "and I have no time for compliments. Will you believe that when I come again after the war I will do what I can to thank you?

"That is, if I come back! There is a vein of evil in the realm that seems to have fixed upon my reign to concentrate itself in individuals. I have not to fight Uras, so much as to protect myself from a faction of my own people. As they say, the snake wears out its own skin.

"But there are not many of these! It must be our business to track them and make them powerless for mischief. And you can help in this.

"If they challenge me to a trail of strength, I am not afraid to meet them. But if you are on my side, you know the risks of it."

Her mouth was set in a proud but winning curve; her voice was measured, though it thrilled sensitively.

"I am your majesty's servant," I said, "now and always." I do not know why I made this declaration. But it sprang to my life.

"Not my servant," she said—irritably, rather—"My own follower, if you like! Now let us discuss the state of affairs. The Uras people, there is no doubt, are in no hurry to attack. They think the plum is ripening nicely. The conspirators here, on the other hand, are clearly anxious for a crisis—were so, anyway, before the other night—"

She went on, laying open before me the network of diplomacy and probabilities, until I saw that the commencement of the armed struggle could not be deferred more than a week or two. Then she questioned me as to how I thought her conclusions fitted in with what I had heard from Opanthë.

When I would have spoken of Opanthë personally, however, the queen avoided the subject, and kept strictly to the matter of our discussion. Having heard from me all she wanted, she dismissed me abruptly. The Arch-Censor, who took charge of me, then carried me off to a much more cheerful apartment, where she developed a plan of campaign against the conspirators, in which she invited me to join.

It promised to be very exciting work, involving, as it did, secret assignations, domiciliary visits, and very considerable risks of a thrust with one of the pointed daggers beloved of the Armerians. I cannot say the reality quite came up to the plan put forward. Detective work may involve these picturesque incidents—but most of our information was gathered in a milder mannered sort of way and rather in drawing room than in domino.

We had some interesting encounters, nevertheless. Particularly I remember one night, when Ilex and I received a message to intercept a conspirator who, we were informed, would leave the house in which she was a resident at a particular hour for a rendezvous. It was of no use following her; that had been done before with no results that were not known already. Our scheme was to detain her, and to observe what came of it, for we strongly suspected that she was the messenger between the faction and their agents.

Amphron, the head of the house, was elderly and never stepped beyond the doors. Her dwelling was a fine building near the outskirts of the town, and on account of the difference in level between front and back, it had the appearance of being two-storied. The garden behind it, thickly planted with shrubberies, merged gradually into a wild tangle forming part of the public possessions. Across this Athlis had been seen, night after night, to steal. She might have spared herself the trouble of dodging from aloe to cactus bush in that fashion,—for she had been tracked regularly. The family was known to be bitterly hostile to the reigning queen, though its members had the reputation of preferring to avoid active participation in dangerous matters. It needed only a little ingenuity, aided by a lucy accident of two, to arrive at the strong suspicions I have mentioned.

So it came about that we found ourselves, soon after dark, sheltering near the back premises of Amphron's mansion. To "mak siccar," two others were with Ilex and me: and six slaves were hidden in a bush not far away. I did not feel (as I had expected I should) like a burglar—at any rate, if my intimations of what a burglar's feelings are like approximate to the truth. I felt that the whole proceedings were laughably like a game of hide and seek. And then I fell to speculating which window the object of our search would appear at; whether she would be dressed in light or dark clothes; and (very dubiously) whether we could silence her before she had time to alarm the house. This wing of the building was certainly quiet. The lower story, appropriated to the slaves, had no large apertures, and the upper, though, brightly lighted, was deserted.

Still, the house was full of sympathisers with Athlis's mission. It was imperative to seize her in quietness. As we kept straining our eyes up at the lighted windows, there appeared a form at one of them. It was impossible to realise for a few seconds that this was veritable the person we were waiting for. One of our companions drew her breath, and the other laughed a warning at her—mirthlessly. The figure at the window above us stepped out on to the colonnade adjoining it, and, after a glance at the starry night, began dexterously to climb down an ancient tree which was trained against the wall.

"Don't lose her! *Don't* lose her!" muttered Iphrûnë, or *enfant terrible*. "Slip to the next bush, nearer the house! She can't miss us that way!"

She led the way, flying rather than running. It was a foolish move, for we had to cross a zone of light. But it was no use getting separated, so we fled helter-skelter, heads down, after her, Ilex indulging in some pointed and beautiful imprecations on the way. What I said on my part I really forget. I flatter myself that we executed that faulty movement noiselessly and well. If someone on our side had blundered, the mistake was never noticed by our quarry.

Now, there was nothing for it but to wait again till she should emerge into the light. This, if only for a moment, she could not help doing somewhere. Seconds seemed hours. Suddenly she appeared quite close to us, not two yards off, looking very substantial and lively. I shrank back; she did not hear the rustle, but pushed calmly on. We let her pass. Then in half a minute it was all over, and we had her secured and speechless in her valetudinarian relative's own garden.

When people are on the other side in a struggle with you, you are apt to give them a good deal less than credit for their good qualities. And it was not until Athlis was safely disarmed, hardly even then, that it began to occur to me that she had scaled the wall and faced the darkness with a good deal of cool agility and courage. We carried her to some distance, and returned to watch for those who might come in search of her.

The sweet, heavy scent of the night flowers came to one across the grass; the red blooms showed distinctly and strangely in the light which streamed from the windows, and the stifled groans, which were all Athlis could put for a cry, sounded weirdly in the near distance.

"Stop that creaking somehow," said Ilex to Iphrûnë. "Tell her you'll kill her if she makes a sound! Or, better: get the slaves to carry her to Viquena's house. Blindfold her, you know, and don't miss the right house, whatever you do!"

We had not long to wait before a stranger appeared on the scene. We were all in high good-humour, for this was no one whom we had suspected; indeed, it was a person none of us even knew. She was a powerfully-built and tall personage, and her movements were in the highest degree suspicious. She glided with remarkable silence from one dark thicket to another, reconnoitered the house carefully, and stood for sometime near the window that Athlis had come out of. Clearly we were on the eve of an important discovery. What was our astounded feeling to observe her produce a ladder, rear it against the wall, and walk into the house! We looked at each other in astonishment.

"Well, of all—" said Oprë.

"Did you see that?" sarcastically inquired Ilex.

"She *must* be intimate with the family," added I.

The question now was, whether to leave the ladder in its place. We decided to take it away. The front entrances were well watched, and anyone going out would be identified or followed. There was a long pause of waiting.

A curious cry, unlike the notes of the other birds, was heard now at intervals.

"That's the *ichone*. It is rather a rare bird," whispered Ilex. Almost immediately after, as we crouched among the leaves of the thicket, we caught sight of a dark figure creeping along by the foot of the house wall. The newcomer looked up at he window intently, and then she made the *ichone's* call, loudly and clearly in groups of three notes, over and over again repeated. She turned impatiently round, and stamped on the ground with obvious vexation. The first stranger appeared at the window: this time with a bulky parcel in her arms. But the bird-caller did not make any attempt to communicate with her; on the contrary, she slid into the shadow of an aloe that was near.

"I'll tell you what, you people," said Oprë *sotto voce*: "That first one isn't in it at all. It's a thief!—An ordinary enterprising thief!"

"Believe you are right, Oprë," returned Ilex. "What shall we do?"

"Bag them both!" said she. "We can, if we go to work properly."

Number one threw down the parcel and descended by the tree,— which was not an easy performance for a person of that weight. Losing her bearings in consequence, she had to search about for the parcel. To our delight, she approached the bush were the bird-caller was hiding. The latter tried toe scape observation; but it was hopeless, and merely served to encourage the thief, who would have otherwise fled.

"What are you doing here at this hour of night, spying about?" inquired the latter insolently.

"It isn't necessary to inquire what *you're* doing, at all events!" said the other.

"Will you wait quietly here, while I find my bundle?"

"Yes!"

"I don't believe you."

"No?"

"Let me fasten you up"—persuasively.

"No, I draw the line there."

"Well, take that, then!"

The thief drew a heavy sword, and aimed a blow at the other, who leapt aside, and, slipping for a moment behind a tree, possessed herself of her own weapon.

"Uhu!" said Oprë, half awestruck and half excited at the duel which followed. Twice the thief looked as if she would have liked to turn and run; but the package caught her eye, with its carbuncles and jasper glittering out of the corners of the wrapping, and she stood her ground. At last two stupid slaves of ours came up in hot haste, inquiring if it was one of us who was fighting, and if they were wanted. The combatants caught sight of them. It was worst for the thief. Her nerve was shaken, and she received the point of her antagonist's steel in the right shoulder.

"Now's our time!" we simultaneously exclaimed, and, leaving the slaves to arrest the burglar, we three proceeded in chase of the other, who surprised us by making no effort to evade us. As we came up to her, we recognised her as the daughter of one of the Gate-Wardens.

"Am I not lucky?" she said, "to have settled the account of that wretched thief! Is it the same that took Scherone's jewels the other day, do you think?"

"It *was* fortunate you were here," said Ilex grimly. "Not many people are here at this time of night! What brough you, Poikelis?"

"Well, what brought *you*?" pertinently responded she.

"Detective work," said Ilex. "And you caught our game for us."

"Very glad, I'm sure—and I hope you will remember me favourably! And noy I must be off."

"Not," said Oprë, "until you answer our question."

She got angry. "By the lightning, I am not to give an account of my movements to you or to anybody! I had a little piece of private business—you understand?—Between myself and Athlis, which third parties have nothing whatever to do with. That is enough for you!—Too much!"

"Yes,—you're too inquisitive, Oprë," said Ilex. "Poikelis has done our work for us. So there's nothing but to say goodnight to her, and take ourselves off to someother job. We must leave that bundle at the house, though."

"Let *me* take it," said Poikelis eagerly.

"Certainly," answered Ilex, pinching Oprë in secret.

As Poikelis stooped to the bundle we easily tripped her up, and had her conveyed to the same house as Athlis. We ourselves waited a considerable time longer; but no further visitors came to the premises. So we repaired to the place where our captives were interned.

First we saw Athlis.

Oprë at once took a high tone with her.

"I suppose you don't know Athlis," she said, "that one of your fellow conspirators has just been found poking round your premises, and has confessed why?"

She said nothing.

"It isn't good for our health," said Oprë, "to hang about at nights like this, and, besides, our time's valuable. So it would be very satisfactory if you could just give us a few particulars about who are in this movement. . . well, if you won't, we can get them from a more accommodating lady down the corridor. And she will get the benefits we proposed to give you."

"Benefits!" laughed Athlis bitterly.

"Yes," returned Oprë briskly. "We have already enough evidence to arraign you and all your family for treason. And our friend that I spoke of will probably give us a little extra. Let me see—there's yourself, Athlis, there's Amphron—well, she's hardly fair game; we'll let her off: she's too ill—but there's still your stepmother, Vrinda, and your intelligent cousin Raina, and your half-sister. Give us the few details we want, and we prosecute none of them. Otherwise, we do!"

I suppose it was necessary, but I could not have stood it much longer; nor could Ilex. The girl was pale and quiet, and only her hard breathing showed what she felt. Her head proud and erect.

"Vrinda, too!" she half murmured.

"Well, she's a very nice person in a private capacity," observed Oprë judicially. "I haven't a word to say against her. But if she *will* go and get mixed up in revolutionary families, she must expect—sooner or later—the dungeons and the Trophy of Victory."

Oprë took two or three turns down the chamber. Ilex and I stood silent, as the lamp flame flickered on the silver chains.

"Now," resumed Oprë, in an encouraging tone, "you're a girl of common sense, Athlis—plenty of sense! Just apply it. Which shall it be?"

Athlis's head sank slowly forward.

"Oh, Vrinda!" she muttered.

"Yes, I'm sure you see it's best," said Oprë. "Vrinda and all of them will be safe if—"

"Oprë, I'm sure she's fainted."

And so she had. Nor can I complete this part of my narrative, as at that moment a white-kilted officer hurried into the room, and whispered to Ilex, who carried me off at once, and walked briskly homewards, informing me of the news as we started.

Ilex's regiment was to proceed to the frontier in the morning, along with several others. The crisis had become acute.

"You will take me with you?" I said.

"I can't! The orders are too strict. Or else I think I would venture it."

"Couldn't you get me a place as servant,—cook,—messenger,—sutler,—correspondent? Or mightn't I volunteer?"

She shook her head.

"The army doesn't deal in those luxuries! But I *will* leave word with the headquarters staff that you are willing to do things of that sort. And I expect they'll be glad to have despatch riders. Can you ride, Mêrê?"

Well, it would have been a pity if I could not! I satisfied her as to that, and she observed:

"Then we shall see each other again before long, because I'll tell Cerene to send you my way. She manages that department. And she said once she would do anything I liked in reason, if only I asked."

"And what shall I do meanwhile?"

"You can look after my house for me. That's one thing. Mira and Darûna and Amphôr and Kâra will be coming with me; perhaps some of the others may be called up, too. So there will be plenty to do at home."

We talked about other things as we walked on through the night. At my room Ilex left me, with her accustomed warm kiss.

"Stop! When do you go, in the morning?" I cried.

"In three hours, or four, I must be going to the armoury."

"Then I'll go," I declared.

"There isn't any need for you to go all that distance," said she. "If you like to see us away at the door—"

"Should I be a nuisance at the armoury?"

"Oh, you couldn't get in. No, that would be no use, I'm afraid. I'll tell Nîa to waken you in time. Take a sleep now!"

I wakened to find the place a scene of bustle and excitement. Horses were trampling about, their hoofs clattering on the tile pavements; slaves were rushing to and fro with requisites for the journey and platters of refreshment; the very domestic animals shared the general stir. The younger children were not disturbed; two or three elder ones had been told what was going on, and they sat apart with rather solemn and anxious faces.

Ilex got beside me for a few minutes.

"I hate a fuss," she said, "and we will just slip off as quietly as we can. I have told Calenda not to let the slave shout at the gates. Sometimes they do, and it always strikes me as so very senseless."

"Will you not salute everybody?"

"My dear! What an absurd procession it would be if we four went solemnly round the household with the due reverences! No, we know each other too well for that."

"In England," I said, "you would. You would say goodbye to me and kiss me."

"And I can do that here," she said, and demonstrated the possibility with efficacy and despatch.

Time pressed. The horses were at the door, and very unostentatiously, our small party of officers left the house and rode down the street.

There was no waving of hats or handkerchiefs; no on shouted messages of good luck, or followed at the horses' bridles; only the little Appthis broke into a passion of tears and could not be induced to restrain them.

"You are just a baby, Appthis!" was the sever pronouncement of Lyphra, who was a year or two older. "Suppose Calenda had gone away as well and Vera and Enschîna and me? I easily might; they wanted a drummer in Chloris's regiment, if I would have joined it. And," she pursued, "supposed I had gone, you would have nobody to help you to make the embankment for the little tortoise pool in the Green Court! We'll go and start it this morning, Appthis."

But the young lady displayed an entire, and, indeed, ostentatious indifference for the time being to embankments and tortoises alike, a fact which had the effect of arousing in Lyphra considerable irritation.

"Don't ask me again to make embankments for you!" she observed with heat and intense scorn. "I ought to know better than play with children like you, who can't keep interested in one thing from one day to another!"

She flew off in just the same palpitating, bird-like fury that, on one memorable occasion, I had noticed seize on Ilex. I did not follow her, for she had probably gone to the best place for her—bed. And Appthis was so much affected by her strictures that she was in danger of becoming hysterical. I gradually got her calmer, and took her to my own room. It was so very early that most of us turned in for a little further rest.

"I do really care about the engineering work and the tortoises," pathetically remarked my little companion, "but I can't think about them. *Will* I ever be able to think about them again, or will my head always be too sore?"

"You are a silly little darling!" I told her. "After breakfast your head and your eyes will feel alright and Lyphra will have forgotten all she said this morning, and you will get a lot done. And I'll come and bring a cushion, and sit and watch you—if you keep yourselves very clean."

She began to smile a little.

"Lyphra *does* say some horrid things somethings. *You* never do, Mêrê."

"No, it would be simply awful if I did. I am a visitor here, you see, and on my best behaviour. And—don't tell Lyphra this!—I think she is very nervous and easily upset, and then she must just say what occurs to her, without having time to think how other people may feel it. People like that are generally vexed most of all with themselves. Try to think it is really herself she is scolding when she does that!"

"I'll think it over," conceded Appthis, in an old-fashioned way.

"Mêrê," she began again hurriedly, "are there many people killed when there is a way?"

"It depends," I said, trying to speak as if there were not an insistent lump in my throat. "They say weapons of precision haven't improved matters much. It depends—I can't really tell. I don't know how they fight here. In Italy, I believe, people were rather shocked at one time anybody was killed at the end of day's battle."

"I think it *can't* be like that here," said Appthis. "Do you know how many people get killed, hunting? Hunting lions and things like that? Because I once heard Arix say, war, as we make it, is very like hunting; you get round the wild beast in tremendous numbers, and then, if it *does* fly out with its claws, there is no chance for it."

"I couldn't tell you, Appthis!"

She got rather restless after this unsatisfactory questioning. Finally she said straight out: "I do hope Ilex and Kâra and Mara and Dạrûna will come back."

"Well, why not?" I asked. "Isn't Ilex a lovely fencer? Do you suppose anybody will have a chance against her, with that damasked sword, with the golden handle?"

"No: but five or six might!" she replied. So seriously that I was forced to laugh.

"But she would have sense not to go near five or six. You have far more sense than those clumsy Uras people! Haven't you?"

"Well—" admitted Appthis, with due modesty. "And Darûna is a better fencer than Ilex. And Kâra is very sharp. I'm afraid Mira will be the worst off. She well always be pushing into places that other people don't care to go to. And she hasn't the least idea of taking care of herself."

The grown up way in which she uttered this observation was again rather laughable.

"But then, you see," I said, "everybody will be wanting to take care of *her*. So I think we may leave all our people in the hands of—" Really I did not know how to fill up the blank.

"Yes, I know—of course," said Appthis. After which she dropped off to sleep.

In the course of the morning, Athroës, by invitation, looked in, sardonically genial as usual. She gave me, I must say, considerable ground for hopefulness as to the result of the conflict. The Uras troops were, according to her, a special class, practically untrained in the use of the sword or in strategy, or, indeed, in anything except idleness and self-conceit. The real strength of the enemy lay in their raw levies; equally unskilled, but not without strength and address.

"And they have this civilised quality," said the doctor, "they know when they are beaten. Show them strongly superior forces surrounding them, and they admit handsomely that they are done for. Some troops would try to do a lot of ineffective damage, and get themselves cut to pieces before giving in. But not they! The only drawback is that they are sometimes too stupid to take in the fact that they are out manœuvred."

She proceeded to remark that she had watched our friend's regiment leave, and added as many details as she could remember, as she saw that it pleased us to know them.

"There were twenty or thirty of us," she said, "standing by the Atalian gate, on the marble platform just inside. Let me see—there was Tirassaphë, Mythë—who else?—Oh, of course, Phanaras! She arrived in Alzôna last night, and she was bound not to miss her one opportunity of seeing Ilex. Indeed, she wants to go on to the camp—but that lies in the hands of the gods,—that is, the Government; and whether she gets permission is more than doubtful, I expect. Well, we waited, and ate a good many more mulberries than were good for us—"

So Phanaras had seen Ilex off—and I hadn't! Certainly she herself had dissuaded me from going to the armoury. But what was there to hinder me from going to the gates? None of the rest of the household had gone. It was surely not necessary for me to model my conduct on theirs! Phanaras!—Beautiful, so they said; assiduous, so it appeared—her anxious, affectionate glance and the wave of her hand would be the last memory Ilex would take with her. Why not?

Well, in the first place, Phanaras was not fit for her—if what I heard was true. In the second, she must think so little of me in comparison! It was simple jealousy, I admitted,—and I did not see why I should be so anxious to stand well with Ilex. The fact remained that I did—intensely: and the vexation I experienced was not the less acute for my inability to understand it. Only I was beginning to recognise that Ilex meant everything to me—that I had come to consider myself and her as especially appropriated to each other—that any interruption for good and all to our constant companionship would be heartbreaking—in short, that she was indispensable to me. I did not in the least think myself indispensable to her: and so I had been content to let matters go on as they had, without thinking of taking advantage of the custom of the country to establish a permanent relationship.

Besides, I never quite got rid of the idea of returning to Europe. So I had taken her friendship as it came, thinking—if I thought at all—that I could let it go if occasion demanded. But now I suddenly found that I could not—not this way, at all events. She was so very charming.

Athroës's voice rang through the chamber (she did not often speak loudly; when she did it was when trying to describe events):

"Then we saw a cloud of dust along the road, and Eronâl—*she* was there, Arix; I thought you said she had gone to Kytôna?—Eronâl turned to me and said, 'Send to your apothecary for some rose water to settle dust with, or else we can't see them.' But I told her that would be a trifle too expensive for my resources, and she said: 'Oh, we would all subscribe!' So then I said people would remark that I was making a good thing out of patriotism—selling rose water by the barrel. And I hardly thought I had enough in stock to produce a very effective improvement. Of course, there was nothing in the way of water needed; there is a good big piece of lawn before you come to the gate. . ."

"Enschîna," I said, under my breath to the beautiful old lady to whom I had learnt to apply in difficulties, "is there anyway of sending letters to the camp? I suppose there is communication?"

"Not except by special messenger," she returned. "We will send one of the slaves every week so long as the camp is fixed. When the regiment begins moving about, we must just trust to luck."

"I forgot something I wanted to tell Ilex," I said. "I suppose I can't send after her?"

"Is it anything very urgent? Because you can have one of the slaves and a horse; and she will do her best to overtake them."

"No, thanks," I answered, rather dismally; reflecting that no explanations would have much chance of being well received if they involved the exhaustion of a horse and slave of the recipient.

The trodden track, with the departing cavalry upon it, kept rising before my mind. Was it not possible to follow them? To see Ilex again and explain? But I saw that it was not possible. I should have to take a horse and guides. She would only be embarrassed—vexed, most likely. There was nothing for it but to cultivate patience; with indifferent success. Fortunately Cydonia was brought in by Pathis, from the morning theatre, and she helped to enliven us. Through her manner, from time to time, verged upon bluntness: so that one would have said that she was irritated at something,—only that she was generally so indifferent to irritations.

"Did you see Chloris away this morning?" I asked, with a little trepidation.

She looked keenly at me, and said shortly:

"No; I saw her last night."

"At your house?"

"Yes."

I did not like to say more. But evidently Cydonia did not care for Chloris as I thought, or else there was a prejudice against leave-takings of any kind *coram publico*. It was not easy to see which. And I did not like to seem a complete barbarian by inquiring.

The weeks dragged slowly on. Everybody was very nice and kind. I was never at a loss for someone to accompany me anywhere I chose. But I missed Ilex's constant devotion, and her glance that used to seem to flash her very heart unwaveringly into mind. The weeks passed on—two strained, anxious weeks—at the end of which the thunderclap came.

At break of day one morning the queen sent for me to the palace. She seemed brighter and more active that I had lately seen her.

"I have a small piece of work for you," she said. "Yes, sit down and let me tell you. Perhaps you know—of course you do—that we have a camp near the frontier, where our massed troops are facing a similar camp of the Urassites? It's a quite easy frontier to cross at any point; except far away, where it passes along a mountainous country, and there it can only be traversed by one difficult pass.

"Now, we have purposely left this pass unguarded. We have posts, none of them very strong, all the way along the line, not for defence, but for observation. But the pass is absolutely denuded. The reason is, that I want to induce them to attack us by that line—as I have cause to think they, in fact, contemplate doing. If they did so without our expecting them, a rapid march on their part would bring them down on our flank like a thunderbolt. But, as we shall be prepared for them, we shall be able to take them at a great disadvantage. It won't do to move off too soon, or they will take alarm, and I am afraid to occupy the pass. My plan will be to push troops as far in its direction as I dare; and to hurry them forward by every earthly method as soon as it is safe.

"You'll see the tremendous importance," she went on, sitting straight up as she spoke, and looking past me out at the window, "in this scheme, of delaying the enemy by making every effort to hold as long as possible the towns that they will come across when they debouch from the pass. Pyramôna is the first of these, and the most important—"

"Pyramôna!—What a pity it is not a stronger place!" I interrupted with uncourtier-like eagerness. "It must be only a fifth-rate town, because it was there that your majesty send Brytas as governor."

Beatrice smiled a little.

"Do you really suppose, then, that I would send my good Brytas to command an insignificant town because of a little trifle that she wasn't to be blamed for? I put Brytas in Pyramôna in order to have a high officer there without attracting suspicion. Did you not watch the Uras Agent? She sent a messenger that very night, I have no doubt, to tell her government that we thought Pyramôna of no importance. But I have secretly sent as many soldiers there as can safely be pushed so far: and the same has been done for nearer towns.

"I want you," she proceeded, "to go to the camp with a word for the Arch-Marshal that the ambassador has handed me a declaration of war. I have not received it yet, but I am certain to do so in the course of the day. You need not press on at any extra speed, because the actual declaration is not of so much moment. What is my real object is sending you, is to put you at the disposition of the Marshal as a messenger to Pyramôna. As a stranger, and one who might well be kept out of harm's way, your desptach will excite less comment than if we sent one of our own officers. The Marshal will send you on when there is a certain intelligence of the enemy's movements. Then, of course, I rely on your celerity!"

She ended by asking me, in a very handsome way, whether I liked to undertake such a responsible and risky business. There was only one answer possible.

"Then my Secretary will see about guides for you. That's all! By the way, Ilex's regiment has gone to Pyramôna. It has had to be moved up by cautions stages and under various blinds and screens. But there it is. You may like to know."

I left the queen with dancing footsteps. Whatever might happen, at Pyramôna, I should again see Ilex. That was enough to make the mission a pleasure excursion!

"Let me see!" observed the Secretary, "about guides. You want somebody, if possible, who knows you can be trusted. It's difficult to give you a good one. Most of our people who know the country well are engaged otherwise."

"I wonder," I said, "if Nîa, my friend, Ilex's slave, would do? I understand she knows the frontier well; she has been with Darûna through one or two mock campaigns there, and I can answer for her trustworthiness."

"Can you?" said the official dubiously, pressing the point of her reed pen against her chin—"Can you? Recollect, the slaves are honeycombed with disaffection. I must say, I dislike—"

"I will put it that Ilex's safety and mine depend upon her, and she's sure not to fail us," I said. "Quite sure. I understand your objections: I quite appreciate them. But they don't apply to Nîa."

"Everybody thinks their own slaves reliable!" murmured the Secretary, with some reason. And I had hard work to convince her that Nîa might safely accompany me. At last I succeeded, so far as to secure her permission to take Nîa if no one else was at liberty by the time of my departure.

"I would rather," she said candidly, "take someone off her other service, and send her with you. But you ought to have some choice in the matter, so I won't stick out. Take care of yourself! And be ready to start a minutes notice."

I WENT STRAIGHT HOME, ARRANGED to have the services of Nîa, and began to prepare for the journey.

"You will want a decent sword apiece, and a stiletto or two—" said Vera.

"Is that all?" I exclaimed. "I was thinking of changes of clothes, and a kettle, and forks, and things like that."

Arix looked at me in pitying bewilderment, and Calêna explained that an Armerian never carried more than could be helped.

"You can always get bananas anywhere," she said, "or something,—and a drink of water. That's enough. One doesn't need to boil a kettle. My advice is—live by the way; the less you have to carry the better. And don't carry any clothes, on any account."

"Are you serious?" I asked, more than half-doubtfully.

"Perfectly," she responded with convincing candour. "An Armerian never carries encumbrances on a journey. You only need to try it!"

"But, Calêna," said Arix, "if she does not start till later, she had better take something to eat with her, because you can't get anything at the first stage."

"That's true," added Vera, "but it's the exception that proves the rule. And it strikes me I'd better go and make a practical application of it by choosing out some extra good things for Mêrê's supper. What will you have, Mêrê? Come with me and choose!"

We departed into the distant recesses of the store chambers. Whilst there, among the fragrant heaps of preserves and spices and the orderly rows of big jars, such as the bandit merchant of Arabian story might have envied, we heard the sound of strange voices talking in the entrance hall. The store chamber, though not easily accessible from the hall, had a long opening near its roof which looked directly into it. Vera climbed up a tier of vats, and peeped through. I felt rather excited. Was it the message for me to leave?

In a moment or two Vera reported:

"It's Cydonia: I forgot she was coming this morning. I asked her to come and see that bird of ours that has such a cough. Well, we'll have to go see her at least, I will. I think we've picked out everything we want?"

"Far too much," I replied; to which she answered lightly:

"Oh no! I wouldn't give you too much. You may be sure of that. Shall you tell Cydonia you are going to the camp?" she continued, as we proceeded along the dark, cool passages.

"I think the less said the better," I answered. "I shall just go out with Nîa this evening without telling more people than is absolutely necessary."

"You're wise," observed Vera empathetically.

We turned into the entrance hall; but it was empty. The party had moved into the room adjoining, where we found them. Vera at once took Cydonia off to see the invalid, and Cydonia pulled my sash, as she passed me, as an invitation to accompany them. While Vera, assisted, or perhaps rather hindered, by one of the children, was trying to perform some mysterious operation about the cage, Cydonia remarked in a low tone:

"The queen tells me you are going to the camp."

I assented.

"Have you a guide?" she said.

"I'm taking Nîa, I expect."

"Oh, thank you very much," she answered gratefully,—indeed, with quite inexplicable gratitude. And then she applied herself with feverish energy to the diagnosis of the feathered thing's complaint. It looked mopish and fretful enough, poor animal, and Cydonia could not but begin to feel a conscientious interest in advising on its treatment. Gradually she grew more methodical and cool.

But when she said the last word on the subject, she suddenly declared that she must go.

"Cydonia, you'll stay and have your midday meal with us now that you're here," invited Vera. "You never *will* stay with us"—(which was hospitable, but not strictly true)—"Mêrê may be away ever so long; you won't have a meal with her for ages. Do stop!"

"I can't indeed," said Cydonia, with a charmingly apologetic look in my direction. "I really have some very important business to see after; and I must get home this very second. So don't keep me."

She was not usually affected with an excess of shyness, and the *soupçon* of embarrassment which she showed for the moment became her. I never thought her so sympathetic as just then.

"Well," returned Vera with real disappointment, "surely you must have your dinner? Ours will be ready in five minutes."

"No," persisted Cydonia, laughing, a little too loudly, "I'll tell you what I'll do. I'll come over again this afternoon and say goodbye to Mêrê. Now I'm off!"

And we saw that she really wanted to go, so we desisted from pressing her.

"I wonder what she wants," observed Vera. "The queen often gets her to do bits of state business—and it might be something of that kind, that she would not care to explain to us."

"Very likely it might," I agreed.

But, notwithstanding her promise to return, Cydonia did not make her appearance until the last moment. Meanwhile, there was a good deal to do, in spite of the scanty preparations that I was unanimously instructed to make. For one thing, Arix spent an hour in teaching me a sword stroke which she told me had saved her for life time and again in her travels. She gave me, besides, a good deal of information about the country and the best modes of foraging. Then there were maps to study, and rough plans to draw; in the midst of this employment there came a slave of Thekla's with a sudden rumour that the advantage-guard of the Uras army had been seen eight miles off. She was wildly excited and hysterical; and we could make no connected story of it not trace her authority. And she would not stop to much be questions, but rushed off to take the pleasing intelligence somewhere else.

"Do you think it safe for Mêrê to go?" inquired Calêna.

"Pî!" said Enschîna. "If the queen thinks it safe, she ought to know better than a silly slave."

"Sometimes the mouse knows what the mistress doesn't!" returned Calêna.

"Beatrice has her cats," was the elderly lady's response.

"I wish," broke in Cyasterix, "that somebody would lay hold of that slave of Thekla's—what do they call her? Cola?—And teach her not to go shivering round the town, terrifying everybody with her stories."

"You couldn't do that," said Pathis. "Look how dangerous it would be. Suppose it were really true! Nobody would dare to say so, for fear of being accused as panic-manufacturers. If there was really a serious crisis, what is there so inspiring and exciting as a few words, broken and wild, from a half-terrified person who had just heard the news? Are we to suppress all that, and say that people must always wait to be certain, and then go quietly and make the announcement as if they were saying, 'Dinner's ready!'"

"Not at all," said Cyasterix. "But it's intolerable that on every flimsy rumour these creatures should think themselves licensed to scour the city like comets with a train of terrifying stories."

"It would be, perhaps," Arix said, "if we were very easily frightened."

"You don't allow," said Cyasterix, "for the wearing effect of this on the nerves. Once is nothing; you wait till you've had a crop of the same sort of visit for breakfast and lunch, with a stampede through the streets by way of desert, for a fortnight or so. Then talk."

The rest were too polite to draw her attention to the fact that she herself had no personal experience of the alarming state of affairs she depicted. Pathis, however, inquired:

"You don't mean to say that if I heard that Alipôras"—a redoubtable Uras leader of horse—"was at the gates, I shouldn't fly out and tell Celôra, and Loutas, and all my neighbors?"

"Certainly, I do," answered Cyasterix. "Where would be the good?"

"Hm!" said Pathis, and the discussion dropped.

"Well," remarked Calêna, "is it quite safe to let Mêrê go? Should someone see the queen?"

"Is it the least likely," said Arix, "that any foreign troops could have got within the distance without our people seeing them? It would be a simple insult to the intelligence of the Intelligence Department! Don't you let stories of this kind matter, Mêrê! I've heard too many such-like!"

"As far as I am concerned, they will not," I said. "Where I'm told to go, I will try to get to."

"Yes, but don't think it isn't perfectly safe," persisted she. "I know just how this kind of nonsensical tale springs up. And those slaves—"

"Those slaves—" echoes Cyasterix.

"—like nothing better than to rush about repeating them."

"Now, wouldn't you," said Cyasterix appealingly—"wouldn't you do something to slave who spread false news like that, out of just mere liking for excitement and vanity and—? Wouldn't you?"

"I should make a good deal of allow for people whose nerves are overstrained at our anxious time. I should not blame them too much for giving way to feelings of excitement and wildness. That is my own personal opinion—a very insignificant little one!" answered Enschîna.

All this argument kept me from thinking much about my journey. And, indeed, it did not trouble me much to leave Alzôna, for was not Ilex to be found elsewhere? Appthis, however, followed me about wistfully, and I felt sorry to leave her.

"*Don't* go, Mêrê," she said, when we were alone for a minute.

"But I must, sweet one! We must do a little work when we can, you know."

"Somebody else might do it!"

"No, nobody else could do this. Isn't it nice for me to think that nobody else quite can?"

"I wish you couldn't—I don't mind your going," she added frankly, "so much as I did the others: because you're not going to fight! Only I *do* mind." And she nestled her head in my dress.

"Suppose I had a chance," I said, "of seeing Darûna and Mira—and Ilex—and getting messages from them, and looking after them—how would that be?"

"Yes! You might," said Appthis, her eyes sparkling. "And Kâra—you forgot Kâra, and she tells such lovely stories! She told me one just the day before she went away, about a deer; and there was a forest, where it lived; and every morning, when the sun shone, it went and heard the birds chirp, and it came to a pool and drank like our little antelope in the garden—only this was much bigger. And Artemis was very fond of it—only it never knew; and—"

The bronzes gates clashed against the side of the portico. In the doorway stood the queen's messenger—the golden sphinx glittering across the dark hall. The porter preceded her towards me; she smiled her recognition, and told me, in a word, that the formal declaration had been received.

"You will take this note to the Arch-Marshal," she added. "If you should be attacked, it is of no consequence, and you need not get rid of it."

"Is that a likely occurrence?" I asked. "Because I have just heard that the enemy is no more than eight miles off."

"I did not mean an attack by horse, foot, and artillery," the messenger responded dryly. "It was private treachery that I was referring to. As for such an absurd report, I need not tell you it is utterly ridiculous."

"Are you absolutely certain?" I said. "It is the unexpected that happens!"

"If it were in the least likely," she repeated, "the Secretary would see that you had a captain's escort."

With which assurance I was satisfied, and, as it proved, rightly. The messenger had not gone ten minutes before I was in the saddle, equipped for the start.

"Where's Nîa?" I said impatiently, and I spied her in a close conversation with Cydonia, who said a word or two to me as Nîa mounted her horse. Our departure was a much more imposing affair than the military ones of a fortnight before had been; most of the family gathered in the doorway, and, with Cydonia, nodded their adieux as we rode off.

Through the streets and gates—across and open, heathy common—then a plunge into a dark forest, into which the rays of the evening sun scarcely penetrated.

X

The Camp

The first stage out of Alzôna brought us for the night to a small hut in the forest—our resting place, for it was impossible for the horses to push on farther, and there was no system of posting. They were tethered, and left to find pasture. Inside, there was only a single room—but a good fire blazed in it, near the warmth of which a traveller was discussing bread and curry.

Nîa gave a shout of welcome. The stranger got up and slapped her on the shoulder affectionately.

"Zoris!" exclaimed Nîa. "Who would have thought to come across you like this? Where are you going?"

"Humph! That's a state secret!—You're looking well, Nîa! What brings you here?"

"I'm showing this stranger the way to Marshal's army. You see, I'm not as close as you! And who's your mistress? By the lighting, it seem a lifetime since we were together in old Zora's keeping!"

"Yes, by my hair! What times we used to have! Nîa, I never thought but we would see each other long before this!"

She regarded the ring with a mixture of admiration and self-importance, her head on one side.

"Pf!" said Nîa, "an errand you don't know the meaning of! Why, I have a ring, too, and I know very well what it means. It is one of my mistress's friend's—Cydonia's—and I am to give it to her *kerôta*, with a letter besides. So there!"

With a mocking smile, she threw down on the table a ring, much like the first, and followed it up with a parchment letter, daintily painted with sprays of ivy. This struck the brown wood with a slam, and, ricocheting pleasantly, it knocked both rings off the table.

"Be careful, Nîa, of mine," grunted Zôcris, but not unamiably.

I picked the rings up and gave them to Nîa.

"Which is which?" I said.

She examined them.

"Well,—do you know?" turning to Zôcris. "I'm bothered if I do! They're as like as two peas. By the lightning, I've got you into a hole, Zôcris!"

"Not a bit," said she. "If they're exactly alike, what matters? Are they?"

"Look at them," said Nîa, crestfallen. "I can't see any difference."

Zôcris put them side by side on the table gain. We three examined them nervously. Beyond trifling differences such as would not be noticed if the two were not together, there seemed nothing to distinguish them from one another. The seals were engraved simply with vandyked bands.

"Come, either'll do," said Zôcris, and as I noted her coolness I did not wonder at her mistress's choice for her a delicate mission. "There's nothing to choose between them."

Nîa's apologies, if rough, were hearty. She made up a bed for me out of the travelling rugs, and the last thing I was conscious of was her voice and Zôcris's talking together, whilst the last embers flickered in reflection against the rafters.

In the morning I looked about the rough interior very early. Early as it was, however Zôcris had gone. Had she been acting fairly with us, I wondered? I wakened Nîa. She did not need to be called twice. Before I was quite certain that I had spoken, she was up and busy about preparing breakfast.

"Have you your ring and letter safe, Nîa?" I asked her.

"Slept with them under my rug!" she answered. "Here they are."

And, lifting up the end of the covering, she showed me them.

"Zôcris has gone," I observed.

"Oh yes! She went as soon as it was light."

"Had no breakfast, then?"

"No. She would eat it on the road."

"Well, Nîa," I said, "we'll do that, too. What do you say?"

For the forlorn aspect of the tent, with the dead embers of last night's fire untidy and ashy in the morning beams, was depressing and comfortless.

"We might get to the camp tonight, if you had a good rest," said Nîa doubtfully. "If you begin in a hurry, you will want long stops throughout the day. It will be very hot in the afternoon, too."

"As you like. I am in your hands," I said. "Only, I must say I should be glad to be in the open air."

Nîa conceded the point.

"Alright. We'll go on, then, but it will be better if we stop and eat in an hour or so, rather than get what we want as we ride."

It was perfectly still as we turned out at the doorway. There seemed to be no bird twittering, even. But there was a fresh scent in the air, and a deep greenness on the trees that were infinitely pleasant. I splashed my face with water at the spring where the horses drank: an operation which Nîa regarded with extreme contempt, mingled with a little disgust; as she considered it an entirely unnecessary display of asceticism.

"Ugh! How your ladyship does give yourself cold shocks!" she observed. "If it were midday, now! But this cold morning! Ugh!"

I shook the drops away, and tried to persuade her to follow my example—but without effect. As we rode through the forest, the strange quietude continued to prevail. Our horses' trampling hoofs,—their champing at the bits,—the clink of their harness as now and again they turned their glossy heads to one another—these, with our own breathing, were the only sounds. We might be alone, Nîa and I, in an enchanted world of trees. Far in the distance, nevertheless, there was a faint tinkling sound; which grew louder as our horses stepped on, daintily avoiding the fallen branches. Gradually it grew into a harmonious chime of metal; and resolved itself into the jingling of the caparison and accoutrements of a gorgeously attired cavalry soldier, who was proceeding in the opposite direction to ourselves at a rapid pace. We gave the customary salutation: but she had hardly passed when Nîa said in a low and excited voice:

"Did you see what was on her saddle in front of her? Zôcris's cloak!"

It was a beautiful cloak—and very likely the property of her mistress—cream-coloured, and embroidered with laurel branches in gold.

"I'll go after her," I declared, "and make some excuse for speaking to her. Then I can try to find out, Nîa, whether she's met Zôcris."

So I trotted back, and, stepping the soldier, I begged for a needle. It was readily give, and I thanked the girl for it.

"Met anybody on the road?" I added, by way of a parting remark.

"Two countryfolks driving a goat; a charcoal-burner: some children:—and a slave on horseback who was riding past me as bold as brass." The soldier gave a short laugh. "I asked her her business. She took no notice. That made me wild, rather, and I tried to bring her to her senses. But I hadn't time to bother with her, so it ended in my snatching this cloak of hers. I will see if they can find out whose it is at Alzôna. Very likely she had stolen it—look at it! It's a valuable cloak: worth the stealing!"

I nodded farewell in response to hers. Nîa was waiting impatiently for me.

"Aha!" she exclaimed, apostrophizing the departing trooper, when I told her the result of my inquiries. "Zôcris would be one too many for you, my lady; she would, indeed! You thought you were going to be so clever. You didn't think that a slave with a sword in her hand might be a match for a cavalry soldier! Now you've learnt a little. Always nice to get to know more!" concluded Nîa, with an air or prim decorum, admirably assumed.

"I can't make out what Zôcris is after," I said. "Why does she make it a secret where she's going to? Is it not permissible to go to Oristhôn?"

Nîa shook her head.

"I can't pretend to say," she answered. "These things are all past my understanding. I am only a slave; and what my mistresses do is their affair. It isn't mine; and I can't make it so."

Nîa constantly harped on this string. Absolutely devoted to individual free people—I had not forgotten the night when she watched outside my room, in the cold, out of pure goodwill—she yet chafed, it was plain to see, at the limitations of her condition. And still she was not fit, any of my friends would have said, to take her place amongst them as an equal. She herself might have admitted it: so that the grievance was rather a sentimental one. It pleased her to entertain it: it did not embitter her, but it made her caustic. It gave her, also, a certain air of detachment, as of one who is merely playing a part in life,—and a part which she does not care about.

We reached a convenient place for a rest, dismounted and commenced our meal.

"Your are very much honoured, Nîa," I observed as we ended. "Cydonia evidently doesn't think me a proper person to be entrusted with her messages!"

"Consider how long she's been accustomed to get me to do little things for her, your ladyship! I have taken all kinds of messages for the ladies in our house, from her and her sisters, since I was seventeen. They see me in the Forum: and it comes—'Nîa, ask Mira to come round this evening,' or 'Nîa, tell Calêna we are going to Vanathis'—that is their country place, you know—'say we're going to Vanathis tomorrow, and ask her to come with us,'—and so on. And I have done more particular things for them than that! Besides, the Lady Cydonia wouldn't want to trouble you with her affairs!"

"At fifteen, did you begin to work?"

"Work! When haven't I worked? It was plenty of work I had when I was being trained. And I came to my mistress at seventeen."

"Had you any choice as to what work you would do? I mean, do they train people specially to be cooks, or weavers, or attendants?"

"Yes," said Nîa rather shortly. "They do train them for this or that work. But they don't often let them choose. It is just if they show themselves likely for it."

"I hope you will see a good deal of Zôcris now that you have come across her," I remarked. Nîa was gratified, and muttered a confused but pleased acknowledgement. Suddenly, however, it occurred to her that we had spent nearly an hour since we halted, and she secured the horses, that we might recommence our journey.

Leaving the forest after a while, we crossed a flat plain, dotted with villages. A guide was scarcely a necessity, for the path was well marked by the small articles which here and there had been dropped by the soldiers of the battalions that had traversed it. In one place of a piece of gold fringe,—in another fragment of a broken jar,—in another the debris of a pomegranate. Nîa viewed these indications with much scorn.

"A nice set these have been!" she said. "If I were in command of their division, they should just go straight back to Alzôna! Except for the horses' hoofs you should never be able to tell that a squadron has gone past. And the same with infantry. Untidy lot!"

"They should give you a commission," I observed. "You could keep them up to the mark! Is it ever possible—" I stopped, afraid of not putting my question delicately enough.

"Possible for one of us to be free? Just! If we are as good as them—as fine, I mean, you know; and as dignified—we have a right, then, to be as free as anybody. But how are we to get to be like that? Fifty or sixty may, perhaps, every year—out of thousands and millions," concluded she, her arithmetical conceptions growing more and more tropical.

"You will, some day, Nîa!"

"No, not me. As likely that my ladies should grow like me! I'll never need think of that." Her face flushed, nevertheless, and she spoke in smothered snatches.

"Not at all as likely," I said. "You know it's far more likely that one should grow better than worse. For one thing, you want to be better, and none of them wants to deteriorate."

"Hm! What you want is exactly what you don't get," remarked Nîa.

This piece of proverbial philosophy ended the conversation for the time being; for we now approached a tiny village, with a single handsome tower, which stood out of the mass of dark green foliage in which the houses were half hidden. Here we stopped and watered our horses; the inhabitants pressing round us with offers of what they had to give in the way of assistance and supplies. Clearly the battalions that had tramped through already must have behaved well to these people, and, indeed, they did not look like a population that it would be safe to treat badly. There was very little of the rustic about their self-reliant and intelligent bearing. Their interest was much involved, naturally, in progress of operations; for they lay right in the most obvious track of an invading army. Leaving the hospitable shelter of their small *forum*, we resumed our way. Nightfall came on, in spite of Nîa prophecy to the contrary, before we reached the camp. We pressed forward, nevertheless; for its lights could be easily distinguished across the level plain. Twinkling through a fringe of palms, they invited us on, like the lights of a city.

The sentries stopped us, and sent us forward with a picket. I had expected to find the Marshal occupying a house as her headquarters, but, after the medieval and classical fashion, she lived under canvas with the rest of the troops. Her tend was lighted, and she received me with quiet cordiality. I did not know her well, and it was sometime before I began to understand her. Perfectly white hair, a thin, wrinkled face, with deep-set, flaming eyes; a tall and erect figure—it was a curious picture that she presented, and one not very easy to interpret. I told her, in a word, my mission; she bowed gravely and motioned me to a seat, at the same time pushing towards me some platters on which were various fruits and loaves of spiced bread.

"You have travelled all day, and you must be hungry," said she. "I never talk with people who are both hungry and tired. I want a few moments' talk with you, so you will do me the favour of trying our camp cookery."

I was not sorry to do so. She left me entirely unnoticed, and plunged into the analysis of a mass of memoranda. After fifteen minutes or so of silence, broken only by the entry of an officer with a report, she looked up.

"Where do you propose to sleep?"

"I had made no arrangements! As the queen's messenger I expected some accommodation," I said with asperity. She did not show any sign of resentment or apology, but continued to look forward quietly, and observed:

"You wish to stay in the camp, then?"

"I am at your service," I said. "I understood that you might find me useful—"

She got up and stood with her back to me, lifting a casket from the hook where it hung at the side of the tent.

"But you would like to see the camp?" she said in rather emphatic and precise tones. "You would naturally, as a stranger, like the opportunity of visiting the place and inspecting the arrangements?"

She spoke so suggestively and with so incisive an intonation that I felt an affirmative reply was imperatively called for, and I gave it—somewhat hesitatingly. Did the Marshal know of the queen's idea that I might be employed as a messenger? It might have been driven out of her mind by the many other things she had to occupy her thoughts. At all events, I could always ask to be permitted to proceed to the town where Ilex's regiment was stationed. These thoughts flew through my brain in a second or two, and gave me a vague sentiment of uneasiness. I did not know then the Marshal's inveterate fondness for "playing dark," and concealing the position of affairs from her most intimate subordinates until the last possible moment.

"If you want to stay, for such purposes," she resumed, "I will attach you at once to one of the sets of people who occupy a tent—if that accommodation will suit you; if you prefer to leave in the morning, I would ask you to accept my couch."

This was rather an overwhelming offer, and I refused it with many thanks.

"Don't think it a sacrifice," she said, with a slow smile. "I shall be up all night, most likely."

But I insisted strongly that I did want most particularly to visit the camp. I even offered to bivouac in the open, if I could only be permitted to do so. The Marshal struck a gong as I spoke, and at once a messenger appeared. A mere child, with big, innocent brown eyes and a wealth of hair, it seemed an oddly incongruous apparition in the veteran's soldier's tent.

"Send the Captain Sôri," said the Marshal.

In a moment the child reappeared with an officer, to whom the chief entrusted me. Under her guidance Nîa, our horses, and myself were soon comfortably quartered with the Valasna Light Cavalry. The tend which I occupied held six. It was absolutely devoid of furniture, and there was very little in the way of superfluous *impedimenta* about it, though a few loose things were to be observed, such as bronze and even silver vessels, weapons, a candelabrum. It was just time to extinguish the light, so I only got a glimpse of the interior before it was plunged in pretty complete darkness. Only from sounds was it possible to judge anything of the occupants.

The Captain guided me to a spot where there was room for me to lie down wrapped in my rugs, and threw herself down beside me. A variety of remarks filled the night air which rushed through the tent.

"Acütha, I can't hear you! Erosythë, for goodness' sake be quiet!"

"Iromár! Can you *not* behave like reasonable beings? Let me say what I want: and then speak one at once,—in order of seniority! I have brought in a visitor—a foreigner. She has leave to see the camp, and her name is Mêrê. She means to stay a few day;—the Marshal wants her to have Lorên's place while she is away."

"Will she do Lorên's drills?" inquired a deep voice from the remote corner.

"Will you never be serious? And you are not quite hospitable, either, to begin by making bad jokes!"

"I apologise for my subordinate," interrupted another voice—clear cut, this, and refined. "Let me introduce myself—Iromár, the senior officer here. Erosythë, my lieutenant,—show yourself awake, Erosythë, and say something!"

The personage addressed responded, as the reporters say, in a brief and appropriate manner."

"Irnisu, who is Sôri's lieutenant—"

"Delighted to see-hear, I mean—you! And, if you don't mind, I will go to sleep now," said Irnisu.

"Acütha, who was so far overcome by sleepiness as to have to be apologized for just now—"

"I am desolated!" said the deep voice. "It's very dreadful to be so unfortunate!"

"And—oh, I forgot: of course, Lorên's away! Now we'll get to know each other better in the morning! I hope you'll just ask us if you want to know anything. By the way, didn't I see you once at the palace?"

Before I could answer, Sôri chimed in from close to me:

"You are not the foreigner that got ride of Galêsa and Opanthë for us?"

I admitted my share in that transaction; and, but that Iromár peremptorily commanded quietude, even Irnisu would have talked about the affair for half the night. As it was, Sôri carried on a whispered conversation until my braid and eyelids refused to hold me any longer from sleep.

The unaccustomed sound of trumpets woke me. A primitive toilet, a plain and lively breakfast, the materials of which were prepared from first to last by ourselves, and then an exodus of the military element, who were due at the parade ground. Nîa and I started to find Chloris's regiment. This was not an easy matter. At length, however, the desired part of the camp was reached. After traversing a wilderness of canvas, intersected by straight lanes of dusty pathway, we came upon the familiar white dresses, with dark red cloaks, the uniform of Chloris's regiment. She herself was to be seen before long, seated on an elevation composed of heaped-up logs of timber, and engaged in superintending, with a fine mixture of irresponsibility and gravity, a mysterious kind of game or tournament which was in progress below. Catching sight of us, she descended from her perch with more quickness and agility than grace, leaving it for the first to occupy who felt the call; and she made at once for where we stood. I fancy she would have liked to embrace me, if not Nîa as well, she came up with such a springing step. But, in fact, it was a very quiet and restrained greeting, though a thoroughly kind one, that she gave us.

"Come into my tent," she said, after the first few words of welcome. "There's nobody there—everybody's out in the sun—and we can have a nice time to ourselves."

Once in the dim canvas shade, the girl's brightness passed from sobriety to positive seriousness. Her ordinary air of light unconcern was quite gone; there was a quick sensitiveness about her mouth, a deep meaning in her eyes, which I had not seen before. She seemed to have risen to a new dignity, as she asked me about the Alzôna people and her own house. I was not sure that I did not like old Chloris better. Nîa kept discreetly in the background, clasping the ring and the missive. With a touch of her impulsive ways, Chloris, as she talked to me, pushed a full beaker of sherbet to the slave.

"Nîa deserves it," I laughed. "She has something for you."

She turned round inquiringly, and Nîa produced the letter, carefully flicking the dust off with her sleeve.

"From the Lady Cydonia," she observed.

Instantaneously, all Chloris's mature dignity had departed. Her eyes sparkled: she seized the letter and caressed it, laughing and scolding Nîa for keeping it so long. She brought from a metal casket scent and cordials and rare fruits, and pressed them on the messenger's acceptance, moving across the ground with dancing feet.

"It *is* pretty!" she said admiringly when she found time to examine the treasure. "When are you going back? I must write—"

"Don't be so anxious to get rid of us," I said. "Most likely we will not go back to Alzôna at all."

She looked at us with a puzzled expression.

"I am not exactly engaged as a letter carrier," I proceeded. "My business was to bring the Marshal the intelligence that war has been formally declared. My next may be to go on someother State business. But," I added, with uncomfortable reminiscences of the Marshal's attitude, "let that be a secret between us, Chloris. I'm very glad Nîan has been able to bring your letter,—but I can't say anything as taking back an answer. I really am sorry!"

"Nevermind—" she began—when Nîa handed her the ring.

I was startled by the sudden revulsion to a statelier manner which she showed. Her colour came and went. She drew herself up, and stood in thought for a moment. Then she looked at the ring carefully. She went to the tent's entrance with it; turned it over and over; looked at it against the light; rubbed its surface; gazed at it with knitted forehead. Then she came slowly back to us, and sat down with a forced little laugh.

"Did you have this ring from Cydonia?" she asked Nîa.

"Yes. Of course I did!"

"From her own hands?"

"Yes. In the street in front of the Lady Ilex's house."

"Well, it is not her ring!"

Nîa would not look at me. There was a moment's silence.

"That isn't remarkable," I said. "Don't be angry, Chloris! The fact is, we met someone on the way who had a ring exactly like it—so we though, though it seems we were mistaken—and they go mixed, as we were comparing them."

"Well, you are a nice pair!" said Chloris, not too pleased, but mollified by the consciousness of having her letter to read. "I must just take Nîa's word for it. But it might have been very awkward."

My guide fell on the ground at Chlori's feet, saying in a choked voice:

"It was all me!"

"Don't be so absurd!" said Chloris. "For goodness' sake, get up, Nîa! Suppose anybody comes in!" For, indeed, a soldier appeared at the tent door, and passed away, after pausing for a moment in extreme astonishment.

In the habit of obedience, Nîa regained her feet, while Chloris considerately turned to me and inquired how the affair happened. I explained to her that it was almost a pure accident—nothing to be vexed about. Quite pleasantly, she agreed, only asking:

"And whose slave was it, then, who went away with the other ring?"

"Zôcris, a slave of the Second Keybearer," I told her.

"That creature!" flamed out Chloris. "To have my Cydonia's— Cydonia's ring! She should not touch it with her fingertip! Mêrê, how can I get it from her?"

"How to get it from the commandant of Oristhôn is the point," I returned.

"Ah-h-h!" said Chloris thoughtfully; "that's delightful! That's charming! It will send their plans all wrong—you see if it doesn't! They won't have the confidence in their slave that I have in you and Nîa. They won't believe the message—won't act on it, at any rate—if they see it's the wrong ring. They'll be certain some trick is being played upon them!"

"Do you think, though," I interposed, as soon as I could get in a word, "that they will even notice the difference? A person of your penetration isn't to be found in every—"

Chloris looked at me in some surprise.

"Why, it only needs a glance," she said. "Look at this—barry dancetté of eight pieces! I know Cydonia's arms very well—four barrulets dancette."

"Where is the difference?"

"Difference! One has seven dividing lines, and the other eight."

"That is not very noticeable, surely!"

"Wait till somebody offers you seven gold crowns in payment of an eight crown score," said she; "then see if eight and seven mean precisely the same thing! And there's this difference also—which you can't see on the rings—that the Keybearer's arms are blue and gold; Cydonia's are silver and black."

She glanced at the letter in her hand. I felt we ought to leave her in peace to read it, so I summoned Nîa to follow me away.

"But you are not going!" exclaimed Chloris.

"Indeed, we must—"

"But you haven't seen the regiment! You haven't had bread and salt with us in this charming dining room! You've not heard the band! Nothing! Oh, I can't let you go yet a while!"

"Oh, yes, Chloris!" I said. "there will be plenty of opportunities, even today. I solemnly promise to attend the afternoon parade, to come and dine with you afterwards, to do everything proper, in short. But I've kept you long enough now."

"Well, will you come back at midday for a meal?"

"After then, please! I hardly like to leave the set I'm quartered with, for the whole day. You won't let them see much more of me after I meet you again, I expect."

"No, indeed!" she said. "You must spend the rest of the day with me"; and she escorted us out of the tent with a highly impressive air of importance.

Nîa and I wandered about not for a very long time, and in due course we regained the cavalry quarters, where we were made welcome by the party of five whose hospitality I claimed. That day and another passed, so far as occupation was concerned, pleasantly and without disturbance. Interesting enough it was to stroll through the camp, observing its manifold activities, and noting its resemblances and unlikenesses to anything of the kind I had seen before. But it was all overshadowed and spoilt by a constant impatience to be away. I could take no time to observe—every moment was devoted to fruitless, hungry speculation as to when I should be sent on, and questionings as to how soon I should apply for leave to start on my Om account, if no orders came. I moved about the place in a dream, hardly conscious of the wonderful, varied panorama that was spread before me; conscious hardly of Chloris's kindness and Nîa's devotion; conscious only of a longing disquietude, rising into overwhelming impatience to be away. It was an unsatisfactory state, and I had not long to remain in it. I could not bring myself, so early, to leave the camp, and, abandoning my hope of an official mission, to find my way to Ilex as best I could. And, fortunately, not three days after my arrival, a message come for me to attend the Arch-Marshal. We were at dinner.

"You'll have to go," said Erosythë. "The Marshal won't be kept waiting. And just when that fig *pâlê* was coming on! Too bad!"

"I'll keep you a small piece," Acütha promised, "about the size of my fingernail; that will just suit a delicate creature like you!"

Irnisu kept up an unremitting attention to her plate. Iromár said:

"Yes, if I were you I'd go at once; there's always oatcake and lemons to be had here—so you won't starve."

Sôri got up, and offered to conduct me. I did not want her to, but she insisted that I could not find my way. So we went together.

The Marshal was surrounded by a number of officers, and took no notice of us; Sôri would not leave me, however, until the commander rose, and signed to me to pass with her into the inner tent. Two splendidly proportioned sentinels, armed with silver-hafted halberds or axes, guarded the entrance. We crossed to the farther side, and sat on a small carpet that was spread there. The chief suddenly became pleasantly familiar.

"Now that you're seated-by the way, have you dined?—You can tell me what you think of our troops. Did you find the Valasna officers hospitable?"

"Yes, indeed! Though I have not seen very much of them—I have been wandering up and down the place, seeing old friends, and so on."

"Old friends," smiled the Marshal, glancing up at the tent-side, where hung four or five heavy swords and a very Scottish-looking circular target. "Surely you don't have any old friends in this country!"

I smiled back. "Comparatively old friends, I mean. Chloris, for instance, I have known nearly ever since I came."

"Ah! Erotris's girl? I have seen her about the palace. And she is in the army? I have often wanted to have a long talk with you about the strange way you came here amongst us," she proceeded, "but I am afraid I shall not have the satisfaction just yet. For I think we ought to send you out of harm's way as soon as may be. Now that war is openly declared, this is far too dangerous a place for you. You won't take an old campaigner's advice, and travel in Oranthë for a few months? That—"

"Oh no, your Excellency," I broke in. "I should not leave Armeria on any account. Indeed, I hoped—"

She silenced me with an uplifted hand.

"Let us talk quietly, please! We cannot be as private here as one would quite like. Well, that is settled. You must be moved away from the scene of action here; and you do us the honour of wanting to remain in the country. In that case, the best thing will be for you to go up to Pyramôna. Start tonight. Now, if you can. And the sooner you get there, the better I shall be pleased! By the way"—she rose, still speaking, and stood before a cabinet, small and bronze-cornered, from which she extracted a small packet—"I should be obliged, since you are going, if you would carry this to the Commandant Brytas. They are papers of some importance, and I must ask you to take considerable care of them."

I did not, in the first glow of satisfied expectancy, exactly understand whether this message, or my removal to a place of safety, or someother motive, was uppermost in the commander's thoughts, but I felt only that I must thank her as gratefully as I knew how.

"It is very good indeed of your Excellency to think of my safety—and to entrust me with these. I will do all I can to let Brytas have them at once. Does it matter if anyone sees them?"

"Ah!" she said dryly, "it would be better not. In fact, if anyone insists—and it might be difficult to persuade a troop of cavalry of their impoliteness in doing so—I should recommend you to go to any lengths rather than let them be seen. Not that there is any risk of anybody being so improper—only, as you know, there are some Alzôna people whom we cannot altogether trust. Perhaps you would rather not—"

"It will be a pleasure if I can try to do the slightest service to the crown," I replied. "I can't thank you sufficiently for giving me the opportunity. It really is far too good and kind of you. I wish I could thank you anything like properly! Perhaps the queen may have mentioned—"

But here the Marshal cut me short.

"Don't oppress me with thanks," she said. "I would rather stand a siege! And my time is taken up; I have the colonel of the Orynthiacs to see now. Ah, Colonel," she said, opening the curtain and dismissing me, "punctual as usual! So is this lady—a civilian, whom I have tried to persuade to leave the country. She will not go—and I am sending her to a quieter corner at Pyramôna."

"Like your sensible self, your Excellency," observed the Colonel, a stiff creature, with a prim voice. "This will be a hot place for a civilian in a day or two."

The Marshal took her in, and I hurried towards my quarters. Nobody was about. Iromár always took a walk after dinner. Erosythë and Irnisu had a lecture to attend, and Sôri and Acütha were nowhere to be seen. There was a miscellaneous collection of eatables set out, with a humorous note from the company. I examined it in high spirits, laughing at its weak jokes, and telling them to Nîa, who was ready to appear at a moment's call.

"Fancy, Nîa! They say, 'We hope you will excuse no bread, as we do not keep anything so common!' and they say, 'We have provided very little lemon juice, you being quite acid enough.'" I stopped to laugh. Soon recollecting myself, I ordered Nîa to have the horses ready at once.

"I will just scribble a line to these absurd creatures," I said, "and by the time I get it finished I expect the horses to be here. Because you must hurry all you can, Nîa. Just think!—We are off tonight to where you will see the Lady Ilex; and the commandant of the town is Brytas, you know. So be your quickest, my good—"

She disappeared as I spoke, with an alacrity that satisfied even myself. In an incredibly short space she was ready at the tent with our two horses.

"Do you want a spare one?" she said.

"Not unless we need it. Do we?"

"I think not."

"Then we'll try to get on without it. How far may we expect to get before nightfall?"

"We must stop at Clazixu, unless your ladyship likes to sleep out."

I deliberated for a few moments.

"Can you keep awake at nights, Nîa?"

"I think I can," she replied modestly.

"And do you think you can find a safe sleeping place?"

"Plenty, your ladyship. Lovely beds of fern, where a regiment might lose itself!"

"And where the horses can be tethered?"

"Oh yes, easily!"

"Well, we may settle to bivouac, then. Take plenty of oatcake, and then we needn't trouble the people anywhere tonight for food."

I left a note on the despatch tray for Chloris; then Nîa and I set out on our journey. I had only the vaguest idea how long it would take. A week, a fortnight, a day—it was all the same. The unsettled, anxious time was over, and it seemed like a year, looking back. We were fairly on our way from the camp. Never had it looked so pretty. very group of stray soldiers seemed fit for an artist to study. The setting—I cannot say the western—sun shone brilliantly on the snowy canvas, and brightened the green of the spots of grass, and glittered on the spears of the picquets and reliefs starling their rounds or the evening. A curious figure, wrapped in rich shawls, and wearing a crowned turban, was passing through one of the side lanes, escorted by several high officers. I believe, from what I afterwards learnt, that this must have been a foreign general, of princely rank in her half-barbarian home, who was permitted to visit the camp.

She was expected to take back an impressive report, no doubt, to her uncivilized Sovereign; but she seemed proud and unmoved enough to please the most exacting mistress, jealous of her envoy's upholding her dignity. Near the limits of the lines we came across another odd sight—a soldier striding along the middle of the way, flourishing her arms with a majestic air, and uttering from time to time loud, unintelligible cries. She was, we saw, the victim of a peculiar kind of disease which seizes occasionally upon these people. Under its influence, while retaining their senses in the main, the persons affected lose control of themselves; they imagine that they are the only people in the world, and they exchange their ordinary polished bearing for an absurd swagger, which frequently culminates in a frenzied dashing about of the limbs, during which stage they are somewhat dangerous. Fortunately they never seize a weapon in such attacks. Like other nervous disorders, the affection is very liable to spread. I was told that by giving way to a frenzy it is possible to render it chronic. This is regarded as criminal, otherwise the *iâca*, or person subject to that attack, is treated as we in Britain might treat anyone wild with neuralgia, or any violent pain.

Passing the *iâca*, who rushed against Nîa's horse, and was promptly recalled to sobriety by a violent stroke with a palm branch switch—a measure often efficacious in the milder stages—we reached the outermost sentinels, and soon we had heard the last notes of the army bugles.

"How long do you think we shall take?" it suddenly occurred to me to demand of Nîa.

"We will do ten miles tonight," said she. "Tomorrow, about this time, we ought to be there."

And she rose to her full height and flicked a leaf off her horse's bridle. For the time she was leader and mistress here; she unconsciously realised it. Perfectly polite, she lost the air of subject deference—"subject" is hardly the right word, but it must do—which was hers before. She dropped into it again, however, when, in the early starlight, she made the arrangements for our night's rest. Quietly and deftly she secured the horses, piled up the dry leaves for a couch, and found a spring of good water. Then she settled herself to watch. I put the precious parcel in my dress folds, well hidden, and lay down.

"You must waken me between midnight and daybreak, so as to get a little sleep yourself," I told her. "Promise me, Nîa."

"Oh, but, your ladyship, I can do very well without sleep," she insisted. "I will sleep for hours and hours at Pyramôna to make up for it."

"How do you know you, will have the chance, Nîa? No, I want you to be fresh, tomorrow particularly. Suppose we meet a few of the enemy? How could you second me With a head like a pumpkin? We won't either of us sleep long, but we must have some rest. Isn't that sensible?"

"A night's rest doesn't make an inch of difference to me," persisted she, her figure just discernible as she crouched a few yards away, with her head erect and alert. "I am quite used to it. 'Course, if your ladyship orders me—" her tone was injured; but I kept to my point, and told her that I did order her. She did not speak again and I fell asleep with her sombre, thoughtful profile in my view. It was rather a tragic guardian that she made in that solitary lair,—but my dreams were of most prosaic things. A tea party in a remote provincial town: the neat table equipage, the talk concerning the gas manager's deficiencies, and the latest additions to the library; and, through the small room's window, glimpses of the harbour, where the waves curled, wildly up past the jetty on to the flat beach—these were the images that raced through my brain. When, however, the waves began to invade the dining room, and to disturb the keen discussion on disestablishment—(in which Mr. Gladstone was taking a prominent part, accompanied on the piano by Mr. George Grossmwith)—by splashing the frames of the pictures, I judged it time to waken. Nîa had come down from the tragic pedestal, and was for the few minutes before she went to sleep, her accustomed self-devoted, outspoken, and a little rough. It was eerie work watching. I had no inclination to doze, but the silence was so profound and dark. No sound came from the horses, even; and I could not guess their whereabouts. The trill of a nocturnal bird burst out very occasionally, and everytime it. sent a shock darting through me, as if its loud, lonely notes were a new and strange thing on the earth. Gradually the darkness lifted; and long before the sun shot above the horizon, I had wakened Nîa and breakfasted. One of the horses, however, was not to be seen. We tracked it for a couple of hours, and at last came across it, peacefully enjoying a meal of rich grass, from which it departed with considerable signs of vexation, so that it was a party of three extremely bad-humoured creatures which, with the other horse, proceeded on the actual journey.

Through a pleasant, flat country we passed, diversified by villages, and here and there a walled ton. Extensive woods were frequent: and by midday we discerned, over the tops of a grove of cedars, the dark blue summits of the range of hills at whose base lay the town towards which we were travelling. We gave our horses little rest, making even the halt at midday a short one.

"Come! we're doing fine!" said Nîa. "Looks as if we would get to the place before night, this does."

"Even with losing all that time over the horse?" I questioned doubtfully.

"I think so. That's Marêzos, that bit of pink wall past those trees. I have passed it later than this, and got to Pyramôna before night."

"At a different time of year, perhaps?"

"Not much later, your ladyship. And it shows we are going at a good pace."

We paused here at a veil. Nîa jumped from the saddle, and scrambled down the sides of the depression at the centre of which it was sunk. It hardly seemed a very safe performance, for the little craggy rocks and shingly gravel, with which the ground was covered, afforded an insecure foothold. She managed to get some water in a gourd; the horses and I were thankful for it, for it was terribly warm. Descending again for a second supply, she was suddenly confronted by a square-set, sullen-browed figure, which rose magically from behind the biggest boulder. The remarks which this personage addressed to Nîa were emphatic and noisy, but I could not catch their meaning. My guide pursued her way imperturbably. She was followed, however, by the stranger, whose loud accents took a decidedly threatening tone. Nîa turned as she neared the well's edge, and ordered the unwelcome attendant away, but to no purpose. The two exchanged sharp words, and, before I knew what was happening, the stranger, who was a powerfully-built peasant, had grasped Nîa by the waist and forced her to the ground. I leapt from my horse in a moment; leaving it in the sole charge of its companion, I made my way down to the scene of the struggle, a good deal more careless than I ought to have been in avoiding collisions with fragments of rock,—as I afterwards found out to my cost. The ruffian had left Nîa on sight of me, and I headed him or her off, my companion following up the chase. She had taken off her sword, so as not to be embarrassed in climbing. However, we were now two to one, and the ill-conditioned disturber of our peace saw fit to stop.

"I should like to know what you mean by falling upon my slave in that way!" I demanded angrily. The reply was a guttural growl which I could not understand.

"Says you have no business to question him," burst out Nîa, adopting the role of interpreter with avidity.

"I give you till I count four to answer," I said. "After then—" I looked at my sword with significance.

"He says it's the Mazêyon well, and not for strangers," said Nîa. "But it's all nonsense! Travellers may always use water."

"However that may be," I said severely, "what right could you have to treat this slave of mine as you did? We will tie him to the bridle, Nîa, and take him to Pyramôna, and see what the Lady Brytas says to a brute who insults the Marshal's messengers!"

Nîa's eyes gleamed fire at this suggestion. The scamp, however, became awkwardly apologetic and humble.

"The lady won't be hard on her servant because of standing up for the town rights! Only my place to watch the well!" he grunted, according to Nîa.

"I can't possibly think anything of an excuse like that," I remarked. "I will certainly take you to Pyramôna. Take the bucket-line, Nîa, and fasten it on him."

He made a quick movement sideways, but stopped when he caught sight of our horses above the brink, and began another deprecatory grumble.

"Oh well," I said, "we can't afford time to bother with him. Listen," I proceed, turning to the obnoxious cause of this further delay, "you deserve—(what shall I tell him, Nîa?)"

"To have his hair and eyebrows cut off and his nose slit!" said Nîa, with pleased alacrity and great distinctness. I repeated the information, which had already produced a further lengthening of the crestfallen features of the villager, with additional emphasis.

"But," I added, "we're on urgent business, and we will be satisfied if you do this. Lie on your face flat on the ground, and my slave will put her foot on your neck, and you will kiss her sandals."

Extremely unfortunate was any Armerian who incurred such a fate! I had unknowingly made the penalty not much lighter than the original one suggested by the active fancy of Nîa. Extremely reluctantly also was it that the villager proceeded to stoop, and slowly to settle in the prescribed manner lengthwise on the ground, with many pauses and inward struggles. For it seemed that the worst class of country people entertain a peculiar prejudice against slaves, whom they regard with hatred and contempt. They think that they themselves ought to possess

IRENE CLYDE

slaves, and they resent the obligation to refrain from meddling with them. Consequently it is a particularly bitter pill when, instead of carrying the exhibition of their feelings to the verge of illegality as usual, they come to be forced by any chance to treat a slave on an equal footing.

I never saw anyone so elated, as Nîa upon this occasion. She threw her right sandal off, and advanced to the prostrate Hetch, who, after all, was a freeman. Her satisfied smile was almost majestic, and so was her carriage. She planted her foot firmly on the peasant's neck, and beamed on me like a child paddling in the sea. I was anxious about the horses, but I could not interfere with her naive enjoyment.

"Mayn't I just cut his hair off?" she entreated, stretching out her hand for my sword. But I drew the line here, and shook my head, commencing at the same time to regain the level ground where the horses stood. I left Nîa to receive the kiss of her sandals without a witness, at the same time impressing upon the prostrate countryman that if he ventured to rise before an hour had passed, he might expect nothing better than to be trotted to Pyramôna.

By the time I was in my saddle, the slave was with me, and we pushed on, tolerably satisfied that no alarm would be raised.

"Hurt, Nîa?" I inquired.

She disclaimed any injury with the air of a princess.

"I thought," I said, feeling rather small, "that the peasant might have hurt you. It was a rough clasp-like a bear's, if you know what such beasts are."

"Indeed, he might have killed me!" she said shortly, turning moist eyes to me. "I can't thank you—it isn't my way. Of course, I ought to, if a lady cared for it!"

"Don't talk that way, Nîa!" I insisted. "You ought to know I care. The only thing is, that there is nothing to be thankful for. If there had been any danger, or any trouble even, it would be different. And why shouldn't I care for your good opinion, just as much as Lyx might, or Zôcris?"

She rode on in silence.

"In the country I come from," I went on, "we hate the idea of slavery, and keeping people in a class apart. There is no such barrier between one man and another there!" And I told her about the British instinct for freedom, while she listened with rapt interest.

"And so nobody looks do, m on anybody else there! And nobody's forced to work. And everybody understands one another. If I could just go for one month, now!"

"Not impossible, perhaps, Nîa. But would you come away again?"

"I would have to!"

"How could anybody make you?"

"What would the Lady Ilex and her honourable sister do without me?"

"Ah, well! If you are so considerate, Nîa! But what is that tall turret?"

It was the most conspicuous feature of the little town of Talusquë, I learnt—a slender square shaft of white marble. Nîa could not tell me to what building it belonged; but I found with satisfaction that she considered that, in spite of all delays, we were making excellent progress. We stopped for a few—a very few—minutes at a tiny village late in the afternoon, to recruit. By this time the line of hills had become distinct and near. They formed a spur of the great Alpine mass which rose farther away, and was itself invisible as yet. Serrated in outline, and wildly precipitous, they formed a much more formidable barrier than their mere height would suggest. The increasing beauty of the scenery, where clusters of dark green-fronded trees rose against the background of this picturesque range, was in tune with our thoughts. Pyramôna, Brytas, Ilex, were not far away!

Miles had to be traversed yet, nevertheless; and the hills, instead of being ahead to the left hand, began to stretch behind us as well. It seemed as if it would be dark before we arrived; and an hour or so past nightfall the moon would fail us. But as we reached the crest of a slight rise in the ground, we overlooked a fine plain, in the midst of which Pyramôna—for there could be no other such town near—lay, gilded by the evening sun. We almost shouted, and urged our horses on, the city in full view all the way, until we came to its gate.

The horses knew, with their strange animal intuition, that there was fodder here, and they made short work of the distance. Myself and Nîa laughed and passed loud remarks apropos of nothing as, we flew along. The vedette outside the walls detached a soldier to accompany us, and we hear d her clattering after us on her mountain pony. A few foot passengers we met, and a band of countryfolk, coming out with baskets and a cart—of all of whom we took little enough notice. At the gate, in the cool shade of its archway, was stationed a guard, who received us with a due mixture of caution and respect, and detailed an officer, who might answer to our sergeants, to conduct me to Brytas, in the citadel. The town teemed, with uniforms, and as, we passed through the darkening streets I tried to distinguish that of Ilex's regiment, but without success. The citadel was a delightful old building, divided from the public square by a courtyard, whose wall was pierced by innumerable great arches. Its principal wing consisted of a massive block of buildings, perfectly plain but for a projecting battlement which frowned at the summit. We entered its main corridor, were received by the town major, who was beginning to talk to me about finding us quarters when Brytas herself came in. She came straight up to me, and, without the least awkwardness, summarily embraced and kissed me, and led me immediately through an antechamber into her room, without speaking a word. Not until we had sat down did she say:

"You have despatches for me?"

I produced them.

"It won't seem discourteous to you if I read them? You know how pleased I am to see you without my saying!"

I assented, with a smile, and waited. The room we sat in was a rather remarkable one. Nearly cubical, its stone walls were unrelieved by any decoration, except that, high up, they were perforated by large quatrefoil openings. Round each side were ranged a profusion of cabinets and bureau—a marked contrast to the Alzôna rooms, which were so sparingly furnished. On the top of most of these chests there were piled maps, and papers, and surveying instruments, and weapons, and the like.

Brytas glanced through the papers, and, remarking absently, "How does it come that you have brought these?" she settled to read them, without waiting for or seeming to expect an answer. So we sat, for half an hour, in silence. Then she pushed the despatches on to a low ebony table at her right hand, and observed in a brisker tone:

"I'm terribly busy, Mêrê! But there's a little room off this, that you can have tonight. Nîa will stable your horses; and, if you don't mind, she had better sleep in that room, too. We can have ten minutes' talk before you go to bed."

She rose, and told an attendant officer to see to my entertainment meanwhile. By the time the horses were seen to, a meal was ready for me, spread in a little gallery, from which I could watch the crowded streets far below.

"Is it possible," I said at the first opportunity to my cicerone, "for me to see the Lady Ilex tonight? She belongs to the White Cavalry."

The adjutant, who was not sharing the meal with me, but was perpetually trimming the lamps, adjusting the situation of the rugs, or otherwise altering things, was a person given to uttering set pronouncements on the least formal occasions. She responded:

"The interview which you desire is entirely impracticable. I am, of course, well acquainted with the Lady Ilex"—why did her pronunciation set my teeth on edge?—"who is, indeed, colonel of her regiment. Unfortunately, these squadrons have been pushed forward to Ylonár,—a small village in the Kerma Pass, some miles away. As the gates are now closed, I confess I see no method of communication with them."

The appetite with which I had begun supper was gone. Neither the adjutant nor I found the other an entertaining companion. The few moments which one had to spend in gazing over the parapet until Brytas was disengaged seemed like a month. At last a shy, pale child appeared, with the intimation that the Commandant could receive me.

"That's right!" said Brytas, as I appeared. "I have just put a spoonful of coffee on to infuse. Sit down on that settle, and think you're at Alzôna again! And so you've come here out of harm's way," she continued, with a comical look. "It was a miscalculated move. The Uras folks are pouring this way in their tens of thousands, and I'm thinking of sending a messenger into the teeth of them—that's to Ylonár, in the mouth of the pass. We've got to hold Ylonár at all risks for as long as may be; and it isn't much to hold. I will send out infantry tomorrow, and the cavalry screen will be withdrawn to Pyramôna here. But I am leaving Ilex as officer in command at Ylonár. If we throw back the Uras people, we relieve Ylonár first thing;—if not—well, if not, it must take its chance, and likely the rest of the kingdom will go down with it. Now, Mêrê, don't say you will if you don't want to! I thought of letting you go first thing in the morning with a verbal message to Ilex. And then you could remain at her disposal."

"The very thing I would have asked!" I exclaimed; and Brytas smiled a little faintly, and said, after a moment's pause:

"It is partly because I think Ilex would like it, that I make the suggestion. Think it over, Mêrê. I'm sorry I can give you no longer than while I make the coffee."

She was silent; but my mind needed no time for reflection. I assured her of that. And when she had finished her preparations, she came over and sat beside me.

"It won't do to have my plans got hold of," she observed, "so I can't put what I have to say in black and white. Let me explain to you exactly what I would like you to tell Ilex. If you should be captured by the Uras scouts, you may tell them anything!"

We spent not more than the ten minutes she had mentioned

in discussing the message. Her explanation of it was so lucid and straightforward that I took in the details without any difficulty.

"Now you must go to bed, and sleep well! I will send Nîa; and the horses will be ready as soon as it is light. You can have breakfast sooner— but my people will see to all that. Perhaps I won't see you in the morning, Mêrê:—Take care of yourself, if I don't!" And with an imitation of the queen she put her hands on my shoulders, and kissed me warmly.

I was tired, and fell asleep before Nîa came in. Early, as usual, she aroused me before Brytas's attendant came. Napoleon was right in defining real courage as—"two o'clock in the morning courage." The very darkness rebukes one, and tells one that decent people ought to be in bed.

The unaccustomed hang of things, the cold air, combine to depress one's spirits. By break of day we were mounted and moving down the street, deserted now. But there was plenty of stir by the gate, where an infantry regiment was drawn up in line, in readiness to leave. The perfect regularity of the formation could not have been exceeded, nor the brilliance of the accoutrements, nor the stillness in the ranks. Suddenly a sharp word of command was given:—the line swung round into column, and filed out at the battlemented archway.

We reined in our horses to let the troops pass, and as they did so their band struck up a march. The ringing rattle of the drums echoed from the walls, wakening one's energies to life again. Our eyes were riveted on the succession of armed and free-stepping figures, until the rearguard closed the line. Moving away towards the gate, we encountered a solitary horseman, who startled me by calling to us. Brytas it proved to be, unrecognisable in a gorgeous helmet with a spreading winged crest.

"See! I *have* met you again," she said. "When next, I wonder? Nevermind, it's sure to be right in the end. Nîa!" she added, making the slave colour with pleasure, "I am very glad Mêrê chose you for a guide. You'll be in Ylonár, Mêrê, before the sun has warmed the ground."

Her horse became a little restive. She waved her hand to us and rode slowly away, her bronze wings quivering with the movement.

As for me, the pink flush on the craggy hilltops shone like a beacon-fire to guide me to the pass; the notes of the grasshoppers were little bugle-calls urging me onwards: I hardly looked at Nîa. Scattered parties of cavalry were to be seen at various points of the plain: passing a wood, we came across a regiment at breakfast, and for a moment I fancied them enemies; but we left them behind us, with nothing to fear from them except keen glances. Nîa steered me silently and circumspectly towards our objective. Ylonár refused to show itself until we had entered the mazes of the rocks; when, turning round an outlying mass of boulders, we came in view of it.

Of course, I was disappointed with it. A single walled enclosure, solitary and lifeless,—with no such plenitude of graceful palms as encircled the lowland cities, it was only too obviously a lonely mountain post, built at the call of absolute necessity. A low dome could just be discerned over the parapet and a truncated cube of a tower. There were rocks in the neighbourhood from which it might have been commanded by rifle-fire: but it stood well enough away to be quite safe against other attacks unless prolonged. A horse somewhere behind the stone walls neighed, and was answered by a chorus of companions. A single mounted soldier rode down to us from the gate, and brought us to the enclosure.

Once inside the gateway one could see the small extent of the place still better. A square building, flush with the wall, occupied most of what room there was. Two or three much smaller erections stood in the remaining space, where a squadron or two of cavalry were assembling under cramped conditions. The trampling legs of the horses as they curveted in the fresh morning air looked so unpleasantly numerous, that it was with relief that I followed the warder up a staircase in the thickness of the wall—and it was medievally thick—to the top. Across a primitive bridge made of a plank she led me, on to the flat roof of the main building.

There sat a figure that I could not mistake.

"Ilex!" I cried, as I hurried over the rough bridge. But my voice was weak, and she did not hear me. As we approached her she looked round, sprang up, and came to me with shining eyes.

"Mêrê: what *are* you doing here?" she exclaimed as she took me in her arms.

"I am the Commandant's messenger," I said. "And I am yours now."

It took a minute or two to make her understand my appearance. Then she dived down a sort of hatchway, accompanied by me, to a roughly comfortable little room, where I delivered the message of Brytas. She listened attentively, and remained lost in thought and the contemplation of travel-stained papers for some length of time.

At last, pushing the papers aside, she threw a bright look at me.

"And now, Mêrê," she said, "you must go. We shall see each other again. Somewhere, if not here: sometime, if it may be long. My regiment is ready to leave;—as soon as the infantry Brytas promises come up, they will go to Pyramôna. And you will be able to go with them." She rose as she spoke.

I told her it was impossible.

She insisted. For a few seconds a curious feeling took possession of my mind. Was it commendable, or right, to risk everything-life, liberty, the possibility of restoration to Europe (or to my senses)—for a being who was, for all I could tell, a phantom of the brain? I brushed the persistent suggestion aside, as best I could. There was no time to argue questions of casuistry. I repeated my refusal. There was a wide curule chair by me. I remember throwing myself back in it and clutching the handles quietly, as I told her I could not go. It was to be with her, that I had come: I could not fancy her sending me away.

"Mêrê, you know what it is?" she said. "It is an awful risk. If it isn't certain that this fort will go down, it's not far from it. I can't let you!"

"What would it matter to me that I was safe if you were not?" I answered, with as much appeal in my voice as I could summon."

I would rather be with you always—"

"You are thinking so just now! But you would forget—and go back to your friends—and live happily—" she said.

"Ilex! Is it likely—?"

She came over to me and put her hand on my shoulder.

"Mêrê, dear, it can't be. I know you would mind it—but not like that."

Her voice caressed me like the south wind. I cannot tell, what I said. Did she want me to go? Did she not care to have me? Was Phanaras, perhaps—

"I know what is right for me to do," said Ilex. "You ought not to be here! Only there is no more time to talk about it. Not a moment, Mêrê, think!"

"If you had told me to go, I might," I answered. "But if I am to think—I have thought!"

She looked at me lingeringly, as, crossing the little room, she stood by a low doorway.

"I can't believe it, Mêrê I! You have not known me two months, and how can—"

I went to her, and took her hand in mine. From that moment I knew that she would say no more to make me leave. She took a deep breath and hurried out, motioning me to follow her. Through dim stone passages, low vaulted chambers, and echoing corridors she preceded me, until we came out into the open air of the courtyard. The clattering squadrons had disappeared, and only a soldier or two was visible. An attendant was waiting with her horse. She mounted and signed to me to do the same. Outside the troops had formed in line: down the slopes of the ascent were seen the crests of the advancing infantry. In a few moments Ilex had given her instructions to her staff to recall the rest of the cavalry, and horses were quickly moving to right and left. She remained busily engaged, until the incoming garrison was close at hand, when she rode to the waiting squadron and despatched them.

The files of horses wheeled one after another; and, as the last moved away, Ilex shot a questioning glance at me. But I would not look at her, and developed my attention to my bridle.

There was endless work to do in despatching bodies of the infantry regiment to occupy advanced posts, and in setting the rest in their quarters. Nîa was impressed into the service, and for myself, I ranged about the fort, seeing what there was to be seen,—which was not much. At last, Ilex had a moment or two to spare, and she took me by the arm to a store-chamber, where we helped ourselves to loaves and dates.

"You know," she said, as we finished a hurried meal, "you make me think things I wouldn't have thought by staying here in this way!"

"What things?" I said, rather alarmed. Did she suspect me of some dark design?

"Well!—That you care for me as much as I do for you!"

"And do you care for me—so much?"

"I never saw anybody like you! And I must love you!"

She said it quickly, with adverted eyes. I think I smiled at her; and so we understood each perfectly. We passed out into the sun; and I heard a veteran, unaccustomed, nevertheless, to such contracted quarters, observe:

"Why does the Colonel bring her *kerôta* here?"

I could have given the growler fifty crowns on the spot.

XI

The Ramparts

In the evening Ilex entertained the officers and two or three acquaintances who were among the companies garrisoning the fort. It was a quiet affair; most of those present realised the gloomy prospect before them—if it is a gloomy fate to be selected to perish in defence of a country one is proud of. At all events, the outlook, if not depressing, was a serious one. And only one or two of the party showed much hilarity in the face of it. I do not reckon the forced spirits of those of us who were very young.

The visitors dropped off early to their unfamiliar quarters. It was past midnight when we were awakened by a rush of spearmen to the gate and a wild knocking with the bosses of swords. I gained the parapet of the flat roof, and saw the sparkle of a beacon fire blazing at the head of the pass. At the same instant a roaring flame shot up from the little square tower not far from where I was. It was easy, now, to see the gate opened, and the eager scouts admitted. Hardly five minutes had passed when a form, running with frantic speed, came into the zone of light, making for the gate. Pursuing were three horsemen, whose javelins twice missed her. I saw one of them reel from her saddle and another rapidly turn her bridle and rush away. The third closed on the fugitive, who was forced to turn and defend herself. At party of our soldiers started to relieve her; but she stumbled forward and fell—when her antagonist galloped back. I saw her dragged in, and I went down to the gate to see if I could be of any assistance. All confusion was over now. The troops were standing in rank, motionless and composed. I could not make out where the wounded soldier had been carried. Ilex was found. So I crept up to the roof again, and peered over the edge, vainly trying to pierce the darkness that lay beyond the region illuminated by the fire.

"She had hard work to make the beacon burn," I heard a voice say from below. "Some of the sticks had been damp."

"Ah!" returned another voice.

"I don't envy whoever left the damp sticks there, Flora!"

"What would happen to them?"

"Happen?" growled the other.

I lost her next few words. "It's cost Quôna's life already."

"Is she gone?"

"Don't ask me! How do I know? But I say—can she live? The state she was in when we pulled her through the gate?"

"Well," said Flora, after a moment, "it's only a bit sooner than the rest of us!"

I heard no more. It was an hour or two before Ilex came and joined me on the parapet. Together we strained our eyes to the darkness; we could see nothing—nothing a light. But we knew that where we looking, the van of the enemy's army must be stealthily streaming past. It was an eerie feeling. Before day broke Ilex insisted on my going downstairs to sleep.

In the morning it was plain to be see that we were regularly invested. I stood with the little groups of officers by the lower tower, and watched the long lines of horse and foot pass by at a respectful distance, near the foot of the hills. Nearer to us, a strong body of spearmen were stationed, and as we looked, a javelin came whistling past us.

Phartis, who is young and new to campaigning, jumped. The rest of us looked at each other and raised our eyebrows.

"It is no use firing back at them," observed Ilex. "That dart wasn't a very good shot; still, we needn't give them such a promising target. Tell the troops not to show themselves, Phynax."

We accordingly lay low. The enemy did not attempt an assault, but contended themselves with keeping us isolated. An odd feeling it was— that all those moving living creatures, flesh and blood like ourselves, were bent on our destruction. It seems so natural to save life; yet there they were palpable, audible, and determined to take it. What quarrel had we with them?

And so now we realised that we were cut off from Pyramôna by miles of country swarming with the Uras people. Like the tide of the sea, the flood of invasion had welled past us, and left us—for how long?—On our pinnacle of rock. Through the day, as we did not molest them, the besiegers became encouraged to approach the walls. Their discipline was not very good. They thronged round the fort in masses on every side, and indulged in provocative language to their hearts' content. I did not understand much of it, but the accompanying gestures were significant enough. At evening they quietened, and their aspect was a good deal more calculated to inspire alarm, as one noted their silent, ferocious glances. It was then that we had a note from the commander—

Arainol—declaring the intention of carrying the fort by assault if it was not surrendered within twelve hours.

"She gives us lots of time. Let them try!" observed Ilex dryly; and she led me to the station at the inner edge of the roof, where on had a good view without being a conspicuous mark for spear-practice. All round, the clustered ranks of the enemy glared upon us. Above, the sun was sinking. A great slanting cloud, leaden itself, but shot with metallic rose, lay over the horizon; two or three bars of the same pearly rose-lustre stretched beneath it, in the yellow-green light of the ebbing day. We were alone with the silent crowd outside, and the silent earth and heavens encompassing them.

I looked at Ilex and she was smiling. I moved backwards, and laid my head on her shoulder. She clasped me close in her arms. My thoughts flew back to the first time when I had quivered at her touch.

"Oh, my sweet!" she said, speaking with tense utterance as her heart beat near mine. "In the whole gamut of human emotion, is there any such trill as that of knowing that one has someone one loves close—close—to one? Wilder, there may be, but anything so satisfying and perfect—no!"

I trembled with delight in her arms. A sparrow, flying home, fluttered past our faces, and recalled to us the fact that it was growing dark. We turned to go to the rooms below, and as we did we met one of the staff.

"I was coming for you, Ilex," she said. "I don't think the girl that lit the beacon can last much longer. But I'm sorry if I disturbed you! You were enjoying a few quiet moments, eh?"

Ilex kept hold of my arm.

"I'm coming Kothrûn, she might be conscious. And there is a good deal else to do."

We passed down the steps, and Ilex would have left me at my chamber.

"It's not a sight for you," she declared. "Her face and neck—poor thing! She is awfully disfigured."

"My dear, I have not been in a hospital for nothing," I replied. "I ought to be used to that! Perhaps you might let me help a bit."

But I saw in a moment that it was not a case for help, when she let me go into the room where the wounded girl lay.

THE NEXT DAY WAS A trying one. Momentarily expecting an assault, we went about such duties as we could find, in a half-hearted kind of manner. We did not doubt that we could repel an attack; but there is always an uneasy feeling that the sentries may be lax or deceived by some stratagem. The presence of an active and determined besieger does not add to the comfort of a garrison, though it may to its entertainment.

And in the evening our spirits received a further depressing shock. Throughout the hostile camp there were signs of jubilation and delight. Groups of grotesque warriors danced wild flings of hilarious joy; spears came whizzing innocuously into the for (where they were assiduously collected and impounded). Loud shots of triumph reached, hoarse or shrill, across our walls, their sound swelling and falling on the breeze.

"Queen Beatrice taken!"

"Marshal Otâris smashed to shivers!"

Asked Phratis: "What are they saying?"

"Listen and you'll hear," responded Kothrûn grimly, flicking the dust off a stone with her sleeve."

"Ten thousand!—Ten thousand prisoners!" roared a voice.

"That's not true," remarked Phynax calmly.

"The way open to Alzôna!"

"The Armerian beasts running like sheep!"

"Slaves for us!—Plenty of slaves for us! I'll have three senators for mine—the three richest!"

"Cheers for Marshal Klên! Shout for the Marshal! Shout for ourselves!"

"Well," remarked one of the staff dryly, "if all this is true ladies, we had better throw up the sponge at once."

Nobody spoke, and we all glared at the unfortunate humorist, who escaped under cover of a forced laugh.

"What do you suppose it really means, Ilex?" said Phratis.

"Maybe they've gained a small success," said she, "maybe a big one. Or it may be just a camp report. It's dull work sitting here, and people are glad of an excuse to excite themselves. I dare say it is nothing, after all, but that. Whatever it is, it makes no difference to us."

Perhaps it should not have, but truth compels me to add that it did.

"WHERE ARE THOSE PRISONERS?" INQUIRED Phynax the next morning, as we sat and peeped between the battlements. "It strikes me, I don't see them."

"They went past in the night, obviously," said Phratis. "Or else they are scaling the perpendicular heights. Or perhaps they are all massacred."

"Of course, the real reason you don't see them is this," urged another, "they daren't bring them past here, for fear we should rescue them."

In spite of this attempt at badinage, we were dull enough. The days wore on, and there was no sign of any check to Uras forces. At last one grew so weary of the monotony of waiting, and the unexplained passage of the days without incident grew so maddening, that we would most of us almost have welcomed clear signs of defeat. But still no change took place in the outlook. The enthusiasm of the besiegers was not repeated. Yet there was no indication of their retreating.

But at night, wild sounds wakened the echoes of the hillsides. Voices, mingled with the clash of steel, the patter of shod feet, the canter of horses—all roused our small garrison to instant activity. Round the fort surged an eddy of feverish movement. But it was impossible to do anything. One of the soldiers offered to be let down over the wall, with a view to getting information, but it was too great a risk.

Before daylight there came a rush of horse, and a tremendous knocking at the gate. The party assured us they were friends, but we did not venture to admit them, though Kothrûn said she was sure she recognised a voice or two she knew.

But when the day broke, we saw from our station on the walls the pass dotted with troops indeed, but unmistakably our own. We burst into a hearty shout of delight, and lost no time in opening the gate to a small party of mounted troops who were demanding an entrance.

Ilex bent her proud head low, before their leader. And then I saw that her helmet was encircled by a golden crown; and all at once, I knew it was the queen.

Her majesty was in excellent spirits.

"I shall not have laurel-wreaths enough!" she declared. "However, here is one for you, Ilex—and give each of your troops a leaf out of this other. In return, I would like some breakfast with hot coffee."

It was not like her to be so jocular, and I guessed that she had been affected more than she cared to show by the events of the past few days. It was not long before we learnt the history of them. The contact between the opposing armies had taken place later than was expected. The manœuvres had been more complicated. But, in its essence, the plan of drawing the enemy though the neglected pass, and falling on them by a telescopic concentration had succeeded, though the losses had been serious.

"It had nearly failed, though," said Beatrice. "Information was sent to Oristhôn by (who do you think it was?—The Second Secretary to the Treasury) which would have warned them at once; if they had believed it!"

The queen took a long drink of coffee.

"But," she went on, laughing, "of course, they didn't believe them! The stupid creatures! And it was really almost a miracle—the wrong ring went. The messenger got hold of the wrong ring, somehow; so they sent one of their people to make inquiries, and clear up matters. She was taken; and so it all came out."

"And I think," I said, "that I can explain to your majesty the miracle of the rings."

So I told her the story of our adventure in the hut. She was in a temper to enjoy the small comedy, and was frankly amused. Glancing up, I caught sight of Nîa, who was serving the table. Her face was set and white; the lips tightly closed.

"Is she not well disposed to the queen?" I thought. "It can't be that she resents my talking about the affair!" Or did she?

It was not until evening, when all was quiet, and the royal party, taking Ilex with them had gone forward to direct the pursuit, that she came to me, still white and trembling, and laid herself on the ground beside me, with her head on my knee.

"What's the matter?" I said, stroking her black, rough hair. "My dear Nîa, you are so easily upset! Pull yourself together!"

"Zôcris!" she murmured—"Zôcris! What can have become of her? No one knows—I have asked everybody who would speak to me. And that girl, Nalmyon, at Oristhôn—oh, I don't care if she is a grandee and a Colonel!—She is the cruelest brute! My lady,—she is in her hands, and when she gave her the wrong ring, and she find out—"

She stopped speaking and her breath came in long, choking gulps, while hot tears dropped on my dress. None of the Armerians had ever cried that I had seen, and Nîa's distress unnerved me not a little.

"Why, Nîa, she won't find out," I said. "They will think the Secretary sent the wrong ring. No doubt she is rogue enough to have plenty of forged signets."

"Oh, you don't know them!" she moaned hoarsely. "If she had nothing whatever to do with the mistake, still, she was mixed up in it, and in their power—and a slave!"

"She's clever, Nîa—she'll manage to outwit them!"

But this well-intentioned remark had the effect of making Nîa breakdown completely.

IRENE CLYDE

"I have got her killed—or worse!" were the only coherent words I could gather.

It was all very far from enlivening; but it kept me from worrying about Ilex, who returned early in the morning with the gratifying intelligence that the enemy was entirely dispersed, and all real danger was over.

"Only," she said, "there are a good many of them supposed to be hiding in the hill-caves, and they will want rooting out. After I have had a sleep, I will try and begin the work."

"And I must go with you?"

"No, Mêrê, I don't want to take you into a bear's den, do I?"

"And you don't want to go into a bear's den yourself. If this kind of bear is good for you to hunt, it's good for me."

"Well, please yourself! I won't be sorry to have you, for I've no surgeon to take with me. I must leave the regimental doctor here; there are some wounded coming in. Only mind—bears have claws!"

Most of the soldiers who had been disabled during the Pursuit had been taken to Pyramôna. But search parties had brought in a few from the hillsides and now a dismal little procession entered at the gate.

"Two civilians dead; three of the Dragon regiment wounded slightly," reported somebody.

"Two civilians?" I heard Ilex say. "Of all the cool pieces of brutality—" And her voice suddenly fell. She spoke to the officer for a minute, gave a hurried direction, and came away.

"Dear, do you know who it was?" she said, her eyes meeting mine, "Phanaras!"

"What! The lady of luxury and affection? The exquisite who never set her foot on the ground? How could *she* come this way? Ah! I see, Ilex: everybody thought this a safe corner till four days ago."

"Yes, I suppose so. Yet she and her companion were apparently wandering about alone, on the hills. Those three soldiers came up when the people who had killed them were plundering them, and they themselves were knocked about, rather. I must say it's unaccountable to me."

I could say nothing. Yet I felt clear in my own mind that somehow, in a wild rush for personal safety, Phanaras had fallen into the fate she had met. Perhaps she had chosen a pleasant refuge among the hills, and, alarmed at the near approach of the enemy, she fled blindly, like a moth, into their arms. I tried to feel sorry for her.

With that dull little group, which Ilex would not let me go near, in my sight, it was not difficult to succeed. So fond of flattery and ease! And she had been cut down by a soldier's broadsword, alone, nearly, on these bleak rocks. Yet, if it had been Opanthë lying there—inconsistent as we are—I should have been more sorry.

Ilex was dull and absorbed as we rode away through the pass.

XII

The Caves

We struck up to the right, after emerging on the far side of the hills.

"It's easy to work to the left," Ilex observed. "They kept together pretty much till they reached the plain, on that side; and we got between them and the mountains. This way, a good many of them must be lurking about—so, if you please, we'll proceed with all due precautions. And we'll leave our horses here, and scramble."

Every now and again our scouts, higher up the hill, signalled to us the existence of places which it was desirable to examine. We constantly came upon bits of caves, ourselves; but in none of them were there any traces of human beings. Still, they all needed exploring; so our progress was slow. And the luxuriant vegetation, which, in contrast to the opposite slope, covered many acres of this side of the mountains, constantly made us lose touch with our outlying links.

"There's Ochônal gone and lost herself again," observed Ilex to me with vexation. "She'll be getting caught one of these days. And I see Thalyssa, who ought to be keeping close to her—look; under those ivied branches."

We were passing under a sheer wall of limestone rock, over which hung festoons of bewildering green creepers and parasites. Above it, one saw Thalyssa, pushing her way cautiously on.

"Nothing in *that* rock, anyway," Ilex began; when the girl who was walking next us suddenly flashed a sword across our path, and stopped us. Then in a whisper she said rapidly:

"Something is moving to the rock through those bushes. It *may* be a panther—but it is too slow, I think!"

I saw nothing but the waving of the grass in the wind. Ilex thought she traced something, however. The rest came scrambling quickly up, and were told to search the patch of bushes. Ilex and I, like the rest, plunged into the thicket. We reached its other side in a minute or two, and there, right before us, was an unmistakable cave-mouth—low and square.

"Whistle for the rest!" said Ilex: but, before the words were well out of her mouth, she seized me and threw me down in the dense grass beside her. A fragment of limestone fell from above, and crashed on the ground among the bushes. It was followed by another, and before we had seen the dust settle, we realised that someone above was bombarding the bushes. Thick and fast the big lumps of rock came leaping into the undergrowth, and making it quite untenable.

"I hope those folks of ours will have the sense to clear out," Ilex said—and she shouted as loudly as possible instructions to that effect.

"Shall I go and tell them?" I said.

"It's no use," she answered. "Whoever's slinging those rocks is taking aim now. And they would knock you down, once stirred. We're safe beside these stones. They'll tired of this game."

"Can't we get out by following the rock side?"

"Sorry we can't. Look at those ridges we would have to cross! They would have us easily there."

"What is to be done, then?"

"Wait developments, and rush out late on! Then we can join the rest. I'll shout and ask if they can reach that unpleasant person up there with the bits of limestone."

So she did, but no answer came back. At the same time the bombardment slackened gradually. We waited for ten minutes or so after it ceased, shouting at intervals, without being answered.

"This is not nice!" said Ilex. "Make a straight run for it now, Mêrê—no, not straight! Zigzag a bit—and keep to the left. I will go rather to the right."

We flew as fast through the undergrowth as possible. Nobody was to be seen.

"Ah! But look!" said my companion, all at once pointing to the white rock. There a limp, loose heap lay, wedged in between a tree root and the precipitous face of the hillside. Above it was a narrow ledge with a broken little quarry behind.

"That isn't any of our people! That's the villain that's given us all the trouble! How in the name of goodness did she get up there? Do you see how she's slipped?"

"Are you sure?" I said. "Isn't it a dummy, perhaps? Or somebody they've pitched over the rocks?"

"My dear! There are easier ways of despatching people. But, now, where have our folks gone?"

"Here's Thalyssa!" I said delightedly, as that lady, panting and quivering, appeared before us.

"My colonel, such a scramble!" she said. "I'm out of breath, getting down that hillside. What made the rest go off at such a rate?"

"Which way did they go?" asked Ilex.

"Back down the way we came, as fast as they could manage," she answered.

"They must have misunderstood me," remarked Ilex, with vexation. "Anyway, we'll have another try at the cave. Have you noticed what's been going on, Thalyssa?"

"I couldn't see much that was close to the cliff. There was a good deal of noise, and that brought me down."

"Well, there's a cave in there; and Mêrê and I are going to search it. You will keep guard outside. You know the signals. . ."

"If Ochônal turns up," added Ilex, looking back, "keep her with you."

"Yes, my colonel," returned Thalyssa, following us slowly as we passed again to the foot of the rock.

It was agreeable enough to walk to its base when once one was satisfied that there was no immediate likelihood of being battered with limestone crags. But when we stopped before the dark, low opening, it did not look exactly inviting. Clearly it was a stronghold of the enemy's. They had not shown themselves—but was that any reason for supposing that there were not any of them there? The thought crossed my mind that Ilex was not showing herself so careful of my safety as she had been when I arrived at Ylonár.

She pushed on to the threshold. The gloom of the cavernous doorway seemed to envelop me, and the inner side of my forearm began to feel cold and damp. I found myself scraping mechanically with my fingernail the grip of the sword I had. We plunged into the cave. The surprising thing was that it was not dark. From an opening high up plenty of subdued light was admitted. It struck me that it must have been by means of this opening that access was obtained to the ledge from which the loose stones were fired. But this was a first impression, though, I believe, a correct one.

Our attention was immediately turned to the inhabitants of the place. At first we thought there were only two—two old persons who, when their first surprise was over, burst into piercing screams. But, in the dimmer, recesses, we saw there was a bed, and a form lying on it.

"Bother those wretches and their screaming!" irritably observed Ilex—and, indeed, the cavern reechoed to the roof. "Be quiet! Or by the lightning—!"

On this, they modified their outcry, which then took the form of mingled malediction and groans: and we approached the pallet in comparative peace.

It was a thin, bony creature that lay there; no associate—we judged—of the well-fed brace of screamers. A coarse garment was all her covering; she breathed heavily, and seemed hardly conscious of our presence.

"I expect," said Ilex, her voice vibrating, "this is someone of ours that these Uras pigs have got hold of! Wait till I talk to that sinner in yellow!"

But the girl opened her eyes with a start, and half up, clutching at Ilex's dress.

"My dear," said she soothingly, placing her arm round her and being to her level, "don't be frightened—don't mind. Nobody will—*Ah*! Thekla!"

"Ilex! What—?"

"Oh, it surely can't—but it *is*! Neith and Artemis!" said Ilex, starting up with blazing eyes and loosening the fingers that held her.

She sprang to the terrified women, then she slowly and contemptuously lowered her point.

"It is no good killing them," she said, returning to me. "I was an idiot to want to. . . it *is* Thekla, isn't it, Mêrê? Ask her?"

But she would only smile faintly and press our hands.

"Look here," said Ilex, "we must take her out of this. Can you lift the bed? (What a wretched palliasse!) So! Thalyssa, go inside and take care that two people there don't escape. Mêrê," as we came into daylight, "it *is* Thekla! What can we do for her?"

I felt her pulse.

"Seems to me she's starved, and has a kind of nervous fever," I said. "Put her in the shade and we'll try to get her some lemon juice. But we could sent for a palanquin to take her to some town—"

"I'll send Thalyssa: and we can watch Thekla and those two."

But there was a rustling noise in the bushes. And the crests of Armerian helmets appeared above them.

"I met your party, Ilex," said a surprised voice, "and they told me you had ordered them to make the best of their way back. They thought you and Mêrê were both captured. But I see," continued he queen, "you have been making captures instead. I must say it doesn't seem very good management. Whom have you got killed there?"

"Oh, she isn't killed," said Ilex anxiously, "Would you like it, if we had seen Thekla, your majesty?"

Beatrice brushed abruptly past her to the bedside. Without a word she sank beside it, and spread her arms over the tired form.

XIII

The Triumph

In striking contrast to the quiet and businesslike way in which the troops had seemingly left Alzôna was the stately splendour of our reception on our return. Met at the gates by the authorities who had been left in charge, the endless line of victorious soldiery followed the queen and her staff through the length of the city, to the palace. Again and again, the way seemed bridle-deep with flowers. The streets were lined with citizens—elderly and very young, many of them—from whom arose a clear, sweet murmur of acclamation. Need I recount the incidents of the progress? How the Sovereign, in compliance with immemorial custom, leapt from her horse an dipped her feet in the basin of the little gold and marble canopied fountain by the Forum—how the children's chosen leader offered her roses and sugared confections and delicate jars of perfume, m a sweet, shy way—how the magicians sallied forth from an unsuspected corner, and chanted hymns of trembling rejoicing—how the populace and the soldiers took up the singing, with more than a suspicion of undue *vibrato*? Or how at last we passed into the Palace, and watched the procession file past beneath the queen's eye? Nor need I detail the little private celebration of our own, that took place when we reached Ilex's house. The place seemed positively full of green branches. Incense was smoking on three low altars. The elders and children abandoned their staid decorum, and met us with tumultuous embraces, in which the very slaves shared.

"And there's Eryto outside!" declared Appthis. "I must go out and pet her! Ilex, how brown you are! We, will have to wash you with buttermilk!"

Ilex laughed till the tears streamed from her eyes.

"That young lady has evidently ruled the house when we were away," she remarked.

"But you *are* brown, all of you," announced Appthis. "I didn't know it was you, Darûna, in the street till Cyasterix told me."

"But I saw *you*," Darûna told her. "And I saw you want to leave Cyasterix and run to us. Wasn't that what you did?"

The child looked up at her from under its eyelashes, and laughed self-consciously, and Darûna discreetly said no more. She was claimed in a moment with an enthusiastic wild rush by someone else. The whirl of it all,—the delicious, friendly unreason that prevailed, and swept us off our feet, and drove every atom of stiffness out of us—of that one cannot hope to convey any idea. It was not disorder. There was not the least extravagance of an objectionable kind. It is indescribable.

It was not until the next day that we saw Cydonia. Chloris we had met as we left the palace. She was with her regiment. Regardless of propriety and a good many other useful things, she darted to us for a moment, and volubly greeted us with an *empressement* which showed that she had learned something in camp.

If a little of her refreshing youngness had gone off, I doubt whether Cydonia liked her any the less on that account. In fact, Cydonia's one theme, when we encountered her, was the interesting intelligence that of her *kerôta*ship with Chloris was now to be openly recognised. It was so like the ways of sweethearts at home, that I half turned my head to smile. Cydonia caught me.

"What *are* you laughing at? You shouldn't. It's most improper. Consider all the people who are killed! Athroës—only think, Mêrê"— her mock remonstrance changing into real concern—"how, just a few weeks since, she had such a lovely day with us! And so many more— Phanaras among them. What a curious thing that was, Ilex!"

"Very," said Ilex.

I was silent.

"I heard," said Cydonia, resuming after a pause, "when I was quartered in Pyramôna, people say that she was inquiring for your regiment everywhere. At last, when she traced it to Ylonár, nothing would satisfy her but to go on at all risks. So, you see, you were an attraction to the end. The more dangers people showed her in the way, the better she was please. Exactly like a month and a torch flame."

"She surely can't have been quite in her right mind," Ilex said, a little lamely.

"Then neither is Mêrê!" replied the daring Cydonia.

"Was that Chloris that crossed the street there?" interposed Ilex. "In sea green?"

"I believe she has a sea green gown," said Cydonia indifferently. "Well, I'll just go and see, to make sure."

She strolled leisurely away for some ten yards, and then put on steam, and was not long in working up to the rate of six and a quarter miles an hour.

When Ilex and I reached home—we had been inquiring after the progress of a slow and uncertain recovery that Thekla was making—I went, as usual, to my little court, and summoned the attendant. Only Lyx came.

"Where is Nîa?" I asked her.

"Nîa is not very well, your ladyship. She would like to see you, if she may come when I have gone."

"Very well, Lyx."

The agile, deft slave brought me water for my feet, changed my robe for a lighter one, and shaded my sunlight, in wonderfully little time. Then she noiselessly slipped away.

I felt a little sleepy, with the unwonted luxury about me. Something or other came into my head—I forget now what—and I was half dreaming the question out, when Nîa stood before me. Her arms were wide-stretched, opening the curtain of my door—her eyes were bent on the ground—her face was like ashes.

"Nîa, you wanted me, did you not?" I said. I felt my own voice harsh and broken.

She took a few steps into the room.

"I ought not," she managed to say, speaking slowly, "to say anything to you about this. But you are very kind to me."

"Surely everybody's kind to you! Darûna, and Ilex—everybody!"

She inclined further and further.

"Yes, everybody—all the ladies! But your ladyship—in a different way!"

"I have found out about Zôcris," she went on, breaking into a rapid torrent of speech, so that I thought she would become hysterical.

"What has happened, don't ask me, my lady—don't ask me! But she will never look me in the face again! Oh, my lady, never see me again! She must not—I must not—"

"Then it's not so bad? She is not killed? I took advantage of the sudden choke in Nîa's utterance to interpose this consideration.

Nîa drew herself up, and almost looked down on me. Her eyebrows were drawn together in one straight, thin line, and what she said came from her lips like little biting morsels of ice.

"Killed! Killed—if only she were! There is a worse thing. If that were all! Why am I not mad? Too good for me, I suppose."

"You don't mean that—she is out of her mind?"

"Oh, can't you understand? Not that—not killed or mad! That would be easy!—Oh, worse than that!"

I felt at a loss. It was so entirely impossible to guess what she meant. The biting, short outbursts began again, while her form, panted under her hot eyes.

"And it is my doing! Could *you* stand it? . . . I did it!—And I was so fond of her! . . . I can't think of it! I don't think of it. But it is there. . . all the same. I can't even tell her! Why did we meet her?"

A few tears burst from her. I spoke again.

"But if she is alive and well, whatever she may have gone through, it is your place to put things right. You can show her that, whatever people have done to her"—Nîa winced as if I had pricked her in the side—"it makes no difference to you. What is your affection worth, if it isn't to be poured out on her at such a time?"

"If I met her in the street," said the girl, "I should turn aside. And she would rather kill me than think I should want to see her!"

"Then let me tell you, Nîa," I returned, "that you are very heartless—cruelly heartless."

She dropped her moist eyes for a moment,—raised them to mine, and would have withdrawn. But I saw her press her hands together, and I reflected that my judgement, in this odd country, might not be quite infallible.

"Don't go," I said. "I dare say I am wrong. If I were to ask Ilex to explain your reason, very likely—"

"For heaven's sake, my lady, let this be between your ladyship and me! Oh, I have no right to ask it—but if you could only keep this last thing from me! Nobody knows but your ladyship and me, and—Let them never fancy anything!"

She was crying freely, now.

"I should have thought," I said, making one last effort, "that you would have liked to have come out and stood beside her, and said, 'There! Whatever people have done, and whatever may be thought of you, I love you always,' wouldn't you?"

"And she? Would she—burning and broken—want to have me patronising her, and saying, 'Never mind dear, if you have been degraded!'—Me, and slave, too? What she wants is never to see anyone—least of all, me! So I shall never see her again. And my doing, too!"

"Nîa, you are a good girl. You have nothing to blame yourself for," I said. "See, sit down by me, and let me give you some rose water."

I led her to a seat, and bathed her face and hands; and then I put my arm round her neck, and told her, in the best way I could, that it would all come right in the end—that the heart of her love was hers forever, if only she cared to keep it fresh—that all affection was one in essence, and that she and her lost lover were eternally united in its harmony. I did not think it would soothe her, but it did. I was sorry I could remember nothing better to say. At last somebody sent Lyx with a message that I was being waited for, and I had to leave my patience. I never knew what Zôcris's fate had been. Something kept me from inquiring—perhaps a sense of loyalty to Nîa—and no one thought it worthwhile to tell me.

This is not a tragedy; and I have no intention of making it such. Nîa is still living. But she never smiles and she never stands up straight.

My own life-union with Ilex was attended with a great deal of ceremony. Not that I wanted it so: but Ilex did; and besides, as she was a high officer of the Court, it appears that it would have been scarcely decent otherwise. Accordingly, one bewildering morning, I found myself standing in the columned hall appropriated to the transaction of such events. Its splendid immensity held, I was dimly conscious, a gathering of citizens and nobles that should have been a very flattering spectacle. Only, the strangeness of the matter made my head swim, so that the assemblage looked to me like nothing but a beautiful display of flowers. Yet I know that the queen was there; and Thekla. Close to us was the Imperial Chancellor. I heard her address me, and by dint of painfully following every word she said with my eyes fastened hard on her lips, I realised that she was asking me a question: and on the prompting of a friendly voice near, I triumphantly, if uncertainly, returned the proper answer. And then I was conscious of Ilex's clasp enfolding me, with its accustomed sweet tenderness: and of very little more, except of smiling at bright faces from that assured shelter, as we passed along, followed by your own people, and preceded by heralds and musicians, to our home.

"You were the shyest *partie* of all that have ever been from the foundation of the word!" announced Chloris, when she next saw me.

"And can you remember so far back!" observed Mîra, with great interest. "I wish you would just sit down and give me a few details of the process. I often thought you must have had a hand in it—things are arranged so badly in some ways!"

She gazed at Chloris, with the critical interest with which thirty regards sixteen.

"Oh!" said the younger lady, nowise discomposed, "you watch me when Cydonia and I have the same pleasure! You'll see me stick up uncommonly straight!"

"That would be a delight indeed! May I ask when the instructive performance is likely to be offered to an expectant public?"

"Well, Cydonia says not until I'm properly grown up—till I leave off eating green quinces," she added, amid inextinguishable laughter.

Chloris's candid opinion of my appearance was counterbalanced, however, by the favourable verdict of a more august authority. A stream of our acquaintances kept arriving all day, and as I watched the slaves moving about amongst them with trays of sweets and coffee, I became aware of an increase of brilliancy on my left hand, and the soft voice of the queen said:

"My dear, I think you will tempt me to break the traditions of my house, and accept a *conjux*! You are so perfectly suited to Ilex! And I hope you did not find your ceremony tiring this morning. I wondered how you could possibly accommodate yourself to it at all. Oh, of course you were nervous. Strange things—especially when they touch our affections—always are a strain, and hard to carry off easily. I must say, I wondered that a foreigner could go through it half so well."

"She isn't a foreigner any longer, your majesty," said Ilex radiantly. "Is she? Isn't she quite one of us?"

"Indeed, if she cars to be, she is," returned the queen warmly. "All the same, you gave her a difficult part to play this morning, Ilex."

"Thekla will be a shyer *conjux* than Mêrê," volunteered with startling distinctness, a small visitor of six. An appalling silence succeeded: the queen's colour came and went, and a momentary flush settled in Thekla's thin cheek. Conversation, after a few seconds, resumed its flow: but the royal party did not stay much longer.

"It was very good of you to come, Thekla," I found a chance to say, "when you are still so far from strong! I hope you will be well soon—and that someone will make you as happy as Ilex has made me today!"

She drew me behind a curtain for a minute.

"I should have come if I had had to be carried in," she said. "did you and Ilex find me—!"

"Oh, somebody would!" I said. "that's not credit to us."

"Don't say that, Mêrê. I like to think of it—and how your two faces and Beatrice's were the first I remember wakening up to. And"—after a restless play of her fingers with an ivory charm that hung from the wall—"please don't talk to me about—having any *conjux*. I never shall!"

"No, Thekla? . . . Will you forgive me, now," I said hurriedly, "if I said I hoped that the queen—"

"Mêrê"—she straightened her languid pose—"the Queen of Armeria is always single. . . She is the people's alone. . ."

"Need she be? Is it a law?"

"It is the custom. I must not stay now. . . Yes my queen, I am here! I am quite ready. Shall we ride?"

"Of course you will, indeed. The idea of your walking! And I can hardly offer to carry you."

They departed in a whirl of waving fans and glittering attendants. But the stream of visitors ebbed and flowed until late at night.

We went straight to rest. The next day would be devoted to a quieter festivity entirely amongst ourselves. Only, as I passed the oldest member of the household, Enschîna, she took me by the hand to the central tripod, where the bridal incense was still smoking faintly, and gave me a stately kiss, with tears in her eyes.

"Now we have a right to call you one of our kin," she said. "Nobody sooner! Tomorrow we will remind you of it!"

I do not think I shall visit Europe. Ilex is charming, and sensible in many ways: but she confesses to an invincible repugnance to embarking on a new sphere of existence, under the auspices of the Arch-Magician. Altogether, I do not blame her. And I am not going to try the experiment alone.

But I have entrusted this manuscript—how funny it seems to be writing in English characters (and I am not sure about my spelling),— to the care of the high official in question, who promises to have it conveyed to a point from which it can be projected without difficulty into Scotland.

Anyone who discovers it will take it to Jessie Keith, 74, Rae Street, Perth—and I am sure she will see to it that they shall not have had their trouble for nothing.

N.B. My friend's manuscript reached me safely. In accordance with the directions appended to it, I am endeavouring to set up communication with her, if her account is a true one. Meanwhile, I fulfil her first wish—that the manuscript itself should be published at the earliest opportunity. Miss Clyde has been good enough to make the necessary arrangement for the press.

—J.R.

A Note About the Author

Irene Clyde (1869–1954) was a pioneering transgender author and lawyer. Orphaned at a young age, Clyde—who also went by their birth name, Thomas Baty—was an exceptionally bright student whose merits allowed them entry to The Queen's College in Oxford. Earning degrees from Trinity College, Oxford and the aforementioned Queen's College, they became an expert in the field of international law. Starting out simply teaching law at a multitude of British universities, Clyde would begin their writing career publishing books on international law. Becoming more interested in publicly addressing their views on sexuality and gender, Clyde would publish *Beatrice the Sixteenth*: *Being the Personal Narrative of Mary Hatherley, M.B., Explorer and Geographer* in 1909. Though largely overlooked in its time, the novel is an early work of feminist science fiction and one of the first to be published by a transgender author. Several years after this, Clyde would work with a small group of editors to put out a privately circulated feminist gender studies journal entitled, *Urania*. In 1915, Clyde would leave for Japan and growing to love the country, would spend their remaining years serving the Japanese government as a foreign legal adviser. Known in their lifetime as a radical feminist and pacifist, Clyde presented themselves outside of gender-conforming norms and would be considered today to be either non-binary or transgender.

A Note from the Publisher

Spanning many genres, from non-fiction essays to literature classics to children's books and lyric poetry, Mint Edition books showcase the master works of our time in a modern new package. The text is freshly typeset, is clean and easy to read, and features a new note about the author in each volume. Many books also include exclusive new introductory material. Every book boasts a striking new cover, which makes it as appropriate for collecting as it is for gift giving. Mint Edition books are only printed when a reader orders them, so natural resources are not wasted. We're proud that our books are never manufactured in excess and exist only in the exact quantity they need to be read and enjoyed. To learn more and view our library, go to minteditionbooks.com

bookfinity & 🦅 MINT EDITIONS

Enjoy more of your favorite classics with Bookfinity,
a new search and discovery experience for readers.
With Bookfinity, you can discover more vintage
literature for your collection, find your Reader Type,
track books you've read or want to read,
and add reviews to your favorite books.
Visit www.bookfinity.com, and click on
Take the Quiz to get started.

Don't forget to follow us
@bookfinityofficial and @mint_editions

9 781513 136219